Frank Richard Stockton

Mrs. Cliff's Yacht

Frank Richard Stockton

Mrs. Cliff's Yacht

ISBN/EAN: 9783337395650

Printed in Europe, USA, Canada, Australia, Japan

Cover: Foto ©Andreas Hilbeck / pixelio.de

More available books at **www.hansebooks.com**

MRS. CLIFF'S YACHT

BY

FRANK R. STOCKTON

ILLUSTRATED BY A. FORESTIER

NEW YORK
CHARLES SCRIBNER'S SONS
1896

CONTENTS

LIST OF ILLUSTRATIONS

MRS. CLIFF'S YACHT

CHAPTER I

ALONE WITH HER WEALTH

On a beautiful September afternoon in a handsome room of one of the grand, up-town hotels in New York sat Mrs. Cliff, widow and millionnaire.

Widow of a village merchant, mistress of an unpretending house in the little town of Plainton, Maine, and, by strange vicissitudes of fortune, the possessor of great wealth, she was on her way from Paris to the scene of that quiet domestic life to which for nearly thirty years she had been accustomed.

She was alone in the hotel; her friends, Captain Horn and his wife Edna, who had crossed the ocean with her, had stayed but a few days in New York and had left early that afternoon for Niagara, and she was here by herself in the hotel, waiting until the hour should arrive when she would start on a night train for her home.

Her position was a peculiar one, altogether new to her. She was absolutely independent, — not only could she do what she pleased, but there was no one to tell

her what it would be well for her to do, wise for her
to do, or unwise.   Everything she could possibly want
was within her reach, and there was no reason why she
should not have everything she wanted.

For many months she had been possessed of enormous
wealth, but never until this moment had she felt herself
the absolute, untrammelled possessor of it.   Until now
Captain Horn, to whom she owed her gold, and the
power it gave her, had been with her or had exercised
an influence over her.   Until the time had come when
he could avow the possession of his vast treasures, it
had been impossible for her to make known her share
in them, and even after everything had been settled, and
they had all come home together in the finest state-rooms
of a great ocean liner, she had still felt dependent upon
the counsels and judgment of her friends.

But now she was left absolutely free and independent, untrammelled, uncounselled, alone with her wealth.

She rose and looked out of the window, and, as she
gazed upon the crowd which swept up and down the
beautiful avenue, she could not but smile as she thought
that she, a plain New England countrywoman, with her
gray hair brushed back from her brows, with hands a
little hardened and roughened with many a year of
household duties, which had been to her as much a
pleasure as a labor, was in all probability richer than
most of the people who sat in the fine carriages or
strolled in their fashionable clothes along the sidewalk.

"If I wanted to do it," she thought, "I could have
one of those carriages with prancing horses and a driver

in knee breeches, or I could buy that house opposite, with its great front steps, its balconies, and everything in it, but there is nobody on this earth who could tempt me to live there."

"Now," said Mrs. Cliff to herself, as she turned from the window and selected a fresh easy chair, and sank down into its luxurious depths, "there is nothing in this world so delightful as to go back rich to Plainton. To be rich in Paris or New York is nothing to me; it would simply mean that I should be a common person there as I used to be at home, and, for the matter of that, a little more common."

As the good lady's thoughts wandered northward, and spread themselves from the railroad station at Plainton all over the little town, she was filled with a great content and happiness to go to her old home with her new money. This was a joy beyond anything she had dreamed of as possible in this world.

But it was the conjunction of the two which produced this delightful effect upon her mind. The money anywhere else, or Plainton without it, would not have made Mrs. Cliff the happy woman that she was.

It pleased her to let her mind wander over the incidents of her recent visit to her old home, the most unhappy visit she had ever made in all her life, but everything that was unpleasant then would help to make everything more delightful in the present home-coming.

She thought of the mental chains and fetters she had worn when she went to Plainton with plenty of money in her purse and a beautiful pair of California blankets in her handsome trunk; when she had been afraid to speak of the one or to show the other; when she had sat quietly and received charity from people whose houses and land, furniture, horses, and cows, she could have bought and given away without feeling their loss; when she had been publicly berated by Nancy Shott for spending money on luxuries which should have been used to pay her debts; when she had been afraid to put her money in the bank for fear it would act as a dynamite bomb and blow up the fortunes of her friends, and when she could find no refuge from the miseries brought upon her by the necessity of concealing her wealth except to go to bed and cover up her head so that she should not hear the knock of some inquiring neighbor upon her front door.

Then when she had made this background as dark and gloomy as it was possible to make it, she placed before it the glittering picture of her new existence in Plainton.

But this new life, bright as it now appeared to her, was not to be begun without careful thought and earnest consideration. Ever since her portion of the golden treasure had been definitely assigned to her, the mind of Mrs. Cliff had been much occupied with plans for her future in her old home.

It was not to be altogether a new life. All the friends she had in the world, excepting Captain and Mrs. Horn, lived in Plainton. She did not wish to lose these friends, — she did not wish to be obliged to make new ones. With simple-minded and honest Willy

Croup, who had long lived with her and for her; with Mrs. Perley, the minister's wife; with all her old neighbors and friends, she wished to live as she had always lived, but, of course, with a difference. How to manage, arrange, and regulate that difference was the great problem in her mind.

One thing she had determined upon: her money should not come between her and those who loved her and who were loved by her. No matter what she might do or what she might not do, she would not look down upon people simply because she was rich, and oh, the blessed thought which followed that! There would be nobody who could look down upon her because she was not rich!

She did not intend to be a fine new woman; she did not intend to build a fine new house. She was going to be the same Mrs. Cliff that she used to be, — she was going to live in the same house. To be sure, she would add to it. She would have a new dining-room and a guest's chamber over it, and she would do a great many other things which were needed, but she would live in her old home where she and her husband had been so happy, and where she hoped he would look down from heaven and see her happy until the end of her days.

As she thought of the things she intended to do, and of the manner in which she intended to do them, Mrs. Cliff rose and walked the floor. She felt as if she were a bird, a common-sized bird, perhaps, but with enormous wings which seemed to grow and grow the more she thought of them until they were able to carry her so far and so high that her mind lost its power of directing them.

She determined to cease to think of the future, of what was going to be, and to let her mind rest and quiet itself with what really existed. Here she was in a great city full of wonders and delights, of comforts, conveniences, luxuries, necessities, and all within her power. Almost anything she could think of she might have; almost anything she wanted to do she might do. A feeling of potentiality seemed to swell and throb within her veins. She was possessed of an overpowering desire to do something now, this moment, to try the power of her wealth.

Near her on the richly papered wall was a little button. She could touch this and order — what should she order? A carriage and prancing pair to take her to drive? She did not wish to drive. A cab to take her to the shops, or an order to merchants to send her samples of their wares that here, in her own room, like a queen or a princess, she might choose what she wanted and think nothing of the cost? But no, she did not wish to buy anything. She had purchased in Paris everything that she cared to carry to Plainton.

She went and stood by the electric button. She must touch it, and must have something! Her gold must give her an instant proof that it could minister to her desires, but what should she ask for? Her mind travelled over the whole field of the desirable, and yet not one, salient object presented itself. There was absolutely nothing that she could think of that she wished to ask for at that moment. She was like a poor girl in a fairy tale to whom the good fairy comes and asks her to make one wish and it shall be granted, and who stands hesitating and trembling, not being able to decide what is the one great thing for which she should ask.

So stood Mrs. Cliff. There was a fairy, a powerful fairy, in her service who could give her anything she desired, and with all her heart she wanted to want something that minute. What should she want?

In her agitation she touched the bell. Half frightened at what she had done, she stepped back and sat down. In a few minutes there was a knock, the door opened, a servant entered. "Bring me a cup of tea," said Mrs. Cliff.

CHAPTER II

WILLY CROUP DOESN'T KNOW

THE next afternoon as the train approached Plainton, Mrs. Cliff found herself a great deal agitated as she thought of the platform at the station. Who would be there, — how should she be met? With all her heart she hoped that there would not be anything like a formal reception, and yet this was not improbable. Everybody knew she was coming; everybody knew by what train she would arrive. She had written to Willy Croup, and she was very sure that everybody

knew everything that she had written. More than
this, everybody knew that she was coming home rich.
How rich they were not aware, because she had not
gone into particulars on this subject, but they knew
that the wealthy Mrs. Cliff would arrive at 5.20 that
afternoon, and what were they going to do about it?

When she had gone home before, all her friends and
neighbors, and even distant acquaintances, — if such
people were possible in such a little town, — had come
to her house to bid her welcome, and many of them
had met her at the station. But then they had come
to meet a poor, shipwrecked widow, pitied by most
of them and loved by many. Even those who neither
pitied nor loved her had a curiosity to see her, for
she had been shipwrecked, and it was not known in
Plainton how people looked after they had been wrecked.

But now the case was so different that Mrs. Cliff
did not expect the same sort of greeting, and she greatly
feared formality. If Mr. Perley should appear on the
platform, surrounded by some of the leading members
of his congregation, and should publicly take her by
the hand and bid her "Welcome home!" and if those
who felt themselves entitled to do so, should come
forward and shake hands with her, while others, who
might feel that they belonged to a different station in
life, should keep in the background and wait until she
came to speak to them, she would be deeply hurt.

After all, Plainton and the people in it were dearer
to her than anything else in the world, and it would
be a great shock if she should meet formality where

she looked for cordial love. She wanted to see Mr. Perley,—he was the first person she had seen when she came home before,—but now she hoped that he would not be there. She was very much afraid that he would make a stiff speech to her; and if he did that, she would know that there had been a great change, and that the friends she would meet were not the same friends she had left. She was almost afraid to look out of the window as the train slowed up at the station.

The minds of the people of Plainton had been greatly exercised about this home-coming of Mrs. Cliff. That afternoon it was probable that no other subject of importance was thought about or talked about in the town, and for some days before the whole matter had been so thoroughly considered and discussed that the good citizens, without really coming to any fixed and general decision upon the subject, had individually made up their minds that, no matter what might happen afterward, they would make no mistake upon this very important occasion which might subsequently have an influence upon their intercourse with their old, respected neighbor, now millionnaire. Each one for himself, or herself, decided—some of them singly and some of them in groups—that as they did not know what sort of a woman Mrs. Cliff had become since the change in her circumstances, they would not place themselves in false positions. Other people might go and meet her at the station, but they would stay at home and see what happened. Even Mr. Perley thought it wise, under the circumstances, to do this.

Therefore it was, that when Mrs. Cliff stepped down upon the platform, she saw no one there but Willy Croup. If Mrs. Cliff was a little shocked and a good deal surprised to find no one to meet her but that simple-minded dependant and relative, her emotions were excited in a greater degree by the manner in which she was greeted by this old friend and companion.

Instead of rushing toward her with open arms, — for Willy was an impulsive person and given to such emotional demonstrations, — Miss Croup came forward, extending a loosely filled black cotton glove. Her large, light-blue eyes showed a wondering interest, and Mrs. Cliff felt that every portion of her visible attire was being carefully scanned.

For a moment Mrs. Cliff hesitated, and then she took the hand of Willy Croup and shook it, but she did not speak. She had no command of words, at least for greeting.

Willy earnestly inquired after her health, and said how glad she was to see her, but Mrs. Cliff did not listen. She looked about her. For an instant she thought that possibly the train had come in ahead of time, but this, of course, was absurd — trains never did that.

"Willy," she said, her voice a little shaken, "has anything happened? Is anybody sick?"

"Oh no!" said Willy; "everybody is well, so far as I know. I guess you are wondering why there is nobody here to meet you, and I have been wondering at that too. They must have thought that you did not want to be bothered when you were attending to your baggage and things. Is anybody with you?"

"With me!" exclaimed Mrs. Cliff; "who could be with me?"

"Oh, I didn't know," replied the other; "I thought perhaps you might have a maidservant, or some of those black people you wrote about."

Mrs. Cliff was on the point of telling Willy she was a fool, but she refrained.

"Here is the baggage-man," said Willy, "and he wants your checks."

As Mrs. Cliff took the little pieces of brass from her purse and handed them to the man, Willy looked on in amazement.

"Good gracious!" she exclaimed. "Seven! I guess you had to pay for extra baggage. Shall I get you a carriage, and where do you want to be driven to — to your own house or the hotel?"

Now Mrs. Cliff could not restrain herself. "What is the matter with you, Willy? Have you gone crazy?" she exclaimed. "Of course I am going to my own house, and I do not want any carriage. Did I ever need a carriage to take me such a short distance as that? Tell the man to bring some one with him to carry the trunks upstairs, and then come on."

"Let me carry your bag," said Willy, as the two walked away from the station at a much greater pace, it may be remarked, than Willy was accustomed to walk.

"No, you shall not carry my bag," said Mrs. Cliff, and not another word did she speak until she had entered the hallway of her home. Then, closing the door behind her, and without looking around at any of the dear objects for a sight of which she had so long been yearning, she turned to her companion.

"Willy," she cried, "what does this mean? Why do you treat me in this way when I come home after having been away so long, and having suffered so much? Why do you greet me as if you took me for a tax collector? Why do you stand there like a — a horrible clam?"

Willy hesitated. She looked up and she looked down.

"Things are so altered," she said, "and I didn't know —"

"Well, know now," said Mrs. Cliff, as she held out her arms. In a moment the two women were clasped in a tight embrace, kissing and sobbing.

"How should I know?" said poor Willy, as she was wiping her eyes. "Chills went down me as I stood on that platform, wondering what sort of a grand lady you would look like when you got out of the car, with two servant women, most likely, and perhaps a butler, and trying to think what I should say."

Mrs. Cliff laughed. "You were born addle-pated, and you can't help it. Now, let us go through this house without wasting a minute!" Willy gazed at her in amazement.

"You're just the same as you always was!" she cried.

"Indeed I am!" said Mrs. Cliff. "Did you clean this dining-room yourself, Willy? It looks as spick and span as if I had just left it."

"Indeed it does," was the proud reply, "and you couldn't find a speck of dust from the ceiling to the floor!"

When Mrs. Cliff had been upstairs and downstairs, and in the front yard, the side yard, and the back yard, and when her happy eyes had rested upon all her dear possessions, she went into the kitchen.

"Now, Willy," she said, "let us go to work and get supper, for I must say I am hungry."

At this Willy Croup turned pale, her chin dropped, a horrible suspicion took possession of her. Could it be possible that it was all a mistake, or that something dreadful had happened; that the riches which everybody had been talking about had never existed, or had disappeared? She might want to go to her old home; she might want to see her goods and chattels, but that she should want to help get supper — that was incomprehensible! At that moment the world looked very black to Willy. If Mrs. Cliff had gone into the parlor, and had sat down in the best rocking-chair to rest herself, and had said to her, "Please get supper as soon as you can," Willy would have believed in everything, but now — !

The grinding of heavy wheels was heard in front of the house, and Willy turned quickly and looked out of the window. There was a wagon containing seven enormous trunks! Since the days when Plainton was a little hamlet, up to the present time, when it contained a hotel, a bank, a lyceum, and a weekly paper, no one had ever arrived within its limits with seven such trunks. Instantly the blackness disappeared from before the mind of Willy Croup.

"Now, you tell the men where to carry them," she cried, "and I will get the supper in no time! Betty Handshall stayed here until this morning, but she went away after dinner, for she was afraid if she stayed she would be in the way, not knowing how much help you would bring with you."

"I wonder if they are all crack-brained," thought Mrs. Cliff, as she went to the front door to attend to her baggage.

That evening nearly all Plainton came to see Mrs. Cliff. No matter how she returned, — as a purse-proud bondholder, as a lady of elegant wealth with her attendants, as an old friend suddenly grown jolly and prosperous, — it would be all right for her neighbors to go in and see her in the evening. There they might suit themselves to her new deportment whatever it might be, and there would be no danger of any of them getting into false positions, which would have been very likely indeed if they had gone to meet her at the station.

Her return to her own house gave her real friends a great deal of satisfaction, for some of them had feared she would not go there. It would have been difficult for them to know how to greet Mrs. Cliff at a hotel, even such an unpretentious one as that of Plainton. All these friends found her the same warm-hearted, cordial

woman that she had ever been. In fact, if there was
any change at all in her, she was more cordial than
they had yet known her. As in the case of Willy
Croup, a cloud had risen before her. She had been
beset by the sudden fear that her money already threatened to come between her and her old friends. "Not if
I can help it!" said Mrs. Cliff to herself, as fervently
as if she had been vowing a vow to seek the Holy Grail;
and she did help it. The good people forgot what they
had expected to think about her, and only remembered
what they had always thought of her. No matter what
had happened, she was the same.

But what had happened, and how it had happened,
and all about it, up and down, to the right and the
left, above and below, everybody wanted to know, and
Mrs. Cliff, with sparkling eyes, was only too glad to
tell them. She had been obliged to be so reserved
when she had come home before, that she was all the
more eager to be communicative now; and it was past
midnight before the first of that eager and delighted
company thought of going home.

There was one question, however, which Mrs. Cliff
successfully evaded, and that was — the amount of her
wealth. She would not give even an approximate idea
of the value of her share of the golden treasure. It
was very soon plain to everybody that Mrs. Cliff was
the same woman she used to be in regard to keeping
to herself that which she did not wish to tell to others,
and so everybody went away with imagination absolutely unfettered.

CHAPTER III

MISS NANCY SHOTT

THE next morning Mrs. Cliff sat alone in her parlor with her mind earnestly fixed upon her own circumstances. Out in the kitchen, Willy Croup was dashing about like a domestic fanatic, eager to get the morning's work done and everything put in order, that she might go upstairs with Mrs. Cliff, and witness the opening of those wonderful trunks.

She was a happy woman, for she had a new dish-pan, which Mrs. Cliff had authorized her to buy that very morning, the holes in the bottom of the old one having been mended so often that she and Mrs. Cliff both believed that it would be very well to get a new one and rid themselves of further trouble.

Willy also had had the proud satisfaction of stopping at the carpenter shop on her way to buy the dish-pan, and order him to come and do whatever was necessary to the back-kitchen door. Sometimes it had been the hinges and sometimes it had been the lock which had been out of order on that door for at least a year, and although they had been tinkering here and tinkering there, the door had never worked properly; and now Mrs. Cliff had said that it must be put in perfect order even if a new door and a new frame were required, and without any regard to what it might cost. This to Willy was the dawn of a new era, and the thought of it excited her like wine.

Mrs. Cliff's mind was not excited; it was disquieted. She had been thinking of her investments and of her deposits, all of which had been made under wise advice, and it had suddenly occurred to her to calculate how much richer she was to-day than she had been yesterday. When she appreciated the fact that the interest on her invested property had increased her wealth, since the previous morning, by some hundreds of dollars, it frightened her. She felt as if an irresistible flood of opulence was flowing in upon her, and she shuddered to think of the responsibility of directing it into its proper courses, and so preventing it from overwhelming her and sweeping her away.

To-morrow there would be several hundred dollars more, and the next day more, and so on always, and what was she doing, or what had she planned to do, to give proper direction to these tidal waves of wealth? She had bought a new dish-pan and ordered a door repaired!

To be sure, it was very soon to begin to think of the expenditure of her income, but it was a question which could not be postponed. The importance of it was increasing all the time. Every five minutes she was two dollars richer.

For a moment she wished herself back in Paris or New York. There she might open some flood-gate which would give instant relief from the pressure of her affluence and allow her time to think; but what could she do in Plainton? At least, how should she begin to do anything?

c

She got up and walked about the room. She was becoming annoyed, and even a little angry. She resented this intrusion of her wealth upon her. She wanted to rest quietly for a time, tò enjoy her home and friends, and not be obliged to think of anything which it was incumbent upon her to do. From the bottom of her heart she wished that her possessions had all been solid gold, or in some form in which they could not increase, expand, or change in any way until she gave them leave. Then she would live for a week or two, as she used to live, without thought of increment or responsibilities, until she was ready to begin the life of a rich woman and to set in motion the currents of her exuberant income.

But she could not change the state of affairs. The system of interest had been set in motion, and her income was flowing in upon her hour by hour, day by day, steadily and irresistibly, and her mind could not be at rest until she had done something — at least, planned something — which would not only prevent her from being overwhelmed and utterly discouraged, but which would enable her to float proudly, on this grand current of absolute power, over the material interests of the world.

Mrs. Cliff was a woman of good sense. No matter how much money she might possess, she would have considered herself its unworthy possessor if she should spend any of it without proper value received. She might spend it foolishly, but she wanted the worth of her money. She would consider it a silly thing, for instance, to pay a thousand dollars for an India shawl, because few people wore India shawls, and she did not care for them; but if she had done so, she would have been greatly mortified if she found that she had paid too much, and that she might have bought as good a shawl for seven hundred and fifty dollars.

Since she had been in that room and thinking about these things, enough interest had come to her to enable her to buy a good silver watch for some deserving person. Now, who was there to whom she could give a plain silver watch? Willy Croup would be glad to have it, but then it would be better to wait a few hours and give her a gold one.

Now it was that Willy came into the room with a disappointed expression upon her countenance.

"I was just coming in to tell you," she said, "that I was ready now to go up and help you open the trunks, but here comes that horrid Miss Shott, and dear knows how long she will stay!"

Nancy Shott was the leading spinster of Plainton. In companies where there were married ladies she was sometimes obliged to take a second place, but never among maidens, old or young. There were very few subjects upon which Miss Shott had not an opinion; and whatever this opinion might be, she considered it her first duty in life to express it. As a rule, the expression was more agreeable to her than to others.

When Mrs. Cliff heard that Miss Shott was approaching, she instantly forgot her wealth and all her perplexities concerning it. Miss Shott had not called upon her the previous evening, but she had not expected her, nor did she expect her now.

On her previous visit to Plainton, Mrs. Cliff had been shamefully insulted by Miss Shott, who had accused her of extravagance, and, by implication, of dishonesty, and in return, the indignant widow had opened upon her such a volley of justifiable retaliation that Miss Shott, in great wrath, had retired from the house, followed, figuratively, by a small coin which she had brought as a present and which had been hurled after her.

But Mrs. Cliff knew that her acrimonious neighbor could never be depended upon to do anything which might be expected of her, and she was not quite so much surprised as she was annoyed. Of course, she had known she must meet Nancy Shott, and she had intended to do nothing which would recall to the mind of any one that she remembered the disagreeable incident referred to, but she had not expected that the meeting would be in private.

She knew that Nancy would do something decidedly unpleasant. If she had stayed away because she wanted a chance to re-open the previous quarrel, that would be bad enough; but if she had determined to drop all resentment and had come prepared to offer honey and sugar, and thus try to make a rich friend out of one she had considered as a poor enemy, that would be still more disagreeable. But by the time the visitor had entered the parlor, Mrs. Cliff had made up her mind to meet her as if nothing unpleasant had ever happened between them, and then to await the course of events. She was not at all pleased with the visit, but, notwithstanding this, she had great curiosity to know what Miss Shott had to say about the change in her circumstances.

Nancy Shott was different from other people. She was capable of drawing the most astounding inferences and of coming to the most soul-irritating conclusions, even on subjects which could not be otherwise than pleasant to ordinary people.

"How do you do?" said Miss Shott, offering her hand. "I am glad to see you back, Mrs. Cliff."

Mrs. Cliff replied that she was quite well and was glad to be back.

"You are not looking as hale as you did," said the visitor, as she seated herself; "you must have lost a good many pounds, but that was to be expected. From what I have heard, South America must be about as unhealthy a place as any part of the world, and then on top of that, living in Paris with water to drink which, I am told, is enough to make anybody sick to look at it, is bound to have some sort of an effect upon a person."

Mrs. Cliff smiled. She was used to this sort of talk from Nancy Shott. "I am better than I was two years ago," she said, "and the last time I was weighed I found that I had gained seven pounds."

"Well, there is no accounting for that," said her visitor, "except as we grow old we are bound to show

it, and sometimes aging looks like bad health, and as
to fat, that often comes as years go on, though as far as
I am concerned, I think it is a great misfortune to have
more to carry, as you get less and less able to carry it."

Mrs. Cliff might have said that that sort of thing
would not be likely to trouble Miss Shott, whose scant-
ily furnished frame was sure to become thinner and
thinner as she became older and weaker, but she merely
smiled and waited to hear what would come next.

"I do not want to worry you," said Miss Shott; "but
several people that were here last night said you was
not looking as they had hoped to see you look, and I
will just say to you, if it is anything connected with
your appetite, with a feeling of goneness in the mornings, you ought to buy a quassia cup and drink the
full of it at least three times a day."

Miss Shott knew that Mrs. Cliff absolutely detested
the taste of quassia. Mrs. Cliff was not annoyed. She
hoped that her visitor would soon get through with
these prefatory remarks and begin to take the stand,
whatever it might be, which she had come there that
morning to take.

"There has been sickness here since you last left,"
said Miss Shott, "and it has-been where it was least
to be expected, too. Barney Thompson's little boy,
the second son, has had the diphtheria, and where he
got it nobody knows, for it was vacation time, and he
did not go to school, and there was no other diphtheria
anywhere in all this town, and yet he had it and had it
bad."

"He did not die?" said Mrs. Cliff.

"Oh no, he got over it, and perhaps it was a bad case and perhaps it was not; but you may be sure I did not go near it, for I considered it my duty to keep away, and I did keep away, but the trouble is — "

"And did none of the other children take it?" asked Mrs. Cliff.

"No, they didn't. But the trouble is, that when diphtheria or anything like it comes up suddenly like this, without any reason that nobody can see, it is just as likely to come up again without any reason, and I am expecting to hear every day of another of them Thompson children being stricken down; and I was very sorry indeed, Mrs. Cliff, to see, this very morning, Willy Croup coming out of Barney Thompson's house and to hear from her afterwards that she had been to order him to come here to put up a new kitchen door, which I do not suppose is absolutely needed, and even if it is, I am sure I would wait a good while before I would have Barney Thompson come into my house with diphtheria, that very minute, perhaps, in the throats of one or maybe more of his children; but of course, if people choose to trifle with their own lives, it is their own business."

"It was not real diphtheria," said Willy Croup, who happened to be passing the open door at this moment; "it was only a bad sore throat, and the child was well in two days."

"I suppose, of course," said Miss Shott, "that if the disease did get into this house, Willy Croup would be the first to take it, because she is such a spongy person that she takes almost anything that is in the air and is not wholesome; but then you would not want to lose her, and after a funeral in the house, no matter whose it may be, things is always gloomy for a long time afterwards, and nobody can feel easy if it was a catchin' disease that the person died of."

Mrs. Cliff was naturally desirous to hear all the domestic news of the town, but she would have liked to have had something pleasant thrown in among the gloomy tidings of which Miss Shott had made herself the bearer, and so she made a little effort to turn the conversation.

"I shall be glad to go about and see my old friends and neighbors," she said, "for I am interested in everything which has happened to them; but I suppose it will be some days before I can settle down and feel ready to go on in the old way. It seems to me as if I had been on the move ever since I left here, although, of course, I was not travelling all the time."

"I suppose nobody has told you," said Miss Shott, "that Edward Darley has ploughed up that little pasture of his and planted it with young apple trees. Now, it does seem to me that for a man like Edward Darley, who comes of a consumptive family, and who has been coughin' regularly, to my certain knowledge, for more than a year, to go and plant apple trees, which he can't expect to live to see bear fruit, is nothing more or less than a wicked waste of money, time, and labor. I suppose if I was to go and tell him so he would not like that, but I do not know as I ought to consider it. There are people in this world who'll never know anything if they're not told!"

Five other topics of the town, each of a doleful nature and each indicating an evident depravity in a citizen of Plainton, were related by Miss Shott, and then she arose to go.

"I hope you'll remember what I told you about Thompson's children," she said, as she walked to the front door, "and if I was you, I'd have that kitchen fumigated after he has put the door in!"

"There now!" said Miss Shott to herself, as she proudly walked down the street. "The Widow Cliff can't say I've done any toadying; and, no matter what she's got, and what she hasn't got, she can't say to herself that I consider her any better able to give me twenty-five cents than she was when she was here before; or that it makes any difference to me whether she has much or little!"

CHAPTER IV

A LAUNCH INTO A NEW LIFE

It required the greater part of two days for Mrs. Cliff and Willy to open the seven trunks, and properly display and dispose of the various articles and goods, astonishing in their variety and beauty, and absolutely amazing when the difference between the price paid for them and what they would have cost in New York was considered.

During these fascinating operations it so happened that at one time or another nearly all of Mrs. Cliff's female friends dropped in, and all were wonderfully impressed by what they saw and what they heard; but although ¯Miss Shott did not come there during the grand opening, it was not long before she knew the price and something of the general appearance of nearly everything that Mrs. Cliff had brought with her.

Among the contents of the trunks were a great many presents for Mrs. Cliff's friends, and whenever Miss Shott heard of one of these gifts, she made a remark to the effect that she had not a doubt in the world that the Widow Cliff knew better than to bring her a present, for she would not want the thing, whatever it was, whether a glass pitcher or a pin-cushion, flung back at her after the fashion that she had set herself at a time when everybody was trying their best to be kind to her.

It was clearly a fact, that through the influence of the seven trunks Mrs. Cliff was becoming a very popular woman, and Miss Shott did not like it at all. She had never had any faith — at least she said so — in those lumps of gold found in a hole in some part of the world that nobody had ever heard of; and had not hesitated to say that fortunes founded on such wild-goose stories as these should not even be considered by people of good sense who worked for their living, or had incomes which they could depend on. But the dress goods, the

ribbons, the gloves, the little clocks, the shoes, the par-
asols, the breast-pins, the portfolios of pictures, the jewelry, the rugs and table covers, and hundreds of other
beautiful and foreign things, were a substantial evi-
dence that Mrs. Cliff's money was not all moonshine.

It was very pleasant for Mrs. Cliff to bring out her
treasures to display them to her enthusiastic friends,
and to arrange them in her house, and to behold the
rapturous delight of Willy Croup from early morn until
bed-time.

But the seven empty trunks had been carried up into
the garret, and now Mrs. Cliff set her mind to the solu-
tion of the question — how was she to begin her new
life in her old home? It must be a new life, for to
live as she had lived even in the days of her highest
prosperity during her husband's life would be absurd
and even wicked. With such an income she must endeavor as far as was possible to her to live in a manner
worthy of it; but one thing she was determined upon —
she would not alienate her friends by climbing to the
top of her money and looking down upon them. None
of them knew how high she would be if she were to
perch herself on the very top of that money, but even
if she climbed up a little way, they might still feel that
they were very small in her sight.

No, the money should always be kept in the background. It might be as high as the sky and as glorious
as a sunset, but she would be on the ground with the
people of Plainton, and as far as was possible, they
should all enjoy the fine weather together.

She could not repress a feeling of pride, for she would be looked upon as one of the principal persons — if not the principal person — in Plainton; but she could not believe that any real friend could possibly object to that.

If her husband had lived and prospered, it was probable he would have been the principal man in Plainton, the minister always excepted; but now there was no reason whatever why any one should object to her being a principal personage, and, in this case, she could not see why the minister's wife should be excepted.

But Plainton was to be her home; the Plainton people were to be her friends. How should she set about using her money in such a way that she should not be driven forth to some large city to live as ordinary wealthy people live, in a fashion to which she was utterly unsuited, and which possessed for her no attractions whatever?

Of course, she had early determined to devote a large sum to charitable purposes, for she would have thought herself a very unworthy woman if her wealth had not benefited others than herself, but this was an easy matter to attend to. The amount she had set aside for charity was not permanently invested, and, through the advice of Mr. Perley, there would be no difficulty in devoting this to suitable objects. Already she had confidentially spoken to her pastor on the subject, and had found him enthusiastic in his desire to help her in every possible way in her benevolent purposes. But who was there who could help her in regard to her-

self? Who was there who could tell her how she
ought to live so as to gain all the good that her money
should give her, and yet not lose that which was to her
the highest object of material existence,—a happy and
prosperous life among her old friends in her native
town?

Should she choose to elevate herself in the social
circle by living as ordinary very rich people live, she
could not hope to elevate her friends in that way,
although she would be glad enough to do it in many
cases, and there would be a gap between them which
would surely grow wider and wider; and yet here was
this money coming in upon her in a steady stream day
by day, and how was she going to make herself happier
with it?

She must do that, or, she believed, it would be her
duty to hand it over to somebody else who was better
adapted by nature to use it.

"If I did not take so much pleasure in things which
cost so little and which are so easy for me to buy,"
said poor Mrs. Cliff to herself, "or if I did not have
so much money, I am sure I should get on a great deal
better."

Mrs. Cliff's belief that she must not long delay in
selecting some sort of station in life, and endeavoring
to live up to it, was soon strengthened by Willy Croup.
During the time of the trunk opening, and for some
days afterwards, when all her leisure hours were occupied with the contemplation and consideration of her
own presents, Willy had been perfectly contented to let

things go on in the old way, or any way, but now the incongruity of Mrs. Cliff's present mode of living, and the probable amount of her fortune, began to impress itself upon her.

"It does seem to me," said she, "that it's a sin and a shame that you should be goin' about this house just as you used to do, helpin' me upstairs and downstairs, as if you couldn't afford to hire nobody. You ought to have a girl, and a good one, and for the matter of that, you might have two of 'em, I suppose. And even if it wasn't too much for you to be workin' about when there's no necessity for it, the people are beginnin' to talk, and that ought to be stopped."

"What are they talking about?" asked Mrs. Cliff.

"Well, it's not everybody that's talkin'," returned Willy, "and I guess that them that does gets their opinions from one quarter, but I've heard people say that it's pretty plain that all you got out of that gold mine you spent in buyin' the things you brought home in your trunks; for if you didn't, you wouldn't be livin' like this, helpin' to do your own housework and cookin'."

In consequence of this conversation, a servant-of-all-work was employed; for Mrs. Cliff did not know what she would do with two women until she had made a change in her household arrangements; and with this as a beginning, our good widow determined to start out on her career as a rich woman who intended to enjoy herself in the fashion she liked best.

She sent for Mr. Thompson, the carpenter, and con-

sulted with him in regard to the proposed additions to
her house, but when she had talked for a time, she
became disheartened. She found that it would be
necessary to dig a new cellar close to her present prem-
ises; that there would be stones, and gravel, and lime,
and sand, and carts and horses, and men, and dirt; and
that it would be some months before all the hammering,
and the sawing, and the planing, and the plastering, and
tinwork could be finished, and all this would be going
on under her eye, and close to her ears during those
first months in which she had proposed to be so happy
in her home. She could not bear to give the word to
dig, and pound, and saw. It was not like building a
new house, for that would not be near her, and the hub-
bub of its construction would not annoy her.

So she determined she would not begin a new dining-
room at present. She would wait a little while until
she had had some good of her house as it was, and then
she would feel better satisfied to live in the midst of
pounding, banging, and all-pervading dust; but she
would do something. She would have the fence which
separated the sidewalk from her front yard newly
painted. She had long wanted to have that done, but
had not been able to afford it.

But when Mr. Thompson went to look at the fence,
he told her that it would be really a waste of money
to paint it, for in many places it was old and decayed,
and it would be much wiser to put up a new one and
paint that.

Again Mrs. Cliff hesitated. If that fence had to be

taken down, and the posts dug up, and new posts put in, and the flower-bed which ran along the inside of it destroyed, it would be just as well to wait until the other work began and have it all done at once; so she told Mr. Thompson he need not send a painter, for she would make the old fence do for a while.

Mrs. Cliff sighed a little as the carpenter walked away, but there were other things to do. There was the pasture lot at the rear of her garden, and she could have a cow, and there was the little barn, and she could have a horse. The idea of the horse pleased her more than anything she had yet thought of in connection with her wealth.

In her days of prosperity it had been her greatest pleasure to drive in her phaeton with her good brown horse, generally with Willy Croup by her side; to stop at shops or to make calls upon friends, and to make those little excursions into the surrounding country in which she and Willy both delighted. They had sometimes gone a long distance and had taken their dinner with them, and Willy was really very good in unharnessing the horse and watering him at a brook, and in giving him some oats.

To return to these old joys was a delightful prospect, and Mrs. Cliff made inquiries about her horse, which had been sold in the town; but he was gone. He had been sold to a drover, and his whereabouts no one knew.

So she went to Mr. Williams, the keeper of the hotel, who knew more about horses than anybody else, and consulted with him on the subject of a new steed. She told him just what she wanted: a gentle horse which she could drive herself, and one which Willy could hold when she went into a house or a shop.

Now, it so happened that Mr. Williams had just such a horse, and when Mrs. Cliff had seen it, and when Willy had come up to look at it, and when the matter had been talked about in all the aspects in which it presented itself to Mrs. Cliff's mind, she bought the animal, and it was taken to her stable, where Andrew Marks, a neighbor, was engaged to take care of it.

The next morning Mrs. Cliff and Willy took a drive a little way out of town, and they both agreed that this horse, which was gray, was a great deal better traveller than the old brown, and a much handsomer animal; but both of them also agreed that they did not believe that they would ever learn to love him as they had their old horse.

Still he was very easy to drive, and he went along so pleasantly, without needing the whip in the least, that Mrs. Cliff said to herself, that for the first time since her return she really felt herself a rich woman.

"If everything," she thought, "should come to me as this horse came to me, how delightful my life would be! When I wanted him, I found him. I did not have to trouble myself in the least about the price; I simply paid it, and ordered him sent home. Now, that sort of thing is what makes a person feel truly rich."

When they had gone far enough, and had reached a wide place in the road, Mrs. Cliff turned and started back to Plainton. But now the horse began to be a

D

different kind of a horse. With his face towards his home, he set out to trot as fast as he could, and when Mrs. Cliff, not liking such a rapid pace, endeavored to pull him in, she found it very hard to do, and when she began to saw his mouth, thinking that would restrain his ardor, he ambled and capered, and Mrs. Cliff was obliged to let him resume his rapid gait.

He was certainly a very hard-mouthed horse, going home, and Mrs. Cliff's arms ached, and Willy Croup's heart quaked, long before they reached the town. When they reached Plainton, Mrs. Cliff began to be afraid that he would gallop through the streets, and she told Willy that if he did, she must not scream, but must sit quietly, and she would endeavor to steer him clear of the vehicles and people.

But although he did not gallop, the ardent gray seemed to travel faster after he entered the town, and Mrs. Cliff, who was getting very red in the face from her steady tugging at the reins, thought it wise not to attempt to go home, but to let her horse go straight to the hotel stables where he had lived.

When Mrs. Cliff had declared to Mr. Williams that that horse would never suit her, that she would not be willing to drive it, and would not even think of going into a house and leaving Willy Croup to hold him, he was very much surprised, and said that he had not a gentler horse in his stable, and he did not believe there was one in the town.

"All horses," said he, "want to go home, especially at dinner-time."

"But the old brown did not," urged Mrs. Cliff. "That is the sort of horse I want."

"Some very old beast might please you better," said he; "but really, Mrs. Cliff, that is not the sort of horse you should have. He would die or break down in a little while, and then you would have to get another. What you should do is to have a good horse and a driver. You might get a two-seated carriage, either open or closed, and go anywhere and everywhere, and never think of the horse."

That was not the thing she longed for; that would not bring back the happy days when she drove the brown through the verdant lanes. If she must have a driver, she might as well hire a cab and be driven about. But she told Mr. Williams to get her a suitable vehicle, and she would have Andrew Marks to drive her; and she and Willy Croup walked sadly home.

As to the cow, she succeeded better. She bought a fairly good one, and Willy undertook to milk her and to make butter.

"Now, what have I done so far?" said Mrs. Cliff, on the evening of the day when the cow came home. "I have a woman to cook, I have a new kitchen door, and I have a cow! I do not count the horse and the wagon, for if I do not drive, myself, I shall not feel that they are mine in the way that I want them to be."

CHAPTER V

A FUR-TRIMMED OVERCOAT AND A SILK HAT

MRS. CLIFF now began to try very hard to live as she ought to live, without pretensions or snobbery, but in a style becoming, in some degree, her great fortune.

There was one thing she determined to do immediately, and that was, to begin a series of hospitalities,—and it made her feel proud to think that she could do this and do it handsomely, and yet do it in the old home where everybody knew she had for years been obliged to practise the strictest economy.

She gave a dinner to which she invited her most select friends. Mr. and Mrs. Perley were there, and the Misses Thorpedyke, two maiden ladies who constituted the family of the highest social pretension of Plainton. There were other people who were richer, but Miss Eleanor Thorpedyke, now a lady of nearly seventy, and her sister Barbara, some ten years younger, belonged to the very best family in that part of the country, and were truly the aristocrats of the place.

But they had always been very friendly with Mrs. Cliff, and they were glad to come to her dinner. The other guests were all good people, and a dinner-party of more distinction could not have been collected in that town.

But this dinner did not go off altogether smoothly. If the people had come merely to eat, they must have been abundantly satisfied, for everything was of the very best and well cooked, Mrs. Cliff and Willy having seen to that; but there were certain roughnesses and hitches in the management of the dinner which disturbed Mrs. Cliff. In her travels and at the hotels where she had lived she had seen a great deal of good service, and she knew what it was.

Willy, who, being a relative, should really have come to the table, had decidedly declined to do so, and had taken upon herself the principal part of the waiting, assisted by the general servant and a small girl who had been called in. But the dining-room was very small, some of the chairs were but a little distance from the wall, and it was evident that Willy had not a true appreciation of the fact that in recent years she had grown considerably rounder and plumper than she used to be; and it made Mrs. Cliff's blood run cold to see how she bumped the back of Mr. Perley's chair, as she thrust herself between it and the wall.

The small girl had to be told almost everything that she must do, and the general servant, who did not like to wait on table, only came in when she was called and left immediately when she had done what she had been called for.

When the guests had gone, Mrs. Cliff declared to Willy that that was the last large dinner she would give in that house. "It was not a dinner which a woman of my means should offer to her friends." Willy was amazed.

"I don't see how it could have been better," said she,

"unless you had champagne, and I know Mr. Perley wouldn't have liked that. Everything on the table was just as good as it could be."

But Mrs. Cliff shook her head. She knew that she had attempted something for which her present resources were insufficient. After this she invited people to dinner once or twice a week, but the company was always very small and suited to the resources of the house.

"I will go on this way for a while," thought the good lady, "and after a time I will begin to spread out and do things in a different style."

Several times she drove over to Harrington, a large town some five miles away, which contained a furniture factory, and there she purchased many articles which would be suitable for the house, always securing the best things for her purposes, but frequently regretting that certain beautiful and imposing pieces of furniture were entirely unsuited to the capacity of her rooms and hallways. But when her dining-room should be finished, and the room above it, she would have better opportunity of gratifying her taste for handsome wood in imposing designs. Then it might be that Harrington would not be able to give her anything good enough.

Her daily mail was now much larger than it ever had been before. Business people sent her cards and circulars, and every now and then she received letters calling her attention to charities or pressing personal needs of the writers, but there were not very many of these; for although it was generally known that Mrs.

Cliff had come into a fortune, her manner of living seemed also a matter of public knowledge. Even the begging letters were couched in very moderate terms; but all these Mrs. Cliff took to Mr. Perley, and, by his advice, she paid attention to but very few of them.

Day by day Mrs. Cliff endeavored to so shape and direct her fortunes that they might make her happy in the only ways in which she could be happy, but her efforts to do so did not always gain for her the approval of her fellow townspeople. There were some who thought that a woman who professed to have command of money should do a good many things which Mrs. Cliff did not do, and there were others who did not hesitate to assert that a woman who lived as Mrs. Cliff should not do a great many things which she did do, among which things some people included the keeping of a horse and carriage. It was conceded, of course, that all this was Mrs. Cliff's own business. She had paid the money she had borrowed to go to South America; she had been very kind to some of the poor people of the town, and it was thought by some had been foolishly munificent to old Mrs. Bradley, who, from being a very poor person threatened with the loss of her home, was now an independent householder, and enjoyed an annuity sufficient to support her.

More than that, Mrs. Cliff had been very generous in regard to the church music. It was not known exactly how much she had given towards this object, but there were those who said that she must have given her means a considerable strain when she made her contribution.   That is, if the things were to be done which Mr. Perley talked about.

When Mrs. Cliff heard what had been said upon this subject,—and Willy Croup was generally very well able to keep her informed in regard to what the people of the town said about her,—she thought that the gossips would have been a good deal astonished if they had known how much she had really given to the church, and that they would have been absolutely amazed if they knew how much Mr. Perley had received for general charities. And then she thought, with a tinge of sadness, how very much surprised Mr. Perley would have been if he had known how much more she was able to give away without feeling its loss.

Weeks passed on, the leaves turned red and yellow upon the trees, the evenings and mornings grew colder and colder, and Mrs. Cliff did everything she could towards the accomplishment of what now appeared to her in the light of a great duty in her life, — the proper expenditure of her income and appropriation of her great fortune.

Her labors were not becoming more cheerful.   Day after day she said to herself that she was not doing what she ought to do, and that it was full time that she should begin to do something better, but what that better thing was she could not make up her mind.   Even the improvements she contemplated were, after all, such mere trifles.

It was a very cold morning in October when Mrs. Cliff went into her parlor and said to Willy that there was one thing she could do,—she could have a rousing, comfortable fire without thinking whether wood was five, ten, or twenty dollars per cord. When Willy found that Mrs. Cliff wanted to make herself comfortable before a fine blazing fire, she seemed in doubt.

"I don't know about the safety of it," she said. "That chimney's in a pretty bad condition; the masons told us so years ago, and nothin' has ever been done to it! There have been fires in it, but they have been little ones; and if I was you, I wouldn't have too large a blaze in that fireplace until the chimney has been made all right!"

Mrs. Cliff was annoyed. "Well then, Willy, I wish you would go for the mason immediately, and tell him to come here and repair the chimney. It's perfectly ridiculous that I can't have a fire in my own parlor when I am able to have a chimney as high and as big as Bunker Hill Monument if I wanted it!"

Willy Croup smiled. She did not believe that Mrs. Cliff really knew how much such a chimney would cost, but she said, "You have got to remember, you know, that we can't have the Cuthberts here to dinner tomorrow if the masons come to work at that chimney. Ten to one they will have to take the most part of it down, and we shall be in a general mess here for a week."

Mrs. Cliff sat down with a sigh. "You need not mind to have the wood brought in," she said; "just give me a few sticks and some kindling, so that I can give things a little air of cheerfulness."

As she sat before the gently blazing little fire, Mrs. Cliff felt that things needed an air of cheerfulness. She had that morning been making calculations, and, notwithstanding all she had bought, all she had done, and even including with the most generous margin all she had planned to do, her income was gaining upon her in a most discouraging way.

"I am not fit for it," she said to herself. "I don't know how to live as I want to live, and I won't live as I don't want to live. The whole business is too big for me. I don't know how to manage it. I ought to give up my means to somebody who knows how to use them, and stay here myself with just enough money to make me happy."

For the fortieth time she considered the question of laying all her troubles before Mr. Perley, but she knew her pastor. The great mass of her fortune would quickly be swallowed up in some grand missionary enterprise; and this would not suit Mrs. Cliff. No matter how much she was discouraged, no matter how difficult it was to see her way before her, no matter how great a load she felt her wealth to be, there was always before her a glimmering sense of grand possibilities. What they were she could not now see or understand, but she would not willingly give them up.

She was an elderly woman, but she came of a long-lived family, all of whom had lived in good health until the end of their days, and if there was any grand, golden felicity which was possible to her, she

THE GENTLEMAN RAISED HIS HAT AND ASKED IF
MRS. CLIFF LIVED THERE

felt that there was reason to believe she would live long to enjoy it when she wanted it.

One morning as Mrs. Cliff sat thinking over these things, there was a knock at the front door, and, of course, Willy Croup ran to open it. No matter where she was, or no matter what she was doing, Willy always went to the door if she could, because she had so great a desire to know who was there.

This time it was a gentleman, a very fine gentleman, with a high silk hat and a handsome overcoat trimmed with fur — fur on the collar, fur on the sleeves, and fur down the front. Willy had never seen such a coat. It was October and it was cool, but there was no man in Plainton who would have worn such a coat as that so early in the season even if he had one.

The gentleman had dark eyes and a very large mustache, and he carried a cane and wore rather bright tan-colored gloves. All these things Willy observed in an instant, for she was very quick in taking notice of people's clothes and general appearance.

The gentleman raised his hat and asked if Mrs. Cliff lived there. Now Willy thought he must be an extraordinary fine gentleman, for how should he know that she was not a servant, and in those parts gentlemen did not generally raise their hats to girls who opened front doors.

The gentleman was admitted and was ushered into the parlor, where sat Mrs. Cliff. She was a little surprised at the sight of this visitor, who came in with his hat on, but who took it off and made her a low bow as soon as he saw her. But she thought she appreciated the situation, and she hardened her heart.

A strange man, so finely dressed, and with such manners, must have come for money, and Mrs. Cliff had already learned to harden her heart towards strangers who solicited. But the hardness of her heart utterly disappeared in her amazement when this gentleman, having pulled off his right glove, advanced toward her, holding out his hand.

"You don't remember me, Mrs. Cliff?" he said in a loud, clear voice. "No wonder, for I am a good deal changed, but it is not the same with you. You are the same as ever — I declare you are!"

Mrs. Cliff took the proffered hand, and looked into the face of the speaker. There was something there which seemed familiar, but she had never known such a fine gentleman as this. She thought over the people whom she had seen in France and in California, but she could not recollect this face.

"It's a mean thing to be puzzlin' you, Mrs. Cliff," said the stranger, with a cheery smile. "I'm George Burke, seaman on the *Castor*, where I saw more of you, Mrs. Cliff, than I've ever seen since; for though we have both been a good deal jumbled up since, we haven't been jumbled up together, so I don't wonder if you don't remember me, especially as I didn't wear clothes like these on the *Castor*. Not by any means, Mrs. Cliff!"

"I remember you," she said, and she shook his hand

warmly. "I remember you, and you had a mate named Edward Shirley."

"Yes, indeed!" said Mr. Burke, "and he's all right, and I'm all right, and how are you?"

The overcoat with the fur trimmings came off, and, with the hat, the cane, and the gloves, was laid upon a chair, and Burke and Mrs. Cliff sat down to talk over old times and old friends.

CHAPTER VI

A TEMPERANCE LARK

As Mrs. Cliff sat and talked with George Burke, she forgot the calculations she had been making, she forgot her perplexities and her anxieties concerning the rapid inroads which her income was making upon her ability to dispose of it, in the recollection of the good-fellowships which the presence of her companion recalled.

But Mr. Burke could give her no recent news of Captain Horn and Edna, she having heard from them later than he had; and the only one of the people of the *Castor* of whom he could tell her was Edward Shirley, who had gone into business.

He had bought a share in a shipyard, and, as he was a man who had a great idea about the lines of a vessel, and all that sort of thing, he had determined to put his money into that business. He was a long-headed fellow, and Burke had no doubt but that he would soon hear of some fine craft coming from the yard of his old shipmate.

"But how about yourself, Mr. Burke? I want to know what has happened to you, and what you intend doing, and how you chanced to be coming this way."

"Oh, I will tell you everything that has happened to me," said Mr. Burke, "and it won't take long; but first let me ask you something, Mrs. Cliff?" and as he spoke he quietly rose and shut the parlor door.

"Now then," said he, as he seated himself, "we have all been in the same box, or, I should say, in the same boxes of different kinds, and although I may not have the right to call myself a friend, I am just as friendly to you as if I was, and feel as if people who have been through what we have ought to stand by each other even after they've got through their hardest rubs.

"Now, Mrs. Cliff, has anything happened to you? Have you had any set-backs? I know that this is a mighty queer world, and that even the richest people can often come down with a sudden thump just as if they had slipped on the ice."

Mrs. Cliff smiled. "Nothing has happened to me," she said. "I have had no set-backs, and I am just as rich to-day,— I should say a great deal richer, than I was on the day when Captain Horn made the division of the treasure. But I know very well why you thought something had happened to me. You did not expect to find me living in this little house."

"No, by the Lord Harry, I didn't!" exclaimed Burke, slapping his knee. "You must excuse me,

Mrs. Cliff, for speaking out in that way, but really I never was so much surprised as when I came into your front yard. I thought I would find you in the finest house in the place until you could have a stately mansion built somewhere in the outskirts of the town, where there would be room enough for a park. But when I came to this house, I couldn't help thinking that perhaps some beastly bank had broke, and that your share of the golden business had been swept away. Things like that do happen to women, you know, and I suppose they always will; but I am mighty glad to hear you are all right!

"But, as you have asked me to tell you my story, I will make short work of it, and then I would like to hear what has happened to you, as much as you please to tell me about it.

"Now, when I got my money, Mrs. Cliff, which, when compared to what your share must have been, was like a dory to a three-mast schooner, but still quite enough for me, and, perhaps, more than enough if a public vote could be taken on the subject, I was in Paris, a jolly place for a rich sailor, and I said to myself,—

"'Now, Mr. Burke,' said I, for I might as well begin by using good manners, 'the general disposition of a sea-faring man with a lot of money is to go on a lark, or, perhaps, a good many larks, and so get rid of it and then ship again before the mast for fourteen dollars per month, or thereabouts.'

"But I made up my mind right there on the spot

that that sort of thing wouldn't suit me. The very idea of shipping again on a merchant vessel made the blood run cold inside of me, and I swore to myself that I wouldn't do it.

"To be sure, I wouldn't give up all notion of a lark. A sailor with money,—and I don't believe there ever was an able-bodied seaman with more money than I had,—who doesn't lark, at least to some degree, has no right to call himself a whole-souled mariner; so I made up my mind to have one lark and then stop."

Mrs. Cliff's countenance clouded. "I am sorry, Mr. Burke," said she, "that you thought it necessary to do that. I do hope you didn't go on one of those horrible —sprees, do they call them?"

"Oh no!" interrupted Burke, "I didn't do anything of that kind. If I'd begun with a bottle, I'd have ended with nothing but a cork, and a badly burnt one at that. No ma'am! drinking isn't in my line. I don't take anything of that sort except at meals, and then only the best wine in genteel quantities. But I was bound to have one lark, and then I would stop and begin to live like a merchant-tailor, with no family nor poor relations."

"But what did you do?" asked Mrs. Cliff. "If it was a lark without liquor, I want to hear about it."

"It was a temperance lark, ma'am," said Burke, "and this is what it was.

"Now, though I have been to sea ever since I was a boy, I never had command of any kind of craft, and it struck me that I would like to finish up my life on the ocean wave by taking command of a vessel. It is generally understood that riches will give you anything you want, and I said to myself that my riches should give me that. I didn't want a sailin' vessel. I was tired of sailin' vessels. I wanted a steamer, and when I commanded a steamer for a little while I would stop short and be a landsman for the rest of my life.

"So I went up to Brest, where I thought I might find some sort of steamer which might suit me, and in that harbor I did find an English steamer, which had discharged her cargo and was expectin' to sail again pretty much in ballast and brandy, so far as I could make out. I went to this vessel and I made an offer to her captain to charter her for an excursion of one week — that was all I wanted.

"Well, I'm not going to bother you, Mrs. Cliff, with all that was said and done about this little business, which seemed simple enough, but which wasn't. There are people in this world who think that if you have money you can buy anything you want, but such people might as well get ready to change their opinions if they ever expect to come into money."

"That is true," said Mrs. Cliff; "every word of it is true, as I have found out for myself!"

"Well," continued Burke, "there had to be a lot of telegraphin' to the owners in London and a general fuss with the officers of the port about papers, and all that, but I got the business through all right; for if money won't get you everything, it's a great help in making things slip along easy. And so one fine afternoon I

E

found myself on board that steamer as commander for one week.

"Of course, I didn't want to give orders to the crew, but I intended to give my orders to the captain, and tell him what he was to do and what he was not to do for one week. He didn't like that very much, for he was inclined to bulldogism, but I paid him extra wages, and he agreed to knuckle under to me.

"So I gave him orders to sail out of the harbor and straight to the Island of Ushant, some twenty-five miles to the west of northwest.

"'There's no use going there,' said the captain,— his name was Dork,— 'there's nothing on that blasted bit of rock for you to see. There's no port I could run this steamer into.'

"I had been studying out my business on the chart, and this little island just suited my idea, and though the name was 'Ushant,' I said to him, 'You shall,' and I ordered him to sail to that island and lay to a mile or two to the westward; and as to the landing, he needn't talk about that until I mentioned it myself.

"So when we got about a couple of miles to the west of Ushant, we lay to. Now I knew we were on the forty-eighth parallel of latitude, for I had looked that out on the chart, so I said to Captain Dork,—

"'Now, sir!' says I, 'I want you to head your vessel, sir, due west, and then to steam straight ahead for a hundred miles, keepin' your vessel just as near as you can on that line of latitude.'"

"I see!" said Mrs. Cliff, very much interested. "If

he once got on that line of latitude and kept sailing west without turning one way or the other, he would be bound to keep on it."

"That's exactly it!" said Mr. Burke. "'Twas pretty near midnight when we started off to run along the forty-eighth parallel, but I kept my eyes on the man at the wheel and on the compass, and I let them know that that ship was under the command of an able-bodied seaman who knew what he was about, and if they skipped to one side of that line or to the other he would find it out in no time.

"I went below once to take a nap, but, as I promised the fellow at the wheel ten shillings if he would keep her head due west, and told him he would be sure to wake me up if he didn't, I felt certain we wouldn't skip the line of latitude.

"Well, that steamer, which was called the *Duke of Dorchester*, and which was a vessel of not more than a thousand tons, wasn't much of a sailer, or perhaps they was saving coal, I don't know which, and, not knowing how much coal ought to be used, I kept my mouth shut on that point; but I had the log thrown a good deal, and I found that we never quite came up to ten knots an hour, and when we took an observation at noon the next day, we saw that we hadn't quite done the hundred miles; but a little before one o'clock we did it, and then I ordered the captain to stop the engine and lay to.

"There was a brig about a mile away, and when she saw us layin' to, she put about and made for us, and

when she was near enough she hailed to know if anything was the matter. She was a French brig, but
Captain Dork understood her, and I told him to bid
her 'Good morning,' and to tell her that nothin' was
the matter, but that we were just stoppin' to rest. I
don't know what he did tell her, but she put about her
helm and was off again on her own business.

"'Now,' said I to Captain Dork, 'I want you to back
this steamer due east to the Island of Ushant.'

"He looked at me and began to swear. He took me
for a maniac,— a wild, crazy man, and told me the best
thing I could do would be to go below and turn in, and
he would take me back to my friends, if I had any.

"I didn't want to tell him what I was up to, but I
found I had to, and so I explained to him that I was
a rich sailor takin' a lark, and the lark I wanted to take
was, to sail on a parallel of latitude a hundred miles in
a steamer, and then to back that steamer along that
same parallel to the place where she started from. I
didn't believe that there was ever a ship in the world
that had done that, and bein' on a lark, I wanted to do
it, and was willin' to pay for it; and if his engineers
and his crew grumbled about backing the steamer for
a hundred miles, he could explain to them how the
matter stood, and tell them that bein' on a lark I was
willin' to pay for all extra trouble I might put them
to, and for any disturbances in their minds which might
rise from sailin' a vessel in a way which didn't seem to
be accordin' to the ordinary rules of navigation.

"Now, when Captain Dork knew that I was a rich

sailor on a lark, he understood me, and he made no more objections, though he said he wouldn't have spent his money in that way; and when he told his crew and his engineers and men about the extra pay, they understood the matter, and they agreed to back her along the forty-eighth parallel just as nigh as they could until they lay to two miles west of Ushant.

"So back we went, and they kept her due east just as nigh as they could, and they seemed to take an interest in it, as if all of them wanted me to have as good a lark as I could for my money, and we didn't skip that parallel very much, although it wasn't an easy job, I can tell you, to keep her head due west and her stern due east, and steam backwards. They had to rig up the compass abaft the wheel, and do some other things that you wouldn't understand, madam, such as running a spar out to stern to take sight by."

"I declare," said Mrs. Cliff, "that sort of sailing must have astonished any ship that saw it. Did you meet any other vessels?"

"Oh yes," said Burke. "After daybreak we fell in with a good many sail and some steamers, and most of them ran close and hailed us, but there wasn't any answer to give them, except that we were returning to port and didn't want no help; but some of the skippers of the smaller crafts were so full of curiosity that they stuck to us, and when we arrived off Ushant, which wasn't until nearly dark the next day, the *Duke of Dorchester* had a convoy of five sloops, two schooners, a brig, eight pilot boats, and four tugs."

Although Mr. Burke had said that he was going to make very short work with his story, it had already occupied a good deal of time, and he was not half through with it; but Mrs. Cliff listened with the greatest interest, and the rich sailor went on with his recital of adventures.

"Now, when I had finished scoring that forty-eighth parallel backward and forward for a hundred miles, I took out my purse and I paid that captain and all the crew what I promised to give them, and then we steamed back to Brest, where I told him to drop anchor and make himself comfortable.

"I stayed on board for a day and a night just to get my fill feeling I was in command of a steamer, before I gave up a sea-faring life forever. I threw up the rest of the week that I was entitled to and went ashore, and my lark was over.

"I went to England and took passage for home, and I had a first-class stateroom, and laid in a lot of good clothes before I started. I don't think I ever had greater comfort in my life than sittin' on deck, smokin' a good cigar, and watchin' the able-bodied seamen at their work.

"I hope I'm not tiring you, madam, but I'm trying to cut things as short as I can. It's often said that a sailor is all at sea when he is on shore, but I was a country fellow before I was a sailor, and land doings come naturally to me when I fix my mind on them.

"I'd made up my mind I was going to build my mother a house on Cape Cod, but when I got home I thought it better to buy her one already built, and that's what I did, and I stayed there with her a little while, but I didn't like it. I'd had a notion of having another house near my mother's, but I gave up that. There's too much sea about Cape Cod.

"Now, she liked it, for she's a regular sailor's mother, but I couldn't feel that I was really a rich fellow livin' ashore until I got out of hearin' of the ocean, and out of smellin' of salt and tar, so I made up my mind that I'd go inland and settle somewhere on a place of my own, where I might have command of some sort of farm.

"I didn't know just exactly what I wanted, nor just exactly where I wanted to go, so I thought it best to look around a little and hold council with somebody or other. I couldn't hold council with my mother, because she wanted me to buy a ship and take command of her. And then I thought of Captain Horn, and goin' to ask him. But the captain is a great man—"

"Indeed he is!" exclaimed Mrs. Cliff. "We all know that!"

"But he is off on his own business," continued Burke, "and what sort of a princely concern he's got on hand I don't know. Anyway, he wouldn't want me followin' him about and botherin' him, and so I thought of everybody I could, and at last it struck me that there wasn't anybody better than you, Mrs. Cliff, to give me the points I wanted, for I always liked you, Mrs. Cliff, and I consider you a woman of good sense down to the keel. And, as I heard you were livin' in sort of a country place, I thought you'd be the very person that I could come and talk to and get points.

"I felt a hankerin', anyway, after some of the old people of the *Castor;* for, after having had all that money divided among us, it made me feel as if we belonged to the same family. I suppose that was one reason why I felt a sort of drawing to you, you know. Anyway, I knew where you lived, and I came right here, and arrived this morning. After I'd taken a room at the hotel, I asked for your house and came straight here."

"And very glad am I to see you, Mr. Burke!" said Mrs. Cliff, speaking honestly from the bottom of her heart.

She had not known Burke very well, but she had always looked upon him as a fine, manly sailor; and now that he had come to her, she was conscious of the family feeling which he had spoken of, and she was very glad to see him.

She saw that Burke was very anxious to know why she was living in a plain fashion in this unpretentious house, but she found it would be very difficult to explain the matter to him. Hers was not a straight-forward tale, which she could simply sit and tell, and, moreover, although she liked Burke and thought it probable that he was a man of a very good heart, she did not believe that he was capable of advising her in the perplexities which her wealth had thrown about her.

Still, she talked to him and told him what she thought she could make him properly understand, and so, from one point to another, she went on until she had given the ex-sailor a very good idea of the state of her mind in regard to what she was doing, and what she thought she ought to do.

When Mrs. Cliff had finished speaking, Burke thrust his hands into his pockets, leaned back in his chair, and looked at the ceiling of the room, the walls, and the floor. He wanted to say something, but he was not prepared to do so. His mind, still nautical, desired to take an observation and determine the latitude and longitude of Mrs. Cliff, but the skies were very much overcast.

At this moment Willy Croup knocked at the parlor door, and when Mrs. Cliff went to her, she asked if the gentleman was going to stay to dinner.

Mrs. Cliff was surprised. She had no idea it was so late, but she went back to Mr. Burke and urged him to stay to dinner. He consented instantly, declaring that this was the first time that anybody, not his mother, had asked him to dinner since he came into his fortune.

When Mrs. Cliff had excused herself to give some directions about the meal, Burke walked about the parlor, carefully examining everything in it. When he had finished his survey, he sat down and shook his head.

"The trouble with her is," he said to himself, "that she's so dreadfully afraid of running ashore that she will never reach any port, that's what's the matter!"

When Mrs. Cliff returned, she asked her visitor if he would like to see her house, and she showed him over it with great satisfaction, for she had filled every room with all the handsome and appropriate things she could get into it. Burke noticed everything, and spoke with approbation of many things, but as he walked behind his hostess, he kept shaking his head.

He went down to dinner, and was introduced to Willy Croup, who had been ordered to go and dress herself that she might appear at the meal. He shook hands with her very cordially, and then looked all around the little dining-room, taking in every feature of its furnishing and adornment. When he had finished, he would have been glad to shake his head again, but this would have been observed.

When the dinner came on, however, Mr. Burke had no desire to shake his head. It was what might have been called a family dinner, but there was such a variety, such an abundance, everything was so admirably cooked, and the elderberry wine, which was produced in his honor, was so much more rich and fragrant to his taste than the wines he had had at hotels, that Mr. Burke was delighted.

Now he felt that in forming an opinion as to Mrs. Cliff's manner of living he had some grounds to stand upon. "What she wants," thought he, "is all the solid, sensible comfort her money can give her, and where she knows what she wants, she gets it; but the trouble seems to be that in most things she doesn't know what she wants!"

When Mr. Burke that afternoon walked back to the hotel, wrapped in his fur-trimmed coat and carefully puffing a fine Havana cigar, he had entirely forgotten his own plans and purposes in life, and was engrossed in those of Mrs. Cliff.

CHAPTER VII

MR. BURKE ACCEPTS A RESPONSIBILITY

WILLY CROUP was very much pleased with Mr. Burke, and she was glad that she had allowed herself to be persuaded to sit at table with such a fine gentleman.

He treated her with extreme graciousness of manner, and it was quite plain to her that if he recognized her in her silk gown as the person who, in a calico dress, had 'opened the front door for him, he had determined to make her feel that he had not noticed the coincidence.

He was a good deal younger than she was, but Willy's childlike disposition had projected itself into her maturer years, and in some respects there was a greater sympathy, quickly perceived by both, between her and Mr. Burke than yet existed between him and Mrs. Cliff. After some of the amusing anecdotes which he told, the visitor looked first towards Willy to see how she appreciated them; but it must not be supposed that he was not extremely attentive and deferential to his hostess.

If Willy had known what a brave, gallant, and daring sailor he was, she would have made a hero of him; but Mrs. Cliff had never said much about Burke, and Willy simply admired him as the best specimen of the urbane man of the world with whom she had yet met.

The two women talked a good deal about their visitor that evening, and Mrs. Cliff said that she hoped he was not going to leave town very soon, for it was possible that she might be of help to him if he wanted to settle down in that part of the country.

The next morning, soon after breakfast, when Willy opened the front gate of the yard and stepped out upon the street with a small covered basket in her hand, she had gone but a very little distance when she met Mr. Burke, with his furs, his cane, and his silk hat. The latter was lifted very high as its owner saluted Miss Croup.

Willy, who was of a fair complexion, reddened somewhat as she shook hands with the gentleman, informed him, in answer to his questions, that Mrs. Cliff was very well, that she was very well; that the former was at home and would be glad to see him, and that she herself was going into the business part of the town to make some little purchases.

She would have been better pleased if she had not been obliged to tell him where she was going, but she could not do otherwise when he said he supposed she was walking for the benefit of the fresh morning air. He added to her discomfiture by requesting to be allowed to walk with her, and by offering to carry her basket. This threw Willy's mind into a good deal of a flutter. Why could she not have met this handsomely dressed gentleman sometime when she was not going to the grocery store to buy such things as stove-blacking and borax ?

It seemed to her as if these commodities must suggest to the mind of any one rusty iron and obtrusive insects, and as articles altogether outside the pale of allusion in high-toned social intercourse.

It also struck her as a little odd that a gentleman should propose to accompany a lady when she was going on domestic errands; but then this gentleman was different from any she had known, and there were many ways of the world with which she was not at all acquainted.

Mr. Burke immediately began to speak of the visit of the day before. He had enjoyed seeing Mrs. Cliff again and he had never sat down to a better dinner.

"Yes," said Willy, "she likes good eatin', and she knows what it is, and if she had a bigger dining-room she would often invite people to dinner, and I expect the house would be quite lively, as she seems more given to company than she used to be, and that's all right, considerin' she's better able to afford it."

Mr. Burke took a deep satisfied breath. The opportunity had already come to him to speak his mind.

"Afford it!" said he. "I should think so! Mrs. Cliff must be very rich. She is worth, I should say — well, I don't know what to say, not knowing exactly and precisely what each person got when the grand division was made."

Willy's loyalty to Mrs. Cliff prompted her to put her in as good a light as possible before this man of the world, and her own self-esteem prompted her to show that, being a friend and relative of this rich lady, she was not ignorant of her affairs in life.

"Oh, she's rich!" said Willy. "I can't say, of course, just how much she has, but I'm quite sure that she owns at least —"

Willy wished to put the amount of the fortune at one hundred thousand dollars, but she was a little afraid that this might be too much, and yet she did not wish to make the amount any smaller than could possibly be helped. So she thought of seventy-five, and then eighty, and finally remarked that Mrs. Cliff must be worth at least ninety thousand dollars. Mr. Burke looked up at the sky and wanted to whistle.

"Ninety thousand dollars!" he said to himself. "I know positively that it was at least four millions at the time of the division, and she says she's richer now than she was then, which is easy to be accounted for by the interest coming in. I see her game! She wants to keep shady about her big fortune because her neighbors would expect her to live up to it, and she knows it isn't in her to live up to it. Now, I'm beginning to see through the fog." "It seems to me," said he, "that Mrs. Cliff ought to have a bigger dining-room."

This remark pulled up the flood-gate to Willy's accumulated sentiments on the subject, and they poured forth in a rushing stream.

Yes, indeed, Mrs. Cliff ought to have a bigger dining-room, and other rooms to the house, and there was the front fence, and no end of things she ought to have, and it was soon made clear to Mr. Burke that Willy had been lying awake at night thinking, and thinking, and thinking about what Mrs. Cliff ought to have and what she did not have.   She said she really and honestly believed that there was no reason at all why she did not have them, except that she did not want to seem to be setting herself up above her neighbors.   In fact, Mrs. Cliff had told Willy two or three times, when there had been a discussion about prices, that she was able to do anything she wanted, and if she could do that, why did she not do it?   People were all talking about it, and they had talked and talked her fortune down until in some families it was not any more than ten thousand dollars.

On and on talked Willy, while Mr. Burke said scarcely a word, but he listened with the greatest attention.   They had now walked on until they had reached the main street of the little town, gone through the business part where the shops were, and out into the suburbs.   Suddenly Willy stopped.

"Oh dear!" she exclaimed, "I've gone too far!   I was so interested in talking, that I didn't think."

"I'm sorry," said Mr. Burke, "that I've taken you out of your way.   Can't I get you what you want and save you the trouble?"

Now Willy was in another flutter.   After the walk with the fur-trimmed coat, and the talk about dollars by thousands and tens of thousands, she could not come down to mention borax and blacking.

"Oh no, thank you!" said she, trying her best to think of some other errand than the one she had come upon. "I don't believe it's finished yet, and it's hardly worth while to stop. There was one of those big cushion covers that she brought from Paris, that was to be filled with down, but I don't believe it's ready yet, and I needn't stop."

Mr. Burke could not but think it a little odd that such a small basket should be brought for the purpose of carrying home a large down cushion, but he said nothing further on the subject. He had had a most gratifying conversation with this communicative and agreeable person, and his interest in Mrs. Cliff was greatly increased.

When he neared the hotel, he took leave of his companion, saying that he would call in the afternoon; and Willy, after she had looked back and was sure he was out of sight, slipped into the grocery store and got her borax and blacking.

Mr. Burke called on Mrs. Cliff that afternoon, and the next morning, and two or three times the day after. They came to be very much interested in each other, and Burke in his mind compared this elderly friend with his mother, and not to the advantage of the latter. Burke's mother was a woman who would always have her own way, and wanted advice and counsel from no one, but Mrs. Cliff was a very different woman.

She was so willing to listen to what Burke said — and his remarks were nearly always on the subject of the proper expenditure of money — and appeared to attach so much importance to his opinions, that he began to feel that a certain responsibility, not at all an unpleasant one, was forcing itself upon him.

He did not think that he should try to constitute himself her director, or even to assume the position of professional suggester, but in an amateur way he suggested, and she, without any idea of depending upon him for suggestions, found herself more and more inclined to accept them as he continued to offer them.

She soon discovered that he was the only person in Plainton who knew her real fortune, and this was a bond of sympathy and union between them, and she became aware that she had succeeded in impressing him with her desire to live upon her fortune in such a manner that it would not interfere with her friendships or associations, and her life-long ideas of comfort and pleasure.

The people of the town talked a great deal about the fine gentleman at the hotel, but they knew he was one of the people who had become rich in consequence of Captain Horn's discovery; and some of them, good friends of Mrs. Cliff, felt sorry that she had not profited to as great a degree by that division as this gentleman of opulent taste, who occupied two of the best rooms in the hotel, and obliged Mr. Williams to send to Harrington, and even to Boston, for provisions suitable to his epicurean tastes, and who drove around the country with a carriage and pair at least once a day.

When Burke was ready to make his suggestions, he

F

thought he would begin in a mild fashion, and see how Mrs. Cliff would take them.

"If I was in your place, madam," said he, "the first thing I would do would be to have a lot of servants. There's nothin' money can give a person that's better than plenty of people to do things. Lots of them on hand all the time, like the crew of a ship."

"But I couldn't do that, Mr. Burke," said she; "my house is too small. I haven't any place for servants to sleep. When I enlarge my house, of course, I may have more servants."

"Oh, I wouldn't wait for that," said he; "until then you could board them at the hotel."

This suggestion was strongly backed by Willy Croup, and Mrs. Cliff took the matter to heart. She collected together a domestic establishment of as many servants as she thought her establishment could possibly provide with work, and, although she did not send them to be guests at the hotel, she obtained lodging for them at the house of a poor woman in the neighborhood.

When she had done this, she felt that she had made a step in the direction of doing her duty by her money.

Mr. Burke made another suggestion. "If I was you," said he, "I wouldn't wait for times or seasons, for in these days people build in winter the same as in summer. I would put up that addition just as soon as it could be done."

Mrs. Cliff sighed. "I suppose that's what I should do," said she. "I feel that it is, but you know how I hate to begin it."

"But you needn't hate it," said he. "There isn't the least reason in the world for any objection to it. I've a plan which will make it all clear sailin'. I've been thinkin' it out, and this is the way I've thought it." Mrs. Cliff listened with great attention.

"Now then," said Burke, "next to you on the west is your own lot that you're going to put your new dining-room on. Am I right there?"

"Yes," said Mrs. Cliff, "you are right there."

"Well, next to that is the little house inhabited by a family named Barnard, I'm told, and next to that there's a large corner lot with an old house on it that's for sale. Now then, if I was you, I'd buy that corner lot and clear away the old house, and I'd build my dining-room right there. I'd get a good architect and let him plan you a first-class, A number one, dining-room, with other rooms to it, above it and below it, and around it; with porticos, and piazzas, and little balconies to the second story, and everything that anybody might want attached to a first-class dining-room."

Mrs. Cliff laughed. "But what good would it be to me away up there at the corner of the next street?"

"The reason for putting it there," said Burke, "is to get clear of all the noise and dirt of building, and the fuss and bother that you dislike so much. And then when it was all finished, and painted, and papered, and the carpets down, if you like, I'd have it moved right up here against your house just where you want it. When everything was in order, and you was ready, you could cut a door right through into the new dining-room, and there you'd be. They've got so in the way of slidin' buildings along on timbers now that they can travel about almost like the old stage coaches, and you needn't have your cellar dug until you're ready to clap your new dining-room right over it."

Mrs. Cliff smiled, and Willy listened with open eyes. "But how about the Barnard family and their house?" said she.

"Oh, I'd buy them a lot somewhere else," said he, "and move their house. They wouldn't object if you paid them extra. What I'd have if I was in your place, Mrs. Cliff, would be a clear lot down to the next street, and I'd have a garden in it with flowers, and gravel walks, and greenhouses, and all that sort of thing."

"All stretching itself out in the sunshine under the new dining-room windows!" cried Willy Croup, with sparkling eyes.

Mrs. Cliff sat and considered, a cheerful glow in her veins. Here, really, was an opportunity of stemming the current of her income without shocking any of her social instincts!

CHAPTER VIII

MR. BURKE BEGINS TO MAKE THINGS MOVE IN PLAINTON

It was not long before Mr. Burke began to be a very important personage in Plainton. It was generally known that he intended to buy land and settle in the neighborhood, and as he was a rich man, evidently inclined to be liberal in his expenditures, this was a matter of great interest both in social and business circles.

He often drove out to survey the surrounding country, but when he was perceived several times standing in front of an old house at the corner of the street near Mrs. Cliff's residence, it was supposed that he might have changed his mind in regard to a country place, and was thinking of building in the town.

He was not long considered a stranger in the place. Mrs. Cliff frequently spoke of him as a valued friend, and there was reason to believe that in the various adventures and dangers of which they had heard, Mr. Burke had been of great service to their old friend and neighbor, and it was not unlikely that his influence had had a good deal to do with her receipt of a portion of the treasure discovered by the commander of the expedition.

Several persons had said more than once that they could not see why Mrs. Cliff should have had any claim upon this treasure, except, perhaps, to the extent of her losses. But if she had had a friend in camp, — and Mr. Burke was certainly a friend, — it was easy to understand why he would do the best he could, at a time when money was so plenty, for the benefit of one whom he knew to be a widow in straitened circumstances.

So Mr. Burke was looked upon not only as a man of wealth and superior tastes in regard to food and personal comfort, but as a man of a liberal and generous disposition. Furthermore, there was no pride about him. Often on his return from his drives, his barouche and pair, which Mr. Williams had obtained in Harrington for his guest's express benefit, would stop in front of Mrs. Cliff's modest residence ; and two or three times he had taken that good lady and Willy Croup to drive with him.

But Mrs. Cliff did not care very much for the barouche. She would have preferred a little phaëton and a horse which she could drive herself. As for her horse and the two-seated wagon, that was declared by most of the ladies of the town to be a piece of absolute extravagance. It was used almost exclusively by Willy, who was known to deal with shops in the most distant part of the town in order that she might have an excuse, it was said, to order out that wagon and have Andrew Marks to drive her.

Of course they did not know how often Mrs. Cliff had said to herself that it was really not a waste of money to keep this horse, for Willy was no longer young; and if she could save her any weary steps, she ought to do it, and at the same time relieve a little the congested state of her income.

Moreover, Mr. Burke was not of an unknown family. He was quite willing to talk about himself, especially to Mr. Williams, as they sat and smoked together in the evening, and he said a good deal about his father, who had owned two ships at Nantucket, and who, according to his son, was one of the most influential citizens of the place.

Mr. Williams had heard of the Burkes of Nantucket, and he did not think any the less of the one who was now his guest, because his father's ships had come to grief during his boyhood, and he had been obliged to give up a

career on shore, which he would have liked, and go to
sea, which he did not like. A brave spirit in poverty
coupled with a liberal disposition in opulence was enough
to place Mr. Burke on a very high plane in the opinions
of the people of Plainton.

Half a mile outside the town, upon a commanding
eminence, there was a handsome house which belonged
to a family named Buskirk. These people were really
not of Plainton, although their post-office and railroad
station were there. They were rich city people who
came to this country place for the summer and autumn,
and who had nothing to do with the town folks, except
in a limited degree to deal with some of them.

This family lived in great style, and their coachman
and footman in knee breeches, their handsome horses
with docked tails, the beautiful grounds about their
house, a feebly shooting fountain on the front lawn, were
a source of anxious disquietude in the mind of Mrs. Cliff.
They were like the skeletons which were brought in at
the feasts of the ancients.

"If I should ever be obliged to live like the Buskirks
on the hill," the good lady would say to herself, "I
would wish myself back to what I used to be, asking
only that my debts be paid."

Even the Buskirks took notice of Mr. Burke. In him
they thought it possible they might have a neighbor. If
he should buy a place and build a fine house somewhere
in their vicinity, which they thought the only vicinity in
which any one should build a fine house, it might be a
very good thing, and would certainly not depreciate the

value of their property. A wealthy bachelor might indeed be a more desirable neighbor than a large family.

The Buskirks had been called upon when they came to Plainton a few years before by several families. Of course, the clergyman, Mr. Perley, and his wife, paid them a visit, and the two Misses Thorpedyke hired a carriage and drove to the house, and, although they did not see the family, they left their cards.

After some time these and other calls were returned, but in the most ceremonious manner, and there ended the social intercourse between the fine house on the hill and the town.

As the Buskirks drove to Harrington to church, they did not care about the Perleys, and although they seemed somewhat inclined to cultivate the Thorpedykes, who were known to be of such an excellent old family, the Thorpedykes did not reciprocate the feeling, and, having declined an invitation to tea, received no more.

But now Mr. Buskirk, who had come up on Saturday to spend Sunday with his family, actually called on Mr. Burke at the hotel. The wealthy sailor was not at home, and the city gentleman left his card.

When Mr. Burke showed this card to Mrs. Cliff, her face clouded. "Are you going to return the visit?" said she.

"Oh yes!" answered Burke. "Some of these days I will drive up and look in on them. I expect they have got a fancy parlor, and I would like to sit in it a while and think of the days when I used to swab the deck. There's nothin' more elevatin', to my mind, than just that sort of thing. I do it sometime when I am eatin' my meals at the hotel, and the better I can bring to mind the bad coffee and hard tack, the better I like what's set before me."

Mrs. Cliff sighed. She wished Mr. Buskirk had kept away from the hotel.

As soon as Mrs. Cliff had consented to the erection of the new dining-room on the corner lot, — and she did not hesitate after Mr. Burke had explained to her how easy it would be to do the whole thing almost without her knowing anything about it, if she did not want to bother herself in the matter, — the enterprise was begun.

Burke, who was of an active mind, and who delighted in managing and directing, undertook to arrange everything. There was no agreement between Mrs. Cliff and himself that he should do this, but it pleased him so much to do it, and it pleased her so much to have him do it, that it was done as a thing which might be expected to happen naturally.

Sometimes she said he was giving her too much of his time, but he scorned such an idea. He had nothing to do, for he did not believe that he should buy a place for himself until spring, because he wanted to pick out a spot to live in when the leaves were coming out instead of when they were dropping off, and the best fun he knew of would be to have command of a big crew, and to keep them at work building Mrs. Cliff's dining-room.

"I should be glad to have you attend to the contracts," said Mrs. Cliff, "and all I ask is, that while you don't waste anything, — for I think it is a sin to waste money no matter how much you may have, — that you will help me as much as you can to make me feel that I really am making use of my income."

Burke agreed to do all this, always under her advice, of course, and very soon he had his crew, and they were hard at work. He sent to Harrington and employed an architect to make plans, and as soon as the general basis of these was agreed upon, the building was put in charge of a contractor, who, under Mr. Burke, began to collect material and workmen from all available quarters.

"We've got to work sharp, for the new building must be moored alongside Mrs. Cliff's house before the first snowstorm."

A lawyer of Plainton undertook the purchase of the land and, as the payments were to be made in cash, and as there was no chaffering about prices, this business was soon concluded.

As to the Barnard family, Mr. Burke himself undertook negotiations with them. When he had told them of the handsome lot on another street, which would be given them in exchange, and how he would gently slide their house to the new location, and put it down on any part of the lot which they might choose, and guaranteed that it should be moved so gently that the clocks would not stop ticking, nor the tea or coffee spill out of their cups, if they chose to take their meals on board during the voyage; and as, furthermore, he promised a handsome sum to recompense them for the necessity of leaving behind their well, which he could not undertake to move, and for any minor inconveniences and losses, their consent to the change of location was soon obtained.

Four days after this Burke started the Barnard house on its travels. As soon as he had made his agreement with the family, he had brought a man down from Harrington, whose business it was to move houses, and had put the job into his hands. He stipulated that at one o'clock P.M. on the day agreed upon the house was to begin to move, and he arranged with the mason to whom he had given the contract for preparing the cellar on the new lot, that he should begin operations at the same hour.

He then offered a reward of two hundred dollars to be given to the mover if he got his house to its destination before the cellar was done, or to the mason if he finished the cellar before the house arrived.

The Barnards had an early dinner, which was cooked on a kerosene stove, their chimney having been taken down, but they had not finished washing the dishes when their house began to move.

Mrs. Cliff and Willy ran to bid them good-bye, and all the Barnards, old and young, leaned out of a back window and shook hands.

Mr. Burke had arranged a sort of gang-plank with a railing if any of them wanted to go on shore — that is, step on terra firma — during the voyage. But Samuel Rolands, the mover, heedful of his special prize, urged upon them not to get out any oftener than could be helped, because when they wished to use the gang-plank he would be obliged to stop.

There were two boys in the family who were able to jump off and on whenever they pleased, but boys are boys, and very different from other people.

Houses had been moved in Plainton before, but never had any inhabitants of the place beheld a building glide along upon its timber course with, speaking comparatively, the rapidity of this travelling home.

Most of the citizens of the place who had leisure, came at some time that afternoon to look at the moving house, and many of them walked by its side, talking to the Barnards, who, as the sun was warm, stood at an open window, very much excited by the spirit of adventure, and quite willing to converse.

Over and over they assured their neighbors that they would never know they were moving if they did not see the trees and things slowly passing by them.

As they crossed the street and passed between two houses on the opposite side, the inhabitants of these gathered at their windows, and the conversation was very lively with the Barnards, as the house of the latter passed slowly by.

All night that house moved on, and the young people of the village accompanied it until eleven o'clock, when the Barnards went to bed.

Mr. Burke divided his time between watching the moving house, at which all the men who could be employed in any way, and all the horses which could be conveniently attached to the windlasses, were working in watches of four hours each, in order to keep them fresh and vigorous, — and the lot where the new cellar was being constructed, where the masons continued their labors at night by the light of lanterns and a blazing bonfire fed with resinous pine.

The excitement caused by these two scenes of activity was such that it is probable that few of the people of the town went to bed sooner than the Barnard family.

Early the next morning the two Barnard boys looked out of the window of their bedroom and saw beneath them the Hastings' barnyard, with the Hastings boy milking. They were so excited by this vision that they threw their shoes and stockings out at him, having no other missiles convenient, and for nearly half an hour he followed that house, trying to toss the articles back through the open window, while the cow stood waiting for the milking to be finished.

On the evening of the third day after its departure from its original position, the Barnard house arrived on the new lot, and, to the disgust of Samuel Rolands, he found the cellar entirely finished and ready for him to place the house upon it. But Mr. Burke, who had been quite sure that this would be the result of the competition, comforted him by telling him that as he had done his best, he too should have a prize equal to that given to the mason. This had been suggested by Mrs. Cliff, because, she said, that as they were both hard-working men with families, and although the house-mover was not a citizen of Plainton, he had once lived there, she was very glad of this opportunity of helping them along.

As soon as this important undertaking had been finished, Mr. Burke was able to give his sole attention to the new dining-room on the corner lot. He and the architect had worked hard upon the plans, and when they were finished they had been shown to Mrs. Cliff. She understood them in a general way, and was very glad to see that such ample provisions had been made in regard to closets, though she was not able to perceive with her mind's eye the exact dimensions of a room nineteen by twenty-seven, nor to appreciate the difference between a ceiling twelve feet high, and another which was nine.

However, having told Mr. Burke and the architect what she wanted, and both of them having told her what she ought to have, she determined to leave the whole matter in their hands. This resolution was greatly approved by her sailor friend, for, as the object of the plan of construction was to relieve her of all annoyance consequent upon building operations, the more she left everything to those who delighted in the turmoil of construction, the better it would be for all.

Everything had been done in the plans to prevent interference with the neatness and comfort of Mrs. Cliff's present abode. The door of the new dining-room was so arranged that when it was moved up to the old house, it would exactly fit against a door in the latter which opened from a side hall upon a little porch. This porch being removed, the two doors would fit exactly to each other, and there would be none of the dust and noise consequent upon the cutting away of walls.

So Mrs. Cliff and Willy lived on in peace, comfort,

and quiet in their old home, while on the corner lot
there was hammering, and banging, and sawing all day.
Mr. Burke would have had this work go on by night,
but the contractor refused. His men would work extra
hours in consideration of extra inducements, but good
carpenter work, he declared, could not be done by lan-
tern light.

The people of Plainton did not at all understand the
operations on the corner lot. Mr. Burke did not tell
them much about it, and the contractor was not willing
to talk. He had some doubts in regard to the scheme,
but as he was well paid, he would do his best. It had
been mentioned that the new building was to be Mrs.
Cliff's dining-room, but this idea soon faded out of the
Plainton mind, which was not adapted to grasp and
hold it.

Consequently, as Mr. Burke had a great deal to do
with the building, and as Mrs. Cliff did not appear to
be concerned in it at all, it was generally believed that
the gentleman at the hotel was putting up a house for
himself on the corner lot. This knowledge was the
only conclusion which would explain the fact that the
house was built upon smooth horizontal timbers, and
not upon a stone or brick foundation. A man who had
been a sailor might fancy to build a house something as
he would build a ship in a shipyard, and not attach it
permanently to the earth.

CHAPTER IX

A MEETING OF HEIRS

WHILE the building operations were going on at such a rapid rate on the corner lot, Mrs. Cliff tried to make herself as happy as possible in her own home. She liked having enough servants to do all the work, and relieve both her and Willy. She liked to be able to drive out when she wanted to, or to invite a few of her friends to dinner or to tea, and to give them the very best the markets afforded of everything she thought they might like; but she was not a satisfied woman.

It was true that Mr. Burke was doing all that he could with her money, and doing it well, she had not the slightest doubt; but, after all, a new dining-room was a matter of small importance. She had fears that even after it was all finished and paid for she would find that her income had gained upon her.

As often as once a day the argument came to her that it would be wise for her to give away the bulk of her fortune in charity, and thus rid herself of the necessity for this depressing struggle between her desire to live as she wanted to live, and the obligations to herself under which her fortune placed her; but she could not consent to thus part with her great fortune. She would not turn her back upon her golden opportunities. As soon as she had so determined her life that the assertion of her riches would not interfere with her domestic and social affairs, she would be charitable enough, she would do good works upon a large scale; but she must first determine what she was to do for herself, and so let her charities begin at home.

This undecided state of mind did not have a good effect upon her general appearance, and it was frequently remarked that her health was not what it used to be. Miss Nancy Shott thought there was nothing to wonder at in this. Mrs. Cliff had never been accustomed to spend money, and it was easy to see, from the things she had bought abroad and put ·into that little house, that she had expended a good deal more than she could afford, and no wonder she was troubled, and no wonder she was looking thin and sick.

Other friends, however, did not entirely agree with Miss Shott. They thought their old friend was entirely too sensible a woman to waste a fortune, whether it had been large or small, which had come to her in so wonderful a manner; and they believed she had money enough to live on very comfortably. If this were not the case, she would never consent to keep a carriage almost for Willy Croup's sole use.

They thought, perhaps, that the example and companionship of Mr. Burke might have had an effect upon her. It was as likely as not that she had borne part of the expense of moving the Barnard house, so that there should be nothing between her and the new building. But this, as they said themselves, was mere surmise. Mr. Burke might fancy large grounds, and he was certainly able to have them if he wanted them.

G

Whatever people said and thought about Mrs. Cliff and her money, it was generally believed that she was in comfortable circumstances. Still, it had to be admitted that she was getting on in years.

Now arose a very important question among the gossips of Plainton: who was to be Mrs. Cliff's heir?

Everybody knew that Mrs. Cliff had but one blood relation living, and that was Willy Croup, and no one who had given any thought whatever to the subject believed that Willy Croup would be her heir. Her husband had some distant relatives, but, as they had had nothing to do with Mrs. Cliff during the days of her adversity, it was not likely that she would now have anything to do with them. Especially, as any money she had to leave did not come through her husband.

But, although the simple-minded Willy Croup was a person who would not know how to take care of money if she had it, and although everybody knew that if Mrs. Cliff made a will she would never think of leaving her property to Willy, still, everybody who thought or talked about the matter saw the appalling fact staring them in their faces — that if Mrs. Cliff died without a will, Willy would inherit her possessions!

The more it was considered, the more did this unpleasant contingency trouble the minds of certain of the female citizens of Plainton. Miss Cushing, the principal dressmaker of the place, was greatly concerned upon this subject, and as her parlor, where she generally sat at her work, was a favorite resort of certain ladies, who sometimes had orders to give, and always had a great deal to say, it was natural that those good women who took most to heart Mrs. Cliff's heirless condition should think of Miss Cushing whenever they were inclined to talk upon the subject.

Miss Shott dropped in there one day with a very doleful countenance. That very morning she had passed Mrs. Cliff's house on the other side of the way, and had seen that poor widow standing in her front yard with the most dejected and miserable countenance she had ever seen on a human being.

"People might talk as much as they pleased about Mrs. Cliff being troubled because she had spent too much money, that all might be, or it might not be, but it was not the reason for that woman looking as if she was just ready to drop into a sick-bed. When people go to the most unhealthy regions in the whole world, and live in holes in the ground like hedgehogs, they cannot expect to come home without seeds of disease in their system, which are bound to come out. And that those seeds were now coming out in Mrs. Cliff no sensible person could look at her and deny."

When Miss Cushing heard this, she felt more strongly convinced than ever of the importance of the subject upon which she and some of her friends had been talking. But she said nothing in regard to that subject to Miss Shott. What she had to say and what she had already said about the future of Mrs. Cliff's property, and what her particular friends had said, were matters which none of them wanted repeated, and when a citizen of Plainton did not wish anything repeated, it was not told to Miss Shott.

But after Miss Shott had gone, there came in Mrs. Ferguson, a widow lady, and shortly afterwards, Miss Inchman, a middle-aged spinster, accompanied by Mrs. Wells and Mrs. Archibald, these latter both worthy matrons of the town. Mrs. Archibald really came to talk to Miss Cushing about a winter dress, but during the subsequent conversation she made no reference to this errand.

Miss Cushing was relating to Mrs. Ferguson what Nancy had told her when the other ladies came in, but Nancy Shott had stopped in at each of their houses and had already given them the information.

"Nancy always makes out things a good deal worse than they are," said Mrs. Archibald, "but there's truth in what she says. Mrs. Cliff is failing; everybody can see that!"

"Of course they can," said Miss Cushing, "and I say that if she has any friends in Plainton, — and everybody knows she has, — it's time for them to do something!"

"The trouble is, what to do, and who is to do it," remarked Mrs. Ferguson.

"What to do is easy enough," said Miss Cushing, "but who is to do it is another matter."

"And what would you do?" asked Mrs. Wells. "If she feels she needs a doctor, she has sense enough to send for one without waiting until her friends speak about it."

"The doctor is a different thing altogether!" said Miss Cushing. "If he comes and cures her, that's

neither here nor there. It isn't the point! But the
danger is, that, whether he comes or not, she is a woman
well on in years, with a constitution breaking down under
her, — that is as far as appearances go, for of course I
can't say anything positive about it, — and she has
nobody to inherit her money, and as far as anybody
knows she has never made a will!"

"Oh, she has never made a will," said Mrs. Wells,
" because my John is in the office, and if Mrs. Cliff had
ever come there on such business, he would know about
it."

" But she ought to make a will," said Miss Cushing.
" That's the long and short of it; and she ought to have
a friend who would tell her so. That would be no more
than a Christian duty which any one of us would owe to
another, if cases were changed."

" I don't look upon Mrs. Cliff as such a very old
woman," said Miss Inchman, " but I agree with you that
this thing ought to be put before her. Willy Croup will
never do it, and really if some one of us don't, I don't
know who will."

"'There's Mrs. Perley,'' said Mrs. Archibald.

" Oh, she'd never do ! " struck in Miss Cushing. " Mrs.
Perley is too timid. She would throw it off on her husband, and if he talks to Mrs. Cliff about a will, her money
will all go to the church or to some charity. I should
say that one of us ought to take on herself this friendly
duty. Of course, it would not do to go to her and blurt
out that we all thought she would not live very long, and
that she ought to make her will; but conversation could

be led to the matter, and when Mrs. Cliff got to consider her own case, I haven't a doubt but that she would be glad to have advice and help from an old friend."

All agreed that this was a very correct view of the case, but not one of them volunteered to go and talk to Mrs. Cliff on the subject. This was not from timidity, nor from an unwillingness to meddle in other people's business, but from a desire on the part of each not to injure herself in Mrs. Cliff's eyes by any action which might indicate that she had a personal interest in the matter.

Miss Cushing voiced the opinion of the company when she said: "When a person has no heirs, relatives ought to be considered first, but if there are none of these, or if they aren't suitable, then friends should come in. Of course, I mean the oldest and best friends of the party without heirs."

No remark immediately followed this, for each lady was thinking that she, probably more than any one else in Plainton, had a claim upon Mrs. Cliff's attention if she were leaving her property to her friends, as she certainly ought to do.

In years gone by Mrs. Cliff had been a very kind friend to Miss Cushing. She had loaned her money, and assisted her in various ways, and since her return to Plainton she had put a great deal of work into Miss Cushing's hands. Dress after dress for Willy Croup had been made, and material for others was still lying in the house; and Mrs. Cliff herself had ordered so much work, that at this moment Miss Cushing had two girls upstairs sewing diligently upon it.

Having experienced all this kindness, Miss Cushing
felt that if Mrs. Cliff left any of her money to her
friends, she would certainly remember her, and that right
handsomely. If anybody spoke to Mrs. Cliff upon the
subject, she would insist, and she thought she had a
right to insist, that her name should be brought in
prominently.

Mrs. Ferguson had also well-defined opinions upon the
subject. She had two daughters who were more than
half grown, had learned all that they could be taught in
Plainton, and she was very anxious to send them away
to school, where their natural talents could be properly
cultivated. She felt that she owed a deep and solemn
duty to these girls, and she had already talked to Mrs.
Cliff about them.

The latter had taken a great deal of interest in the
matter, and although she had not said she would help
Mrs. Ferguson to properly educate these girls, for she
had not asked her help, she had taken so much interest
in the matter that their mother had great hopes. And if
this widow without any children felt inclined to assist
the children of others during her life, how much more
willing would she be likely to be to appropriate a portion of what she left behind her to such an object!

Mrs. Wells and Mrs. Archibald had solid claims upon
Mrs. Cliff. It was known that shortly after the death
of her husband, when she found it difficult to make col-
lections and was very much in need of money for immediate expenses, they had each made loans to her. It
is true that even before she started for South America

she had repaid these loans with full legal interest. But the two matrons could not forget that they had been kind to her, nor did they believe that Mrs. Cliff had forgotten what they had done, for the presents she had brought them from France were generally considered as being more beautiful and more valuable than those given to anybody else, — except the Thorpedykes and the Perleys. This indicated a very gratifying gratitude upon which the two ladies, each for herself, had every right to build very favorable hopes.

Miss Inchman and Mrs. Cliff had been school-fellows, and when they were both grown young women there had been a good deal of doubt which one of them William Cliff would marry. He made his choice, and Susan Inchman never showed by word or deed that she begrudged him to her friend, to whom she had always endeavored to show just as much kindly feeling as if there had been two William Cliffs, and each of the young women had secured one of them. If Mrs. Cliff, now a widow with money enough to live well upon and keep a carriage, was making out her will, and was thinking of her friends in Plainton, it would be impossible for her to forget one who was the oldest friend of all.

So it is easy to see why she did not want to go to Mrs. Cliff and prejudice her against herself, by stating that she ought to make a will for the benefit of the old friends who had always loved and respected her.

Miss Cushing now spoke. She knew what each member of the little company was thinking about, and she felt that it might as well be spoken of.

"It does seem to me," said she, "and I never would have thought of it, if it hadn't been for the talk we had, — that we five are the persons that Mrs. Cliff would naturally mention in her will, not, perhaps, regarding any money she might have to leave — "

" I don't see why ! " interrupted Mrs. Ferguson.

" Well, that's neither here nor there," continued Miss Cushing. "Money is money, and nobody knows what people will do with it when they die, and if she leaves anything to the church or to charity, it's her money! but I'm sure that Mrs. Cliff has too much hard sense to order her executors to sell all the beautiful rugs, and table-covers, and glass, and china, and the dear knows what besides is in her house at this moment! They wouldn't bring anything at a sale, and she would naturally think of leaving them to her friends. Some might get more and some might get less, but we five in this room at this present moment are the old friends that Mrs. Cliff would naturally remember. And if any one of us ever sees fit to speak to her on the subject, we're the people who should be mentioned when the proper opportunity comes to make such mention."

" You're forgetting Willy Croup," said Mrs. Wells.

"No," answered Miss Cushing, a little sharply, "I don't forget her, but I'll have nothing to do with her. I don't suppose she'll be forgotten, but whatever is done for her or whatever is not done for her is not our business. It's my private opinion, however, that she's had a good deal already ! "

" Well," said Mrs. Ferguson, " I suppose that what

you say is all right, — at least I've no objections to any of it; but whoever's going to speak to her, it mustn't be me, because she knows I've daughters to educate, and she'd naturally think that if I spoke I was principally speaking for myself, and that would set her against me, which I wouldn't do for the world. And whatever other people may say, I believe she will have money to leave."

Miss Cushing hesitated for a moment, and then spoke up boldly.

"It's my opinion," said she, "that Miss Inchman is the proper person to speak to Mrs. Cliff on this important subject. She's known her all her life, from the time when they were little girls together, and when they were both grown she made sacrifices for her which none of the rest of us had the chance to make.

"Now, for Miss Inchman to go and open the subject in a gradual and friendly way would be the right and proper thing, no matter how you look at it, and it's my opinion that we who are now here should ask her to go and speak, not in our names perhaps, but out of good-will and kindness to us as well as to Mrs. Cliff."

Mrs. Wells was a lady who was in the habit of saying things at the wrong time, and she now remarked, "We've forgotten the Thorpedykes! You know, Mrs. Cliff — "

Miss Cushing leaned forward, her face reddened. "Bother the Thorpedykes!" she exclaimed. "They're no more than acquaintances, and ought not to be spoken of at all. And as for Mrs. Perley, if any one's thinking of her, she's only been here four years, and that gives her no claim whatever, considering that we've been life-long friends and neighbors of Sarah Cliff.

"And now, in behalf of all of us, I ask you, Miss Inchman, will you speak to Mrs. Cliff?"

Miss Inchman was rather a small woman, spare in figure, and she wore glasses, which seemed to be of a peculiar kind, for while they enabled her to see through them into surrounding space, they did not allow people who looked at her to see through them into her eyes. People often remarked that you could not tell the color of Miss Inchman's eyes when she had her spectacles on.

Thus it was that although her eyes were sometimes brighter than at other times, and this could be noticed through her spectacles, it was difficult to understand her expression and to discover whether she was angry or amused.

Now Miss Inchman's eyes behind her spectacles brightened very much as she looked from Miss Cushing to the other members of the little party who had consti-tuted themselves the heirs of Mrs. Cliff. None of them could judge from her face what she was likely to say, but they all waited to hear what she would say. At this moment the door opened, and Mrs. Cliff entered the parlor.

CHAPTER X

THE INTELLECT OF MISS INCHMAN

IT was true that on that morning Mrs. Cliff had been
standing in her front yard looking as her best friends
would not have liked her to look. There was nothing
physically the matter with her, but she was dissatisfied
and somewhat disturbed in her mind. Mr. Burke was
so busy nowadays that when he stopped in to see her it
was only for a few minutes, and Willy Croup had
developed a great facility in discovering things which
ought to be attended to in various parts of the town, and
of going to attend to them with Andrew Marks to drive
her.

Not only did Mrs. Cliff feel that she was left more to
herself than she liked, but she had the novel experience
of not being able to find interesting occupation. She
was glad to have servants who could perform all the
household duties, and could have done more if they had
had a chance. Still, it was unpleasant to feel that she
herself could do so little to fill up her unoccupied moments. So she put on a shawl and went into her front
yard, simply to walk about and get a little of the fresh
air. But when she went out of the door, she stood still
contemplating the front fence.

Here was a fence which had been an eyesore to her
for two or three years! She believed she had money
enough to fence in the whole State, and yet those shabby

palings and posts must offend her eye every time she
came out of her door! The flowers were nearly all dead
now, and she would have had a new fence immediately,
but Mr. Burke had dissuaded her, saying that when the
new dining-room was brought over from the corner lot
there would have to be a fence around the whole prem-
ises, and it would be better to have it all done at once.

"There are so many things which I can afford just as
well as not," she said to herself, "and which I cannot
do!" And it was the unmistakable doleful expression
upon her countenance, as she thought this, which was
the foundation of Miss Shott's remarks to her neighbors
on the subject of Mrs. Cliff's probable early demise.

Miss Shott was passing on the other side of the street,
and she was walking rapidly, but she could see more out
of the corner of her eye than most people could see when
they were looking straight before them at the same
things.

Suddenly Mrs. Cliff determined that she must do
something. She felt blue, — she wanted to talk to somebody. And, feeling thus, she naturally went into the
house, put on her bonnet and her wrap, and walked down
to see Miss Cushing. There was not anything in particular that she wanted to see her about, but there was
work going on and she might talk about it; or, it might
happen that she would be inclined to give some orders.
She was always glad to do anything she could to help
that hard-working and kind-hearted neighbor!

When Mrs. Cliff entered the parlor of Miss Cushing,
five women each gave a sudden start. The dressmaker

was so thrown off her balance that she dropped her sewing on the floor, and rising, went forward to shake her visitor by the hand, a thing she was not in the habit of doing to anybody, because, as is well known to all the world, a person who is sewing for a livelihood cannot get up to shake hands with the friends and acquaintances who may happen in upon her. At this the other ladies rose and shook hands, and it might have been supposed that the new-comer had just returned from a long absence. Then Miss Cushing gave Mrs. Cliff a chair, and they all sat down again.

Mrs. Cliff looked about her with a smile. The sight of these old friends cheered her. All her blues were beginning to fade, as that color always fades in any kind of sunshine.

"I'm glad to see so many of you together," she said. "It almost seems as if you were having some sort of meeting. What is it about, — can't I join in?"

At this there was a momentary silence which threatened to become very embarrassing if it continued a few seconds more, and Miss Cushing was on the point of telling the greatest lie of her career, trusting that the other heirs would stand by her and support her in whatever statements she made, feeling as they must the absolute necessity of saying something instantly. But Miss Inchman spoke before any one else had a chance to do so.

"You're right, Mrs. Cliff," said she, "we are considering something! We didn't come here on purpose to talk about it, but we happened in together, and so we thought we would talk it over. And we all came to the conclusion that it was something which ought to be mentioned to you, and I was asked to speak to you about it."

Four simultaneous gasps were now heard in that little parlor, and four chills ran down the backs of four self-constituted heirs.

"I must say, Susan," remarked Mrs. Cliff, with a good-humored smile, "if you want me to do anything, there's no need of being so wonderfully formal about it! If any one of you, or all of you together, for that matter, have anything to say to me, all you had to do was to come and say it."

"They didn't seem to think that way," said Miss Inchman. "They all thought that what was to be said would come better from me because I'd known you so long, and we had grown up together."

"It must be something out of the common," said Mrs. Cliff. "What in the world can it be? If you are to speak, Susan, speak out at once! Let's have it!"

"That's just what I'm going to do," said Miss Inchman.

If Mrs. Cliff had looked around at the four heirs who were sitting upright in their chairs, gazing in horror at Miss Inchman, she would have been startled, and, perhaps, frightened. But she did not see them. She was so much interested in what her old friend Susan was saying, that she gave to her her whole attention.

But now that their appointed spokeswoman had announced her intention of immediately declaring the object of the meeting, each one of them felt that this was no place for her! But, notwithstanding this feeling, not one of them moved to go. Miss Cushing, of course, had no excuse for leaving, for this was her own house; and although the others might have pleaded errands, a power stronger than their disposition to fly — stronger even than their fears of what Mrs. Cliff might say to them when she knew all — kept them in their seats. The spell of self-interest was upon them and held them fast. Whatever was said and whatever was done they must be there! At this supreme moment they could not leave the room. They nerved themselves, they breathed hard, and listened!

"You see, Sarah," said Miss Inchman, "we must all die!"

"That's no new discovery," answered Mrs. Cliff, and the remark seemed to her so odd that she looked around at the rest of the company to see how they took it; and she was thereupon impressed with the idea that some of them had not thought of this great truth of late, and that its sudden announcement had thrown them into a shocked solemnity.

But the soul of Miss Cushing was more than shocked, — it was filled with fury! If there had been in that room at that instant a loaded gun pointed towards Miss Inchman, Miss Cushing would have pulled the trigger. This would have been wicked, she well knew, and contrary to her every principle, but never before had she been confronted by such treachery!

"Well," continued Miss Inchman, "as we must die, we

ought to make ourselves ready for it in every way that we can. And we've been thinking — "

At this moment the endurance of Mrs. Ferguson gave way. The pace and the strain were too great for her. Each of the others had herself to think for, but she had not only herself, but two daughters. She gave a groan, her head fell back, her eyes closed, and with a considerable thump she slipped from her chair to the floor. Instantly every one screamed and sprang towards her.

"What in the world is the matter with her?" cried Mrs. Cliff, as she assisted the others to raise the head of the fainting woman and to loosen her dress.

"Oh, I suppose it's the thought of her late husband!" promptly replied Miss Inchman, who felt that it devolved on her to say something, and that quickly. Mrs. Cliff looked up in amazement.

"And what has Mr. Ferguson to do with anything?" she asked.

"Oh, it's the new cemetery I was going to talk to you about," said Miss Inchman. "It has been spoken of a good deal since you went away, and we all thought that if you'd agree to go into it — "

"Go into it!" cried Mrs. Cliff, in horror.

"I mean, join with the people who are in favor of it," said Miss Inchman. "I haven't time to explain, — she's coming to now, if you'll all let her alone! All I've time to say is, that those who had husbands in the old grave-yard and might perhaps be inclined to move them and put up monuments, had the right to be first spoken to.

Although, of course, it's a subject which everybody doesn't care to speak about, and as for Mrs. Ferguson, it's no wonder, knowing her as we do, that she went off in this way when she knew what I was going to say, although, in fact, I wasn't in the least thinking of Mr. Ferguson!"

The speaker had barely time to finish before the unfortunate lady who had fainted, opened her eyes, looked about her, and asked where she was. And now that she had revived, no further reference could be made to the unfortunate subject which had caused her to swoon.

"I don't see," said Mrs. Cliff, as she stood outside with Miss Inchman, a few minutes later, "why Mr. Ferguson's removal — I'm sure it isn't necessary to make it if she doesn't want to — should trouble Mrs. Ferguson any more than the thought of Mr. Cliff's removal troubles me. I'm perfectly willing to do what I can for the new cemetery, and nobody need think I'm such a nervous hysterical person that I'm in danger of popping over if the subject is mentioned to me. So when you all are ready to have another meeting, I hope you will let me know!"

When Mrs. Ferguson felt herself well enough to sit up and take a glass of water, with something stimulating in it, she was informed of the nature of the statements which had been finally made to Mrs. Cliff.

"You know, of course," added Miss Cushing, still pale from unappeased rage, "that that Susan Inchman began as she did, just to spite us!"

"It's just like her!" said Mrs. Archibald. "But I

never could have believed that such a dried codfish of a woman could have so much intellect ! "

CHAPTER XI

THE ARRIVAL OF THE NEW DINING-ROOM

THE little meeting at the house of Miss Cushing resulted in something very different from the anticipations of those ladies who had consulted together for the purpose of constituting themselves the heirs of Mrs. Cliff.

That good lady being then very much in want of something to do was so pleased with the idea of a new cemetery that she entered into the scheme with great earnestness. She was particularly pleased with this opportunity of making good use of her money, because, having been asked by others to join them in this work, she was not obliged to pose as a self-appointed public benefactor.

Mrs. Cliff worked so well in behalf of the new cemetery and subscribed so much money towards it, through Mr. Perley, that it was not many months before it became the successor to the little crowded graveyard near the centre of the town; and the remains of Mr. Cliff were removed to a handsome lot and overshadowed by a suitable monument.

Mrs. Ferguson, however, in speaking with Mrs. Cliff upon the subject, was happy to have an opportunity of assuring her that she thought it much better to devote her slender means to the education of her daughters than to the removal of her late husband to a more eligible resting-place.

"I'm sure he's done very well as he is for all these years," she said, "and if he could have a voice in the matter, I'm quite sure that he would prefer his daughters' education to his own removal."

Mrs. Cliff did not wish to make any offer which might hurt Mrs. Ferguson's very sensitive feelings, but she said that she had no doubt that arrangements could be made by which Mr. Ferguson's transfer could be effected without interfering with any plans which might have been made for the benefit of his daughters; but, although this remark did not satisfy Mrs. Ferguson, she was glad of even this slight opportunity of bringing the subject of her daughters' education before the consideration of her friend.

As to the other would-be heirs, they did not immediately turn upon Miss Inchman and rend her in revenge for the way in which she had tricked and frightened them, for there was no knowing what such a woman would do if she were exasperated, and not for the world would they have Mrs. Cliff find out the real subject of their discussion on that unlucky morning when she made herself decidedly one too many in Miss Cushing's parlor.

Consequently, all attempts at concerted action were dropped, and each for herself determined that Mrs. Cliff should know that she was a true friend, and to trust to

the good lady's well-known gratitude and friendly feeling
when the time should come for her to apportion her
worldly goods among the dear ones she would leave
behind her.

There were certain articles in Mrs. Cliff's house for
which each of her friends had a decided admiration, and
remarks were often made which it was believed would
render it impossible for Mrs. Cliff to make a mistake
when she should be planning her will, and asking herself to whom she should give this, and to whom that ?

It was about a week after the events in Miss Cushing's parlor, that something occurred which sent a thrill
through the souls of a good many people in Plainton,
affecting them more or less according to their degree of
sensibility.

Willy Croup, who had been driven about the town
attending to various matters of business and pleasure,
was informed by Andrew Marks, as she alighted about
four o'clock in the afternoon at the house of an acquaintance, that he hoped she would not stop very long because he had some business of his own to attend to that
afternoon, and he wanted to get the horse cared for and
the cow milked as early as possible, so that he might
lock up the barn and go away. To this Willy answered
that he need not wait for her, for she could easily walk
home when she had finished her visit.

But when she left the house, after a protracted call,
she did not walk very far, for it so happened that Mr.
Burke, who had found leisure that afternoon to take a
drive in his barouche, came up behind her, and very

naturally stopped and offered to take her home. Willy, quite as naturally, accepted the polite proposition and seated herself in the barouche by the side of the fur-trimmed overcoat and the high silk hat.

Thus it was that the people of the town who were in the main street that afternoon, or who happened to be at doors or windows; that the very birds of the air, hopping about on trees or house-tops; that the horses, dogs, and cats; that even the insects, whose constitutions were strong enough to enable them to buzz about in the autumn sunlight, beheld the startling sight of Willy Croup and the fine gentleman at the hotel riding together, side by side, in broad daylight, through the most public street of the town.

Once before these two had been seen together out of doors, but then they had been walking, and almost any two people who knew each other and who might be walking in the same direction, could, without impropriety walk side by side and converse as they went; but now the incident was very different.

It created a great impression, not all to the advantage of Mr. Burke, for, after the matter had been very thoroughly discussed, it was generally conceded that he must be no better than a fortune-hunter. Otherwise, why should he be paying attention to Willy Croup, who, as everybody knew, was not a day under forty-five years old, and therefore at least ten years older than the gentleman at the hotel.

In regard to the fortune which he was hunting, there was no difference of opinion; whatever Mrs. Cliff's fortune might be, this Mr. Burke wanted it. Of course, he would not endeavor to gain his object by marrying the widow, for she was entirely too old for him; but if he married Willy, her only relative, that would not be quite so bad as to age, and there could be no doubt that these two would ultimately come into Mrs. Cliff's fortune, which was probably more than had been generally supposed. She had always been very close-mouthed about her affairs, and there were some who said that even in her early days of widowhood she might have been more stingy than she was poor. She must have considerable property, or Mr. Burke would not be so anxious to get it.

Thus it happened that the eventful drive in the barouche had a very different effect upon the reputations of the three persons concerned. Mr. Burke was lowered from his position as a man of means enjoying his fortune, for even his building operations were probably undertaken for the purpose of settling himself in Mrs. Cliff's neighborhood, and so being able to marry Willy as soon as possible.

Willy Croup, although everybody spoke of her conduct as absolutely ridiculous and even shameful, rose in public estimation simply from the belief that she was about to marry a man who, whatever else he might be, was of imposing appearance and was likely to be rich.

As to Mrs. Cliff, there could be no doubt that the general respect for her was on the increase. If she were rich enough to attract Mr. Burke to the town, she was probably rich enough to do a good many other things, and after all it might be that that new house at the corner was being built with her money.

Miss Shott was very industrious and energetic in expressing her opinion of Mr. Burke. "There's a chambermaid at the hotel," she said, "who's told me a lot of things about him, and it's very plain to my mind that he isn't the gentleman that he makes himself out to be! His handkerchiefs and his hair-brush aren't the kind that go with fur overcoats and high hats, and she has often seen him stop in the hall downstairs and black his own boots! Everybody knows he was a sailor, but as to his ever having commanded a vessel, I don't believe a word of it! But Willy Croup and that man needn't count on their schemes coming out all right, for Sarah Cliff isn't any older than I am, and she's just as likely to outlive them as she is to die before them!"

The fact that nobody had ever said that Burke had commanded a vessel, and that Miss Shott had started the belief that Mrs. Cliff was in a rapid decline, entirely escaped the attention of her hearers, so interested were they in the subject of the unworthiness of the fine gentleman at the hotel.

Winter had not yet really set in when George Burke, who had perceived no reason to imagine that he had made a drop in public estimation, felt himself stirred by emotions of triumphant joy. The new building on the corner lot was on the point of completion!

Workmen and master-workmen, mechanics and laborers, had swarmed in, over, and about the new edifice in such numbers that sometimes they impeded each other.

Close upon the heels of the masons came the carpenters, and following them the plumbers and the plasterers; while the painters impatiently restrained themselves in order to give their predecessors time to get out of their way.

The walls and ceilings were covered with the plaster which would dry the quickest, and the paper-hangers entered the rooms almost before the plasterers could take away their trowels and their lime-begrimed hats and coats. Cleaners with their brooms and pails jostled the mechanics, as the latter left the various rooms, and everywhere strode Mr. Burke. He had made up his mind that the building must be ready to move into the instant it arrived at its final destination.

It was a very different building from what Mrs. Cliff had proposed to herself when she decided to add a dining-room to her old house. It was so different indeed, that after having gone two or three times to look upon the piles of lumber and stone and the crowds of men, digging, and hammering, and sawing on the corner lot, she had decided to leave the whole matter in the hands of Mr. Burke, the architect, and the contractor. And when Willy Croup endeavored to explain to her what was going on, she always stopped her, saying that she would wait until it was done and then she would understand it.

Mr. Burke too had urged her, especially as the building drew near to completion, not to bother herself in the least about it, but to give him the pleasure of presenting it to her entirely finished and ready for occupancy. So even the painting and paper-hanging had been left to a professional decorator, and Mrs. Cliff assured Burke that she was perfectly willing to wait for the new dining-room until it was ready for her.

This dining-room, large and architecturally handsome, was planned, as has been said, so that one of its doors should fit exactly against the side hall door of the little house, but the other door of the dining-room opened into a wide and elegant hall, at one end of which was a portico and spacious front steps. On the other side of this hall was a handsome drawing-room, and behind the drawing-room and opening into it, an alcove library with a broad piazza at one side of it. Back of the dining-room was a spacious kitchen, with pantries, closets, scullery, and all necessary adjuncts.

In the second and third stories of the edifice were large and beautiful bedrooms, small and neat bedrooms, bath-rooms, servants' rooms, trunk-rooms, and every kind of room that modern civilization demands.

Now that the building was finished, Mr. Burke almost regretted that he had not constructed it upon the top of a hill in order that he might have laid his smooth and slippery timbers from the eminence to the side of Mrs. Cliff's house, so that when all should be ready he could have knocked away the blocks which held the building, so that he could have launched it as if it had been a ship, and could have beheld it sliding gracefully and rapidly from its stocks into its appointed position. But as this would probably have resulted in razing Mrs. Cliff's old house to the level of the ground, he did not long regret that he had not been able to afford himself the pleasure of this grand spectacle.

The night before the day on which the new building was to be moved, the lot next to Mrs. Cliff's house was covered by masons, laborers, and wagons hauling stones, and by breakfast-time the next morning the new cellar was completed.

Almost immediately the great timbers, which, polished and greased, had been waiting for several days, were put in their places, and the great steam engines and windlasses, which had been ready as long a time, were set in motion. And, as the house began to move upon its course, it almost missed a parting dab from the brush of a painter who was at work upon some final trimming.

That afternoon, as Mrs. Cliff happened to be in her dining-room, she remarked to Willy that it was getting dark very early, but she would not pull up the blind of the side window, because she would then look out on the new cellar, and she had promised Mr. Burke not to look at anything until he had told her to do so. Willy, who had looked out of the side door at least fifty times that day, knew that the early darkness was caused by the shadows thrown by a large building slowly approaching from the west.

When Mrs. Cliff came downstairs the next morning she was met by Willy, very much excited, who told her that Mr. Burke wished to see her.

"Where is he?" said she. "At the dining-room door," answered Willy, and as Mrs. Cliff turned towards the little room in which she had been accus-

tomed to take her meals, Willy seized her hand and
led her into the side hall. There, in the open doorway, stood Mr. Burke, his high silk hat in one hand,
and the other outstretched towards her.

"Welcome to your new dining-room, madam!" said
he, as he took her hand and led her into the great room,
which seemed to her, as she gazed in amazement about
her, like a beautiful public hall.

We will not follow Mrs. Cliff, Willy, and the whole
body of domestic servants, as they passed through the
halls and rooms of that grand addition to Mrs. Cliff's
little house.

"Carpets and furniture is all that you want, madam!"
said Burke, "and then you're at home!"

When Mrs. Cliff had been upstairs and downstairs,
and into every chamber, and when she had looked out
of the window and had beheld hundreds of men at work
upon the grounds and putting up fences; and when Mr.
Burke had explained to her that the people at the back
of the lot were beginning to erect a stable and carriage
house, — for no dining-room such as she had was complete, he assured her, without handsome quarters for
horses and carriages, — she left him and went downstairs by herself.

As she stood by the great front door and looked up at
the wide staircase, and into the lofty rooms upon each
side, there came to her, rising above all sentiments of
amazement, delight, and pride in her new possessions, a
feeling of animated and inspiring encouragement. The
mists of doubt and uncertainty, which had hung over her,

began to clear away. This noble edifice must have cost grandly! And, for the first time, she began to feel that she might yet be equal to her fortune.

CHAPTER XII

THE THORPEDYKE SISTERS

THE new and grand addition to Mrs. Cliff's house, which had been so planned that the little house to which it had been joined appeared to be an architecturally harmonious adjunct to it, caused a far greater sensation in Plainton than the erection of any of the public buildings therein.

Its journey from the corner lot was watched by hundreds of spectators, and now Mrs. Cliff, Willy, and Mr. Burke spent day and evening in exhibiting and explaining this remarkable piece of building enterprise.

Mr. Burke was very jolly. He took no credit to himself for the planning of the house, which, as he truthfully said, had been the work of an architect who had suggested what was proper and had been allowed to do it. But he did feel himself privileged to declare that if every crew building a house were commanded by a person of marine experience, things would move along a good deal more briskly than they generally did, and to this assertion he found no one to object.

Mrs. Cliff was very happy in wandering over her new rooms, and in assuring herself that no matter how grand they might be when they were all furnished and fitted up, nothing had been done which would interfere with the dear old home which she had loved so long. It is true that one of the windows of the little dining-room was blocked up, but that window was not needed.

Mr. Burke was not willing to give Mrs. Cliff more than a day or two for the contemplation of her new possessions, and urged upon her that while the chimneys were being erected and the heating apparatus was being put into the house, she ought to attend to the selection and purchase of the carpets, furniture, pictures, and everything which was needed in the new establishment.

Mrs. Cliff thought this good advice, and proposed a trip to Boston; but Burke did not think that would do at all, and declared that New York was the only place where she could get everything she needed. Willy, who was to accompany Mrs. Cliff, had been to Boston, but had never visited New York, and she strongly urged the claims of the latter city, and an immediate journey to the metropolis was agreed upon.

But when Mrs. Cliff considered the magnitude and difficulties of the work she was about to undertake, she wished for the counsel and advice of some one besides Willy. This good little woman was energetic and enthusiastic, but she had had no experience in regard to the furnishing of a really good house.

When, in her mind, she was running over the names of those who might be able and willing to go with her and assist her, Mrs. Cliff suddenly thought of the Thorpedyke ladies, and there her mental category stopped as she announced to Willy that she was going to ask these ladies to go with them to New York.

Willy thought well of this plan, but she had her doubts about Miss Barbara, who was so quiet, domestic, and unused to travel that she might be unwilling to cast herself into the din and whirl of the metropolis. But when she and Mrs. Cliff went to make a call upon the Thorpedykes and put the question before them, she was very much surprised to find that, although the elder sister, after carefully considering the subject, announced her willingness to oblige Mrs. Cliff, Miss Barbara agreed to the plan with an alacrity which her visitors had never known her to exhibit before.

As soon as the necessary preparations could be made, a party of five left Plainton for New York, and a very well-assorted party it was! Mr. Burke, who guided and commanded the expedition, supplied the impelling energy; Mrs. Cliff had her check book with her; Willy was ready with any amount of enthusiasm; and the past life of Miss Eleanor Thorpedyke and her sister Barbara had made them most excellent judges of what was appropriate for the worthy furnishing of a stately mansion.

Their youth and middle life had been spent near Boston, in a fine old house which had been the home of their ancestors, and where they had been familiar with wealth, distinguished society, and noble hospitality. But when they had been left the sole representatives of their family, and when misfortune after misfortune had come down upon them and swept away their estates and nearly all of their income, they had retired to the little town of Plainton where they happened to own a house.

There, with nothing saved from the wreck of their prosperity but their family traditions, and some of the old furniture and pictures, they had settled down to spend in quiet the rest of their lives.

For two weeks our party remained in New York, living at one of the best hotels, but spending nearly all their time in shops and streets.

Mrs. Cliff was rapidly becoming a different woman from the old Mrs. Cliff of Plainton. At the time she stepped inside of the addition to her house the change had begun, and now it showed itself more and more each day. She had seen more beautiful things in Paris, but there she looked upon them with but little thought of purchasing. In New York whatever she saw and desired she made her own.

The difference between a mere possessor of wealth and one who uses it became very apparent to her. Not until now had she really known what it was to be a rich woman. Not only did this consciousness of power swell her veins with a proud delight, but it warmed and invigorated all her better impulses. She had always been of a generous disposition, but now she felt an intense good-will toward her fellow-beings, and wished that other people could be as happy as she was.

She thought of Mrs. Ferguson and remembered what she had said about her daughters. To be sure, Mrs. Ferguson was always trying to get people to do things for

her, and Mrs. Cliff did not fancy that class of women,
but now her wealth-warmed soul inclined her to overlook
this prejudice, and she said to herself that when she got
home she would make arrangements for those two girls
to go to a good school; and, more than that, she would
see to it that Mr. Ferguson was moved. It seemed to
her just then that it would be a very cheerful thing to
make other people happy.

The taste and artistic judgment of the elder Miss
Thorpedyke, which had been dormant for years, simply
because there was nothing upon which they could exercise
themselves, now awoke in their old vigor, and with Mrs.
Cliff's good sense, reinforced by her experience gained
in wandering among the treasures of Paris, the results of
the shopping expedition were eminently satisfactory.
And, with the plan of the new building, which Mr. Burke
carried always with him, everything which was likely to
be needed in each room, hall, or stairway, was selected
and purchased, and as fast as this was done, the things
were shipped to Plainton, where people were ready to
put them where they belonged.

Willy Croup was not always of service in the purchasing expeditions, for she liked everything that she saw,
and no sooner was an article produced than she went into
ecstasies over it; but as she had an intense desire to see
everything which New York contained, she did not at all
confine herself to the shops and bazaars. She went
wherever she could and saw all that it was possible for
her to see; but in the midst of the sights and attractions
of the metropolis she was still Willy Croup.

I

One afternoon as she and Miss Barbara were passing along one of the side streets on their return from an attempt to see how the poorer people lived, Willy stopped in front of a blacksmith's shop where a man was shoeing a horse.

"There!" she exclaimed, her eyes sparkling with delight, "that's the first thing I've seen that reminds me of home!"

"It is nice, isn't it!" said gentle Miss Barbara.

CHAPTER XIII

MONEY HUNGER

DURING the latter part of their sojourn in the city, Willy went about a good deal with Miss Barbara because she thought this quiet, soft-spoken lady was not happy and did not take the interest in handsome and costly articles which was shown by her sister. She had been afraid that this noisy bustling place would be too much for Miss Barbara, and now she was sure she had been right.

The younger Miss Thorpedyke was unhappy, and with reason. For some months a little house in Boston which had been their principal source of income had not been rented. It needed repairs, and there was no money with which to repair it. The agent had written that some one might appear who would be willing to take it as it stood, but that this was doubtful, and the heart of Miss Barbara sank very low. She was the business woman of the family. She it was who had always balanced the income and the expenditures. This adjustment had now become very difficult indeed, and was only accomplished by adding a little debt to the weight on the income scale.

She had said nothing to her sister about this sad change in their affairs because she hoped against hope that soon they might have a tenant, and she knew that her sister Eleanor was a woman of such strict and punctilious honor that she would insist upon living upon plain bread, if their supply of ready money was insufficient to buy anything else. To see this sister insufficiently nourished was something which Miss Barbara could not endure, and so, sorely against her disposition and her conscience, she made some little debts; and these grew and grew until at last they weighed her down until she felt as if she must always look upon the earth and could never raise her head to the sky. And she was so plump, and so white, and gentle, and quiet, and peaceful looking that no one thought she had a care in the world until Willy Croup began to suspect in New York that something was the matter with her, but did not in the least attribute her friend's low spirits to the proper cause.

When Miss Barbara had favored so willingly and promptly the invitation of Mrs. Cliff, she had done so because she saw in the New York visit a temporary abolition of expense, and a consequent opportunity to lay up a little money by which she might be able to satisfy for a time one of her creditors who was beginning to suspect that she was not able to pay his bill, and was therefore pressing her very hard. Even while she had been in

New York, this many-times rendered bill had been forwarded to her with an urgent request that it be settled.

It was not strange, therefore, that a tear should sometimes come to the eye of Miss Barbara when she stood by the side of her sister and Mrs. Cliff and listened to them discussing the merits of some rich rugs or pieces of furniture, and when she reflected that the difference in price between two articles, one apparently as desirable as the other, which was discussed so lightly by Mrs. Cliff and Eleanor, would pay that bill which was eating into her soul, and settle, moreover, every other claim against herself and her sister. But the tears were always wiped away very quickly, and neither Mrs. Cliff nor the elder Miss Thorpedyke ever noticed them.

But although Willy Croup was not at all a woman of acute perceptions, she began to think that perhaps it was something more than the bustle and noise of New York which was troubling Miss Barbara. And once, when she saw her gazing with an earnest eager glare — and whoever would have thought of any sort of a glare in Miss Barbara's eyes — upon some bank-notes which Mrs. Cliff was paying out for a carved cabinet for which it was a little doubtful if a suitable place could be found, but which was bought because Miss Eleanor thought it would give an air of distinction in whatever room it might be placed, Willy began to suspect the meaning of that unusual exhibition of emotion.

"She's money hungry," she said to herself, "that's what's the matter with her!" Willy had seen the signs of such hunger before, and she understood what they meant.

That night Willy lay in her bed, having the very unusual experience of thinking so much that she could not sleep. Her room adjoined Miss Barbara's, and the door between them was partly open, for the latter lady was timid. Perhaps it was because this door was not closed that Willy was so wakeful and thoughtful, for there was a bright light in the other room, and she could not imagine why Miss Barbara should be sitting up so late. It was a proceeding entirely at variance with her usual habits. She was in some sort of trouble, it was easy to see that, but it would be a great deal better to go to sleep and try to forget it.

So after a time Willy rose, and, softly stepping over the thick carpet, looked into the other room. There was Miss Barbara in her day dress, sitting at a table, her arms upon the table, her head upon her arms, fast asleep. Upon her pale face there were a great many tear marks, and Willy knew that she must have cried herself to sleep. A paper was spread out near her.

Willy was sure that it would be a very mean and contemptible thing for her to go and look at that paper, and so, perhaps, find out what was troubling Miss Barbara, but, without the slightest hesitation, she did it. Her bare feet made no sound upon the carpet, and as she had very good eyes, it was not necessary for her to approach close to the sleeper.

It was a bill from William Bullock, a grocer and provision dealer of Plainton. It contained but one item, —

'To bill rendered,' and at the bottom was a statement in Mr. Bullock's own handwriting to the effect that if the bill was not immediately paid he would be obliged to put it into the hands of a collector.

Willy turned and slipped back into her room. Then, after sitting down upon her bed and getting up again, she stepped boldly to the door and knocked upon it. Instantly she heard Miss Barbara start and push back her chair.

"What are you doing up so late?" cried Willy, cheerfully. "Don't you feel well?"

"Oh, yes," replied the other, "I accidentally fell asleep while reading, but I will go to bed instantly."

The mind of Willy Croup was a very small one and had room in it for but one idea at a time. For a good while she lay putting ideas into this mind, and then taking them out again. Having given place to the conviction that the Thorpedykes were in a very bad way indeed, — for if that bill should be collected, they would not have much left but themselves, and Mr. Bullock was a man who did collect when he said he would, — she was obliged to remove this conviction, which made her cry, in order to consider plans of relief; and while she was considering these plans, one at a time, she dropped asleep.

The first thing she thought of when she opened her eyes in the morning was poor Miss Barbara in the next room, and that dreadful bill; and then, like a flash of lightning, she thought of a good thing to do for the Thorpedykes. The project which now laid itself out, detail after detail, before her seemed so simple, so sensible, so absolutely wise and desirable in every way, that she got up, dressed herself with great rapidity, and went in to see Mrs. Cliff.

That lady was still asleep, but Willy awakened her, and sat on the side of the bed. "Do you know what I think?" said Willy.

"How in the world should I!" said Mrs. Cliff. "Is it after breakfast-time?"

"No," said Willy; "but it's this! What are you going to do in that big house, with all the bedrooms, parlor, library, and so forth? You say that you are going to have one room, and that I'm to have another, and that we'll go into the old house to feel at home whenever we want to; but I believe we'll be like a couple of flies in a barrel! You're going to furnish your new house with everything but people! You ought to have more people! You ought to have a family! That house will look funny without people! You can't ask Mr. Burke, because it would be too queer to have him come and live with us, and besides, he'll want a house of his own. Why don't you ask the Thorpedykes to come and live with us? Their roof is dreadfully out of repairs. I know to my certain knowledge that they have to put tin wash-basins on every bed in the second story when it rains, on account of the holes in the shingles! If they had money to mend those holes, they'd mend them, but as they don't mend them, of course they haven't the money. And it strikes me that they aren't as well off as they used to be, and they'll have a hard time gettin' through this winter. Now, there isn't any piece of furniture that you can put in your house that will give it 'such an air of distinction,' as Miss Eleanor calls it, as she herself will give it if you put her there! If you could persuade Miss Eleanor to come and sit in your parlor when you are having company to see you, it would set you up in Plainton a good deal higher than any money can set you up."

"They would never agree to anything of the kind," said Mrs. Cliff, "and you know it, Willy!"

"I don't believe it," said Willy. "I believe they'd come! Just see how willing they were to come here with you! I tell you, Sarah, that the older and older those Thorpedyke ladies get, the more timid they get, and the more unwilling to live by themselves!

"If you make Miss Eleanor understand that it would be the greatest comfort and happiness to both of us if she would come and spend the winter with you, and so help you to get used to your great big new house; and more than that, if they'd bring with them some of their candle-sticks and pictures on ivory and that sort of thing, which everybody knows can't be bought for money, it would be the great accommodation to you and make your house look something like what you would like to have it. I believe that old-family lady would come and stay with you this winter, and think all the time that she was giving you something that you ought to have and which nobody in Plainton could give you but herself. And as to Miss Barbara, she'd come along as quick as lightning!"

"Willy," said Mrs. Cliff, very earnestly, "have you any good reason to believe that the Thorpedykes are in money trouble?"

"Yes, I have," said Willy, "I'm positive of it, and what's more, it's only Miss Barbara who knows it!"

Mrs. Cliff sat for some minutes without answering, and then she said, "Willy, you do sometimes get into your head an idea that absolutely sparkles!"

CHAPTER XIV

WILLY CROUP AS A PHILANTHROPIC DIPLOMATIST

MRS. CLIFF was late to breakfast that day, and the reason was that thinking so much about what Willy had said to her she had been very slow in dressing. As soon as she had a chance, Mrs. Cliff took Willy aside and told her that she had determined to adopt her advice about the Thorpedykes.

"The more I think of the plan," she said, "the better I like it! But we must be very, very careful about what we do. If Miss Eleanor suspects that I invite them to come to my house because I think they are poor, she will turn into solid stone, and we will find we cannot move her an inch, — but I think I can manage it! When we go home, I will tell them how pleasant we found it for us all to be together, and speak of the loneliness of my new big house. If I can get Miss Eleanor to believe that she is doing me a favor, she may be willing to come ; but on no account, Willy, do you say a word to either of them about this plan. If you do, you will spoil everything, for that's your way, Willy, and you know it!"

Willy promised faithfully that she would not interfere in the least; but although she was perfectly satisfied with this arrangement, she was not happy. How could she be happy knowing what she did about Miss Barbara? That poor lady was looking sadder than ever, and Willy was very much afraid that she had had another letter from that horrid Mr. Bullock, with whom, she was delighted to think, Mrs. Cliff had never dealt.

It would be some days yet before they would go home and make the new arrangement, and then there would be the bill and the collector, and all that horrid business, and if Miss Eleanor found out the condition of affairs, — and if the bill was not paid, she must find out, — she would never come to them. She would probably stay at home and live on bread!

Now, it so happened that Willy had in her own possession more than enough money to pay that wretched Bullock bill. Mrs. Cliff made her no regular allowance, but she had given her all the money that she might reasonably expect to spend in New York, and Willy had spent but very little of it, for she found it the most difficult thing in the world to select what it was she wanted out of all the desirable things she saw.

It would rejoice her heart to transfer this money to Miss Barbara; but how in the world could she do it? She first thought that she might offer to buy something

that was in the Thorpedyke house, but she knew
this idea was absurd. Then she thought of mentioning, in an off-hand way, that she would like to put
some money out at interest, and thus, perhaps, induce
Miss Barbara to propose a business transaction. But
this would not do. Even Miss Barbara would suspect some concealed motive. Idea after idea came
to her, but she could think of no satisfactory plan
of getting that money into Miss Barbara's possession.

She did not go out with the party that morning, but
sat in her room trying in vain to solve this problem.
At last she gave it up and determined to do what she
wanted to do without any plan whatever.

She went into Miss Barbara's room and placed upon
the table, in the very spot where the bill had been lying,
some bank-notes, considerably more than sufficient to
pay the amount of the bill, which amount she well
remembered. It would not do to leave just money
enough, for that would excite suspicion. And so placing
Miss Barbara's hair-brush upon the bank-notes, so that
she would be sure not to overlook them, for she would
not think of going down to luncheon without brushing
her hair, Willy retired to her own room, nearly closing
the door, leaving only a little crack through which she
might see if any servant entered the room before Miss
Barbara came back.

Then Willy set herself industriously to work hemming
a pocket handkerchief. She could not do this very well,
because she was not at all proficient in fine sewing, but

she worked with great energy, waiting and listening for Miss Barbara's entrance.

At last, after a long time, Willy heard the outer door of the other room open, and glancing through the crack, she saw Miss Barbara enter. Then she twisted herself around towards the window and began to sew savagely, with a skill much better adapted to the binding of carpets than to any sort of work upon cambric handkerchiefs.

In a few minutes she heard a little exclamation in the next room, and then her door was opened suddenly, without the customary knock, and Miss Barbara marched in. Her face was flushed.

"Willy Croup," said she, "what is the meaning of that money on my table?"

"Money?" said Willy, turning towards her with as innocent an expression as her burning cheeks and rapidly winking eyes would permit; "what do you mean by — money?"

Miss Barbara stood silent for some moments while Willy vainly endeavored to thread the point of her needle.

"Willy," said Miss Barbara, "did you come into my room last night, and look at the bill which was on my table?"

Now Willy dropped her needle, thread, and handkerchief, and stood up.

"Yes, I did!" said she. Miss Barbara was now quite pale.

"And you read the note which Mr. Bullock had put at the bottom of it?"

"Yes, I read it!" said Willy.

"And don't you know," said the other, "that to do such a thing was most — "

"Yes, I do!" interrupted Willy. "I knew it then and I know it now, but I don't care any more now than I did then! I put it there because I wanted to! And if you'll take it, Miss Barbara, and pay it back to me any time when you feel like it, — and you can pay me interest at ten per cent if you want to, and that will make it all right, you know; and oh, Miss Barbara! I know all about that sort of bill, because they used to come when my father was alive. And if you'd only take it, you don't know how happy I would be!"

At this she began to cry, and then Miss Barbara burst into tears, and the two sat down beside each other on a lounge and cried earnestly, hand in hand, for nearly ten minutes.

"I'm so glad you'll take it!" said Willy, when Miss Barbara went into her room, "and you may be just as sure as you're sure of anything that nobody but our two selves will ever know anything about it!"

Immediately after luncheon Miss Barbara went by herself to the post-office, and when she came back her sister said to her that New York must just be beginning to agree with her.

"It is astonishing," said Miss Eleanor, "how long it takes some people to get used to a change, but it often happens that if one stays long enough in the new place, great benefit will be experienced, whereas, if the stay is short, there may be no good result whatever!"

That afternoon Mrs. Cliff actually laughed at Miss Barbara—a thing she had never done before. They were in a large jewelry store where they were looking at clocks, and Miss Barbara, who had evinced a sudden interest in the beautiful things about her, called Mrs. Cliff's attention to a lovely necklace of pearls.

"If I were you," said Miss Barbara, "I would buy something like that! I should not want to wear it, perhaps, but it would be so delightful to sit and look at it!"

The idea of Miss Barbara thinking of buying necklaces of pearls! No wonder Mrs. Cliff laughed.

When the party returned to Plainton, Mrs. Cliff was amazed to find her new house almost completely furnished; and no time was lost in proposing the Thorpedyke project, for Mrs. Cliff felt that it would be wise to make the proposition while the sense of companionship was still fresh upon them all.

Miss Thorpedyke was very much surprised when the plan was proposed to her, but it produced a pleasant effect upon her. She had much enjoyed the company she had been in; she had always liked society, and lately had had very little of it, for no matter how good and lovable sisters may be, they are sometimes a little tiresome when they are sole companions.

As to Barbara, she trembled as she thought of Mrs. Cliff's offer: trembled with joy, which she could not repress; and trembled with fear that her sister might not accept it. But it was of no use for her to say anything, —and she said nothing. Eleanor always decided such questions as these.

After a day's consideration Miss Thorpedyke came to a conclusion, and she sent Miss Barbara with a message to Mrs. Cliff to the effect that as the winters were always lonely, and as it would be very pleasant for them all to be together, she would, if Mrs. Cliff thought it would be an advantage to her, come with her sister and live in some portion of the new building which Mrs. Cliff did not intend to be otherwise occupied, and that they would pay whatever board Mrs. Cliff thought reasonable and proper; but in order to do this, it would be necessary for them to rent their present home. They would offer this house fully furnished, — reserving the privilege of removing the most valuable heirlooms which it now contained, and, as soon as such an arrangement could be made, they would be willing to come to Mrs. Cliff and remain with her during the winter.

When Miss Barbara had heard this decision her heart had fallen! She knew that it would be almost impossible to find a tenant who would take that house, especially for winter occupancy, and that even if a tenant could be found, the rent would be very little. And she knew, moreover, that having come to a decision Eleanor could not be moved from it.

She found Mr. Burke and Willy with Mrs. Cliff, but as he knew all about the project and had taken great interest in it, she did not hesitate to tell her message before him. Mrs. Cliff was very much disappointed.

"That ends the matter!" said she. "Your house cannot be rented for the winter!"

"I don't know about that!" exclaimed Mr. Burke.

"By George! I'll take the house myself! I want a house, — I want just such a house; I want it furnished, — except I don't want to be responsible for old heirlooms, and I'm willing to pay a fair and reasonable rent for it; and I'm sure, although I never had the pleasure of being in it, it ought to bring rent enough to pay the board of any two ladies any winter, wherever they might be!"

"But, Mr. Burke," Miss Barbara said, her voice shaking as she spoke, "I must tell you, that the roof is very much out of repair, and —"

"Oh, that doesn't matter at all!" said Burke. "A tenant, if he's the right sort of tenant, is bound to put a house into repair to suit himself. I'll attend to the roof if it needs it, you may be sure of that! And if it doesn't need it, I'll leave it just as it is! That'll be all right, and you can tell your sister that you've found a tenant. I'm getting dreadfully tired of living at that hotel, and a house of my own is somethin' that I've never had before! But one thing I must ask of you, Miss Thorpedyke: don't say anything to your sister about tobacco smoke, and perhaps she will never think of it!"

CHAPTER XV

MISS NANCY MAKES A CALL

It was a day or two after the most satisfactory arrangement between the Thorpedykes, Mrs. Cliff, and Mr. Burke had been concluded, and before it had been made public, that Miss Nancy Shott came to call upon Mrs. Cliff.

As she walked, stiff as a grenadier, and almost as tall, she passed by the new building without turning her head even to glance at it, and going directly up to the front door of the old house, she rang the bell.

As Mrs. Cliff's domestic household were all engaged in the new part of the building, the bell was not heard, and after waiting nearly a minute, Miss Shott rang it again with such vigor that the door was soon opened by a maid, who informed her that Mrs. Cliff was not at home, but that Miss Croup was in.

"Very well," said Miss Shott, "I'll see her!" and, passing the servant, she entered the old parlor. The maid followed her.

"There's no fire here," she said. "Won't you please walk into the other part of the house, which is heated? Miss Croup is over there."

"No!" said Miss Shott, seating herself upon the sofa. "This suits me very well, and Willy Croup can come to me here as well as anywhere else!"

Presently Willy arrived, wishing very much that she also had been out.

"Do come over to the other parlor, Miss Shott!" said she. "There's no furnace heat here because Mrs. Cliff didn't want the old house altered, and we use this room so little that we haven't made a fire."

"I thought you had the chimney put in order!" said Miss Shott, without moving from her seat. "Doesn't it work right?"

Willy assured her visitor that the chimney was in good condition so far as she knew, and repeated her

I

invitation to come into a warmer room, but to this Miss Shott paid no attention.

"It's an old saying," said she, "that a bad chimney saves fuel!—I understand that you've all been to New York shopping?"

"Yes," said Willy, laughing. "It was a kind of shopping, but that's not exactly what I'd call it!" And perceiving that Miss Shott intended to remain where she was, she took a seat.

"Well, of course," said Miss Shott, "everybody's got to act according to their own judgments and consciences! If I was going to buy winter things, I'd do what I could to help the business of my own town, and if I did happen to want anything I couldn't get here, I'd surely go to Harrington, where the people might almost be called neighbors!"

Willy laughed outright. "Oh, Miss Shott," she said, "you couldn't buy the things we bought, in Harrington! I don't believe they could be found in Boston!"

"I was speaking about myself," said Miss Nancy. "I could find anything I wanted in Harrington, and if my wants went ahead of what they had there, I should say that my wants were going too far and ought to be curbed! And so you took those poor old Thorpedyke women with you. I expect they must be nearly fagged out. I don't see how the oldest one ever stood being dragged from store to store all over New York, as she must have been! She's a pretty old woman and can't be expected to stand even what another woman, younger than she is, but old enough, and excited by having

money to spend, can stand! It's a wonder to me that
you brought her back alive!"

"Miss Eleanor came back a great deal better than she
was when she left!" exclaimed Willy, indignantly.
"She'll tell you, if you ask her, that that visit to New
York did her a great deal of good!"

"No, she won't!" said Miss Shott, "for she don't
speak to me. It's been two years since I had anything
to do with her!"

Willy knew all about the quarrel between the Thorpedyke ladies and Nancy, and wished to change the
subject.

"Don't you want to go and look at the new part of the
house?" she said. "Perhaps you'd like to see the things
we've bought in New York, and it's cold here!"

To this invitation and the subsequent remark Miss
Shott paid no attention. She did not intend to give
Willy the pleasure of showing her over the house, and
it was not at all necessary, for she had seen nearly
everything in it.

During the absence of Mrs. Cliff she had made many
visits to the house, and, as she was acquainted with the
woman who had been left in charge, she had examined
every room, from ground to roof, and had scrutinized
and criticised the carpets as they had been laid and the
furniture as it had been put in place.

She saw that Willy was beginning to shiver a little,
and was well satisfied that she should feel cold. It
would help take the conceit out of her. As for herself,
she wore a warm cloak and did not mind a cold room.

"I'm told," she said, "that Mrs. Cliff's putting up a new stable. What was the matter with the old one?"

"It wasn't big enough," said Willy.

"It holds two horses, don't it, and what could anybody want more than that, I'd like to know!"

Willy was now getting a little out of temper.

"That's not enough for Mrs. Cliff," she said. "She's going to have a nice carriage and a pair of horses, and a regular coachman, not Andrew Marks!"

"Well!" said Miss Shott, and for a few moments she sat silent. Then she spoke. "I suppose Mrs. Cliff's goin' to take boarders."

"Boarders!" cried Willy. "What makes you say such a thing as that?"

"If she isn't," said Miss Shott, "I don't see what she'll do with all the rooms in that new part of the house."

"She's goin' to live in it," said Willy. "That's what she's goin' to do with it!"

"Boarders are very uncertain," remarked Miss Shott, "and just as likely to be a loss as a profit. Mr. Williams tried it at the hotel summer after summer, and if he couldn't make anything, I don't see how Mrs. Cliff can expect to."

"She doesn't expect to take boarders, and you know it!" said Willy.

Miss Shott folded her hands upon her lap.

"It's goin' to be a dreadful hard winter. I never did see so many acorns and chestnuts, and there's more cedar berries on the trees than I've ever known in all my life!

I expect there'll be awful distress among the poor, and
when I say 'poor' I don't mean people that's likely to
suffer for food and a night's lodging, but respectable
people who have to work hard and calculate day and
night how to make both ends meet. These're the folks
that're goin' to suffer in body and mind this winter; and
if people that's got more money than they know what to
do with, and don't care to save up for old age and a
rainy day, would think sometimes of their deserving
neighbors who have to pinch and suffer when they're
going round buyin' rugs that must have cost at least as
much as twenty dollars apiece and which they don't need
at all, there bein' carpet already on the floor, it would be
more to their credit and benefit to their fellow-beings.
But, of course, one person's conscience isn't another person's, and we've each got to judge for ourselves, and be
judged afterwards!"

Now Willy leaned forward in her chair, and her eyes
glistened. As her body grew colder, so did her temper
grow warmer.

"If it's Mrs. Cliff you're thinkin' about, Nancy Shott,"
said she, "I'll just tell you that you're as wrong as you
can be! There isn't a more generous and a kinder person in this whole town than Mrs. Cliff is, and she isn't
only that way to-day, but she's always been so, whether
she's had little or whether she's had much!"

"What did she ever do, I'd like to know!" said Miss
Nancy. "She's lined her own nest pretty well, but
·what's she ever done for anybody else—"

"Now, Nancy Shott," said Willy, "you know she's

been doin' for other people all her life whenever she could! She's done for you more than once, as I happen to know, — and she's done for other neighbors and friends. And, more than that, she's gone abroad to do good, and that's more than anybody else in this town's done, as I know of!"

"She didn't go to South America to do good to anybody but herself," coolly remarked the visitor.

"I'm not thinking of that!" said Willy. "She went there on business, as everybody knows! But you remember well enough when she was in the city, and I was with her, when the dreadful cholera times came on! Everybody said that there wasn't a person who worked harder and did more for the poor people who were brought to the hospital than Sarah did.

"She worked for them night and day; before they were dead and after they were dead! I did what I could, but it wasn't nothin' to what she did! Both of us had been buyin' things, and makin' them up for ourselves, for cotton and linen goods was so cheap then. If it hadn't been for the troubles which came on, we'd had enough to last us for years! But Sarah Cliff isn't the kind of woman to keep things for herself when they're wanted by others, and when she had given everything that she had to those poor creatures at the hospitals, she took my things without as much as takin' the trouble to ask me, for in times like that she isn't the woman to hesitate when she thinks she's doin' what ought to be done, and at one time, in that hospital, there was eleven corpses in my night-gowns!"

"Horrible!" exclaimed Miss Shott, rising to her feet. "It would have killed me to think of such a thing as that!"

"Well, if it would have killed you," said Willy, "there was another night-gown left."

"If you're going to talk that way," said Miss Shott, "I might as well go. I supposed that when I came here I would at least have been treated civilly!"

CHAPTER XVI

MR. BURKE MAKES A CALL

Mrs. Cliff now began her life as a rich woman. The Thorpedykes were established in the new building; her carriage and horses, with a coachman in plain livery, were seen upon the streets of Plainton; she gave dinners and teas, and subscribed in a modestly open way to appropriate charities; she extended suitable aid to the members of Mrs. Ferguson's family, both living and departed; and the fact that she was willing to help in church work was made very plain by a remark of Miss Shott, who, upon a certain Sunday morning at the conclusion of services, happened to stop in front of Mrs. Cliff, who was going out of the church.

"Oh," said Miss Shott, suddenly stepping very much to one side, "I wouldn't have got in your way if I'd remembered that it was you who pays the new choir!"

Mr. Burke established himself in the Thorpedyke

house, which he immediately repaired from top to bottom; but although he frequently repeated to himself and to his acquaintances that he had now set up housekeeping in just the way that he had always wished for, with plenty of servants to do everything just as he wanted it done, he was not happy nevertheless. He felt the loss of the stirring occupation which had so delighted him, and his active mind continually looked right and left for something to do.

He spoke with Mrs. Cliff in regard to the propriety of proposing to the Thorpedykes that he should build an addition to their house, declaring that such an addition would make the old mansion ever so much more valuable, and as to the cost, he would arrange that so that they would never feel the payment of it. But this suggestion met with no encouragement, and poor Burke was so hard put to it for something to occupy his mind that one day he asked Mrs. Cliff if she had entirely given up her idea of employing some of her fortune for the benefit of the native Peruvians, stating that if she wanted an agent to go down there and to attend to that sort of thing, he believed he would be glad to go himself.

But Mrs. Cliff did not intend to send anything to the native Peruvians. According to the arrangements that Captain Horn had made for their benefit they would have as large a share of the Incas' gold as they could possibly claim, and, therefore, she did not feel herself called upon to do anything. "If we had kept it all," she said, "that would have been a different thing!"

In fact, Mrs. Cliff's conscience was now in a very easy and satisfied condition. She did not feel that she owed anything to her fellow-beings that she was not giving them, or that she owed anything to herself that she was not giving to herself. The expenses of building and of the improvements to her spacious grounds had been of so much assistance in removing the plethora of her income that she was greatly encouraged. She felt that she now had her fortune under control, and that she herself might be able to manage it for the future. Already she was making her plans for the next year.

Many schemes she had for the worthy disposition of her wealth, and the more she thought of them and planned their details, the less inclined she felt to leave for an hour or two her spacious and sumptuous apartments in the new building and go back to her little former home where she might think of old times and relieve her mind from the weight of the novelty and the richness of her new dining-room and its adjuncts.

Often as she sat in her stately drawing-room she longed for her old friend Edna, and wished that she and the Captain might come and see how well she had used her share of the great fortune.

But Captain Horn and his wife were far away. Mrs. Cliff had frequent letters from Edna, which described their leisurely and delightful travels in the south and west. Their minds and bodies had been so strained and tired by hard thinking and hard work that all they wanted now was an enjoyment of life and the world as restful and as tranquil as they could make it. After a time they would choose some happy spot, and make for themselves a home. Three of the negroes, Maka and Cheditafa and Mok, were with them, and the others had been left on a farm where they might study methods of American agriculture until the time should come when the Captain should require their services on his estate.

Ralph was in Boston, where, in spite of his independent ideas in regard to his education, he was preparing himself to enter Harvard.

"I know what the Captain means when he speaks of settling down!" said Burke when he heard of this. "He'll buy a cañon and two or three counties and live out there like a lord! And if he does that, I'll go out and see him. I want to see this Inca money sprouting and flourishing a good deal more than it has done yet!"

"What do you mean?" asked Mrs. Cliff. "Don't you call this splendid house and everything in it a sign of sprouting and flourishing?"

"Oh, my dear madam," said Burke, rising from his seat and walking the floor, "if you could have looked through the hole in the top of the mound and have seen under you cartloads and cartloads of pure gold, and had let your mind rest on what might have grown out of it, a house like this would have seemed like an acorn on an oak tree!"

"And you think the Captain will have the oak tree?" she asked.

"Yes," said Burke; "I think he's the sort of man to want it, and if he wants it he'll have it!"

There were days when the weather was very bad and time hung unusually heavy upon Mr. Burke's hands, when he thought it might be a good thing to get married. He had a house and money enough to keep a wife as well as any woman who would have him had any reason to expect. But there were two objections to this plan. In the first place, what would he do with his wife after he got tired of living in the Thorpedyke house; and secondly, where could he find anybody he would like to marry?

He had female acquaintances in Plainton, but not one of them seemed to have the qualifications he would desire in a wife. Willy Croup was a good-natured and pleasant woman, and he always liked to talk to her, but she was too old for him. He might like to adopt her as a maiden aunt, but then that would not be practicable, for Mrs. Cliff would not be willing to give her up.

At this time Burke would have gone to make a visit to his mother, but there was also an objection to this. He would not have dared to present himself before her in his fur-trimmed overcoat and his high silk hat. She was a true sailor's mother, and she would have laughed him to scorn, and so habituated had he become to the dress of a fine gentleman that it would have seriously interfered with his personal satisfaction to put on the rough winter clothes in which his mother would expect to see him.

The same reason prevented him from going to his old friend Shirley. He knew very well that Shirley did not wear a high silk hat and carry a cane, and he had a sufficient knowledge of human nature and of himself to know that if his present personal appearance were made the subject of ridicule, or even inordinate surprise, it would not afford him the same stimulating gratification which he now derived from it.

Fortunately the weather grew colder, and there was snow and excellent sleighing, and now Burke sent for a fine double sleigh, and, with a fur cap, a great fur collar over his overcoat, fur gloves, and an enormous lap-robe of fur, he jingled and glided over the country in great delight, enjoying the sight of the fur-garbed coachman in front of him almost as much as the glittering snow and the crisp fresh air.

He invited the ladies of the Cliff mansion to accompany him in these sleigh-rides, but although the Misses Thorpedyke did not fancy such cold amusement, Mrs. Cliff and Willy went with him a few times, and once Willy accompanied him alone.

This positively decided the opinion of Plainton in regard to his reason for living in that town. But there were those who said that he might yet discover that his plans would not succeed. Mrs. Cliff now seemed to be in remarkably good health, and as it was not likely that Mr. Burke would actually propose marriage to Willy until he saw some signs of failing in Mrs. Cliff, he might have to wait a long, long time; during which his intended victim would probably grow so wrinkled and old that even the most debased of fortune-hunters would refuse to have her. Then, of course, the fine gentleman would find out that he had lost all the time he had spent scheming here in Plainton.

The Buskirks were spending this winter in their country home, and one afternoon Mr. Burke thought he would drive up in his sleigh and make a call upon them. He had been there before, but had seen no one, and some weeks afterward Mr. Buskirk had dropped in at the hotel, but had not found him. This sort of visiting did not suit our friend Burke, and he determined to go and see what a Buskirk was really like.

Having jingled and pranced up to the front of the handsome mansion on the hill, and having been informed that the gentleman of the house was not at home, he asked for his lady, and, as she was in, he was ushered into a parlor. Here, having thrown aside some of his superincumbent furs, George Burke sat and looked about him. He had plenty of time for observation, for it was long before Mrs. Buskirk made her appearance.

With the exception of Mrs. Cliff's house, with which he had had so much to do, Burke had never before been inside a dwelling belonging to a very rich person, and the Buskirk mansion interested him very much. Although he was so little familiar with fine furniture, pictures, and bric-a-brac, he was a man of quick perceptions and good judgment, and it did not take him long to discover that the internal furnishings of the Buskirk house were far inferior to those of the addition to Mrs. Cliff's old home.

The room in which he sat was large and pretentious, but when it had been furnished there had been no lady of good family accustomed to the furnishings of wealth and culture, and with an artistic taste gained in travel at home and abroad, to superintend the selection of these pictures, this carpet, and the coverings of this furniture!

He laughed within himself as he sat, his fur cape on his knees and his silk hat in his hand, and he was so elated and pleased with the knowledge of the superiority of Mrs. Cliff's home over this house of the proud city people who had so long looked down upon Plainton, that he entirely forgot his intention of recalling, as he sat in the fine parlor of the Buskirks, the olden times when he used to get up early in the morning and swab the deck.

"These people ought to come down and see Mrs. Cliff's house," thought Burke, "and I'll make them do it if I can!"

When Mrs. Buskirk, a lady who had always found it necessary to place strong guards around her social position, made her appearance, she received her visitor with an attentive civility. She had been impressed by his appearance when she had seen him grandly careering in his barouche or his sleigh, and she was still more impressed as she saw him in her parlor with additional furs. She had heard he had been a sailor, but now as she talked to him, the belief grew upon her that he might yet make a very good sailor. He was courteous, entirely at his ease, and perhaps a little too bland, and Mrs. Buskirk thought that although her husband might like to sit and smoke with this well-dressed, sun-burned man, he was not a person very desirable for the society of herself and daughters.

But she was willing to sit and talk to Mr. Burke, for she wanted to ask him some questions about Mrs. Cliff. She had heard about that lady's new house, or rather the improvement to her old one, and she had driven past it, and she did not altogether understand the state of affairs.

She had known that Mrs. Cliff was a widow of a store-keeper of the town, and that she had come into posses-sion of a portion of a treasure which had been discovered somewhere in the West Indies or South America, but those portions of treasures which might be allotted to the widow of a storekeeper in a little country town were not likely to be very much, and Mrs. Buskirk was anx-ious to know something definite about Mrs. Cliff's pres-ent circumstances.

Burke felt a little embarrassed in regard to his an-swers. He knew that Mrs. Cliff was very anxious not to appear as a millionnaire in the midst of the friends and associations of her native town, — at least, that she did not desire to do so until her real financial position had been gradually understood and accepted. Nothing she would dislike so much as to be regarded as the people in her social circle regarded the Buskirks on the hill.

So Burke did not blaze out as he would have liked to do with a true and faithful statement of Mrs. Cliff's great wealth, — far in excess, he was very sure, of that of the fine lady with whom he was talking, — but he said everything he could in a modest way, or what seemed so to him, in regard to his friend's house and belongings.

"But it seems to me," said Mrs. Buskirk, "that it's a

very strange thing for any one to build a house, such as the one you describe, in such a neighborhood, when there are so many desirable locations on the outskirts of the town. The houses on the opposite side of the street are very small, some of them even mean; if I am not mistaken there is a little shop somewhere along there! I should consider that that sort of thing would spoil any house, no matter how good it might be in itself!"

"Oh, that makes no difference whatever!" said Burke, with a wave of his hand, and delighted to remember a proposition he had made to Mrs. Cliff and which she had viewed with favor. "Mrs. Cliff will soon settle all that! She's going to buy that whole block opposite to her and make a park of it. She'll clear away all the houses and everything belonging to them, and she'll plant trees, and lay out lawns and driveways, and have a regular landscape gardener who'll superintend everything. And she's going to have the water brought in pipes which will end in some great rocks, which we'll have hauled from the woods, and from under these rocks a brook will flow and meander through the park. And there'll be flowers, and reeds, and rushes, and, very likely, a fountain with the spare water.

"And that'll be a public park for the use of the whole town, and you can see for yourself, madam, that it'll be a grand thing to look out from Mrs. Cliff's windows on such a beautiful place! It will be fitted up and railed off very much after the style of her own grounds, so that the whole thing will be like a great estate right in the middle of the town. She's thinkin' of callin' the park

'The Grove of the Incas.' That sounds nice; don't you think so, madam?"

"It sounds very well indeed," said Mrs. Buskirk. She had heard before of plans made by people who had suddenly come into possession of money.

Burke saw that he had not yet made the impression that he desired. He wanted, without actually saying so, to let this somewhat supercilious lady know that if the possession of money was a reason for social position, — and he knew of no other reason for the Buskirks' position, — Mrs. Cliff would be aft, talking to the Captain while the Buskirks would be walking about by themselves amidship.

But he did not know how to do this. He knew it would be no use to talk about horses and carriages, and all that sort of thing, for these the Buskirks possessed, and their coachman wore top boots, — a thing Mrs. Cliff would never submit to. He was almost on the point of relinquishing his attempt to make Mrs. Buskirk call upon the widow of the storekeeper, when the lady helped him by asking in a casual way if Mrs. Cliff proposed living winter and summer in her new house.

"No," said Burke, "not in the summer. I hear Plainton is pretty hot in the summer, and she'll go — " (Oh, a radiant thought came to him!) "I expect she'll cruise about in her yacht during the warm weather."

"Her yacht!" exclaimed Mrs. Buskirk, for the first time exhibiting marks of actual interest. "Has Mrs. Cliff a yacht?"

L.

"She's going to have one," said Burke to himself, "and I'll put her up to it before I go home this day."

"Yes," he said aloud, "that is, she hasn't got it yet, but she's going to have it as soon as the season opens. I shall select it for her. I know all about yachts and every other kind of craft, and she'll have one of the very finest on this coast. She's a good sailor, Mrs. Cliff is, for I've cruised with her! And nothing will she enjoy better in hot weather than her noble yacht and the open sea!"

Now this did make an impression upon Mrs. Buskirk. A citizen of Plainton who possessed a yacht was not to be disregarded. After this she was rather abstracted, and the conversation fell off. Burke saw that it was time for him to go, and as he had now said all he cared to say, he was willing to do so.

In parting with him Mrs. Buskirk was rather more gracious than when she received him. "I hope when you call again," she said, "that you may find my husband at home. I know he will be glad to see you!"

As Burke jingled and pranced away he grinned behind his great fur collar. "She'll call!" said he to himself. "She'll call on the yacht if she doesn't call on anything else!"

CHAPTER XVII

MRS. CLIFF'S YACHT

WHEN the interview with Mrs. Buskirk was reported that afternoon to Mrs. Cliff, the good lady sat aghast. "I've decided about the park," she said, "and that is all very well. But what do you mean by a yacht? What could be more ridiculous than to talk about me and a yacht!"

"Ridiculous!" exclaimed Burke. "It's nothing of the kind! The more I think of the idea, the better I like it, and if you'll think of it soberly, I believe you'll like it just as much as I do! In the first place, you've got to do something to keep your money from being dammed up and running all over everything. This house and furniture cleared away things for a time, but the whole business will be just as much clogged up as it was before if you don't look out. I don't want to give advice, but it does strike me that anybody as rich as you are oughtn't to feel that they could afford to sit still here in Plainton, year in and year out, no matter how fine a house they might have! They ought to think of that great heap of gold in the mound and feel that it was their duty to get all the grand and glorious good out of it that they knew how!"

"But it does seem to me," said Mrs. Cliff, "that a yacht would be an absolute extravagance and waste of money. And, you know, I have firmly determined I will not waste my money."

"To call sittin' in a beautiful craft, on a rollin' sea,

with a spankin' breeze, a waste of money, is something I can't get into my brain!" said Mr. Burke. "But you could do good with a yacht. You could take people out on cruises who would never get out if you didn't take them! And now I've an idea! It's just come to me. You might get a really big yacht. If I was you, I'd have a steam yacht, because you'd have more control over that than you'd have over a sailin'-vessel, and besides a person can get tired of sailin'-vessels, as I've found out myself. And then you might start a sort of summer shelter for poor people; not only very poor people, but respectable people, who never get a chance to sniff salt air. And you might spend part of the summer in giving such people what would be the same as country weeks, only you'd take them out to sea instead of shipping them inland to dawdle around farms. I tell you that's a splendid idea, and nobody's done it."

Day after day, the project of the yacht was discussed by Mrs. Cliff and Burke, and she was beginning to view its benevolent features with a degree of favor when Mrs. Buskirk called. That lady's visit was prompted partly by a curiosity to see what sort of a woman was the widow of the Plainton storekeeper who would cruise the next summer in her yacht; and partly by a feeling that to such a person a certain amount of respect was due even from a Buskirk.

But when she entered the house, passed through the great hall, and seated herself in the drawing-room, she saw more than she had expected to see. She saw a house immeasurably better fitted out and furnished than her own. She knew the value of the rugs which Miss Shott had declared must have cost at least twenty dollars each, and she felt, although she did not thoroughly appreciate, the difference in artistic merit between the pictures upon her walls and the masterly paintings which had been selected by the ladies Thorpedyke for the drawing-room of Mrs. Cliff.

The discovery startled her. She must talk to her husband about it as soon as he reached home. It was not only money, but a vast deal of money, and something more, which had done all this.

She had asked for the ladies, knowing that Mrs. Cliff did not live alone, and all the ladies were at home. Amid those surroundings, the elder Miss Thorpedyke, most carefully arrayed, made an impression upon Mrs. Buskirk very different from that she had produced on the occasion of their single former interview in the darkened little parlor of the Thorpedyke house.

Mrs. Cliff, in a costume quite simple, but as rich as her conscience would allow, felt within herself all the uplifting influence of her wealth, as she stepped forward to salute this lady who had always been so uplifted by her wealth.

In the course of the conversation, the yacht was mentioned. The visitor would not go away without being authoritatively informed upon this subject.

"Oh yes," said Mrs. Cliff, promptly, "I shall have a yacht next summer. Mr. Burke will select one for me, and I know it will be a good one, for he thoroughly understands such matters."

Before she left, Mrs. Buskirk invited Mrs. Cliff, the Misses Thorpedyke, and Miss Croup to take luncheon with her quite informally on the following Tuesday. She would have made it a dinner, but in that case her husband would have been at home, and it would have been necessary to invite Mr. Burke, and she was not yet quite sure about Mr. Burke.

This invitation, which soon became known throughout the town, decided the position of Mrs. Cliff at Plainton. When that lady and her family had gone, with her carriage and pair, to the mansion of the Buskirks on the hill, and had there partaken of luncheon, very informally, in company with three of the most distinguished ladies of Harrington, who had also been invited very informally; and when the news of the magnificent repast which had been served on the occasion, with flowers from the greenhouse nearly covering the table, with everything tied up with ribbons which could possibly be so decorated, and with a present for each guest ingeniously concealed under her napkin, floated down into the town, there was no woman in that place who could put her hand upon her heart and honestly declare that hereafter Mrs. Cliff could look up to anybody in Plainton.

This recognition, which soon became obvious to Mrs. Cliff, was a source of genuine gratification to that good lady. She had never been inclined to put herself above her neighbors on account of her fortune, and would have been extremely grieved if she had been convinced that her wealth would oblige her to assume a superior position, but when that wealth gradually and easily, without creating any disturbance or commotion in her circle, raised her of itself, without any action on her part, to the peak of social eminence in her native place, her genuine satisfaction was not interfered with in the least degree by her conscience. Her position had come to her, and she had assumed it as if she had been born to it.

But whenever she thought of her preëminence, — and she did not think of it nearly so often as other people thought of it, — she determined that it should make no difference to her; and when next she gave a high tea, — not the grand repast to which she intended to invite the Buskirks on the hill, — she invited Miss Cushing. Now, there were people in Plainton who did not invite the dressmaker to their table, but Mrs. Cliff had asked her when they were all poor together, and she would have her now again when they were not all poor together.

As the winter went on, Burke became more and more interested in Mrs. Cliff's yacht, and if he had not had this subject to talk about, and plan about, and to go at all hours to see Mrs. Cliff about, it is likely that he would have been absolutely obliged to leave Plainton for want of occupation. But the idea of commanding a steam yacht was attraction enough to keep him where he could continually consider it.

He assured Mrs. Cliff that it was not at all necessary to wait until pleasant weather before undertaking this great enterprise. As soon as the harbors were reasonably free of ice it would be well for him to go and look at yachts, and then when he found one which suited him,

Mrs. Cliff could go and look at it, and if it suited her, it could be immediately put into commission. They could steam down into southern waters, and cruise about there. The spring up here in the north was more disagreeable than any other season of the year, and why should they not go and spend that season in the tranquil and beautiful waters of Florida or the West Indies?

Mrs. Cliff had now fully determined to become the owner of a yacht, but she would not do so unless she saw her way clear to carry out the benevolent features of the plan which Mr. Burke had suggested.

"What I want," said Mrs. Cliff, "is to have the whole thing understood! I am perfectly willing to spend some of the pleasant months sailing about the coast and feeling that I'm giving health and pleasure to poor and deserving people, especially children, but I am not willing to consider myself a rich woman who keeps an expensive yacht just for the pleasure of cruising around when she feels like it! But I do like the plan of giving country weeks at sea."

"Very good, madam," he said, "and we can fix that thing so that nobody can possibly make any mistake about it. What do you say to calling your yacht the *Summer Shelter?* We'll paint the name in white letters on the bows and stern, and nobody can take us for idle sea-loafers with more money than we know what to do with!"

"I like that!" said Mrs. Cliff, her face brightening. "You may buy me a yacht as soon as you please, and we'll call her the *Summer Shelter!*"

In consequence of this order, Mr. Burke departed from Plainton the next day, and began a series of expeditions to the seaport towns on the Atlantic coast in search of a steam yacht for sale.

The winter grew colder, and the weather was very bad; there were heavy snows and drifts, and many hardships. There were cases of privations and suffering, and never did she hear of one of these cases that a thankful glow did not warm the heart of Mrs. Cliff as she thought that she was able to relieve it.

But Mrs. Cliff knew, and if she had not known she would have soon found out, that it was often very difficult to relieve distress of body without causing distress of mind, but she and Willy and the Misses Thorpedyke had known all phases of the evil which has its root in the want of money, and they always considered people's sensibilities when they held charitable councils. There was one case in which Mrs. Cliff felt that she must be very careful indeed.

Old Nancy Shott was not standing the winter well. She had a bad cold, and was confined to her bed, and one day Miss Inchman mentioned, during a call on Mrs. Cliff, that she did not believe the poor old thing was able to keep herself warm. She had been to see her, and the coverings on her bed were very insufficient she thought.

The Shotts never did keep a warm house, nor did they care to spend their money upon warm clothes; but although that sort of thing might do very well while they were in health and were constantly on the move, it did

not do when they were sick in bed. When Miss Inchman had gone, Mrs. Cliff called Willy.

"Where are we using those California blankets which
I brought home with me?" she asked.

"Using them!" exclaimed Willy. "We aren't using
them anywhere! I'm sure nobody would think of using
such blankets as those, except when some extra company
might happen to come. It ought to be a long time
before those blankets would have to go into the wash,
and I've kept them covered up on the top shelf of the
linen closet!"

"Well, I wish you would go and get them," said Mrs.
Cliff, "and then wrap them up and take them to Miss
Shott as a present from me."

"Take them to Nancy Shott!" cried Willy. "I
never heard of such a thing in my life! She's able to
buy blankets, dozens of them if she wants them, and to
take to her such blankets as the ones you brought from
California, — why it takes my breath away to think of
it!"

"But you must take them to her," said Mrs. Cliff.
"She may be stingy, but she is suffering, and I want her
to have those blankets because they are the very best
that I could possibly send her. You can get Andrew
Marks to drive you there, but stop two or three doors
from the house. She will think you are putting on airs
if you drive up to the door. And I wish you would give
her the blankets just as if it was a matter of course that
anybody would send things to a sick person."

"Oh yes!" said Willy. "As if you hadn't a pot of

jelly to spare and so sent her these blankets fit for an Emperor on his throne!"

That very evening the reluctant Willy took the blankets to Miss Shott, for Mrs. Cliff knew it was going to be a very cold night, and she wanted her to have them as soon as possible.

When Nancy Shott beheld the heavy and beautiful fabrics of fine wool which Willy spread out upon her bed in order that she might better examine them, the eyes of the poor old woman flashed with admiring delight.

"Well," said she, "Sarah Cliff has got a memory!"

"What do you mean?" asked Willy.

"Why, she remembers," said Miss Shott, "that I once joined in to give her a pair of blankets!"

"Good gracious!" exclaimed Willy, and she was on the point of speaking her mind in regard to the salient points in the two transactions, but she refrained. The poor old thing was sick, and she must not say anything to excite her.

"I suppose," said Miss Shott, after lifting a corner of a blanket and rubbing and pinching it, "that these are all wool!"

Then Willy thought herself privileged to speak, and for some minutes she dilated on the merits of those superb blankets, the like of which were not to be found in the whole State, and, perhaps, not in any State east of the Rocky Mountains.

"Well," said Miss Shott, "you may tell her that I will not throw her present back at her as she once threw one back at me! And now that you're here, Willy Croup, I may as well say to you what I've intended to say to you the next time I saw you. And that is, that when I was at your house you told me an out and out falsehood, — I won't use any stronger word than that, — and how you could sleep after having done it I'm sure I don't know!"

"Falsehood!" cried Willy. "What do you mean?"

"You told me," said Nancy, "that Mrs. Cliff wasn't goin' to take boarders, — and now look at those Thorpe-dykes! Not two days after you tried to deceive me they went there to board! And now what have you got to say to that?"

Willy had not a word to say. She sprang to her feet, she glared at the triumphant woman in the bed, and, turning, went downstairs.

CHAPTER XVIII

THE DAWN OF THE GROVE OF THE INCAS

A MAN may have command of all the money necessary, and he may have plenty of knowledge and experience in regard to the various qualities of sea-going vessels, but even with these great advantages he may find it a very difficult thing to buy, ready to his hand, a suitable steam yacht. The truth of this statement was acknowledged by Mr. Burke after he had spent nearly a month in Boston, New York, and various points between these cities, and, after advertising, inquiring, and investigating the subject in all possible ways, found nothing which he could recommend Mrs. Cliff to purchase.

He wrote to her a great many letters during this period, all of which were interesting, although there were portions of many of them which she did not quite understand, being expressed in a somewhat technical fashion. Burke liked to write letters. It was a novel experience for him to have time to write and something to write about. He had been better educated than the ordinary sailor, and his intelligence and habits of observation enabled him to supplement to a considerable extent what he had learned at school. His spelling and grammar were sometimes at fault, but his handwriting was extremely plain and distinct, and Willy Croup, who always read his letters, declared that it was much better to write plainly than to be always correct in other respects, for what was the good of proper spelling and grammar if people could not make out what was written?

Mrs. Cliff was not at all disturbed by the delay in the purchase of a yacht; for, according to her idea, it would be a long time yet before it was pleasant to sail upon the sea, and if it was interesting to Mr. Burke to go from place to place and have interviews with ship-owners and sea-faring people, she was glad that she was able to give him an opportunity to do so.

As for herself, she was in a pleasant state of feminine satisfaction. Without any sort of presumption or even effort on her part she had attained a high and unquestioned position among her fellow-citizens, and her mind

was not set upon maintaining that position by worthy
and unoffensive methods of using her riches.

She now had a definite purpose in life. If she could
make herself happy and a great many other people
happy, and only a few people envious or jealous, and,
at the same time, feel that she was living and doing
things as a person of good common sense and great wealth
ought to live and do things, what more could be expected
of her in this life ?

Thus backed up by her conscience and her check-book,
she sat, morning after morning, before a cheerful fire of
hickory logs and outlined her career. This was in the
parlor of her old house, which she now determined to
use as an office or business-room. She could afford the
warmest fire of the best seasoned wood; her chimney
was in perfect order, and she was but fifty-five years old
and in excellent health ; — why should she not enjoy the
exhilarating blaze, and plan for years of exhilarating
occupation.

Soon after Mr. Burke left Plainton Mrs. Cliff began
work upon the new park. This 'she could do without
his assistance, and it was work the mere contemplation of which delighted her. She had legal assistance
in regard to the purchase of the grounds and buildings
of the opposite block, and while this was in the hands
of her lawyers, she was in daily consultation with an
eminent landscape-constructor who had come to Plainton
for the purpose. He lodged at the hotel, and drew most
beautiful plans of the proposed park.

In the happy morning hours during which Mrs. Cliff's

mind wandered over the beautiful drives, or stood upon the rustic bridges which crossed the stream dashing among its rocks and spreading itself out into placid pools; or when, mentally, she sat in the shade of the great trees and looked out upon the wide stretches of verdant lawn, relieved by the brilliant colors of the flower-beds, she often felt it was almost the same thing as if it were actually summer, and that she really saw the beautiful grass and flowers, heard the babbling of the stream, and felt the refreshing breezes which rustled the great limbs of the trees.

She did not selfishly keep these pleasures to herself, but often on the stormy evenings, she and Willy and the Misses Thorpedyke would go over the brilliantly colored plans of the Incas' Grove, admire what had been proposed, and suggest things which they thought would be desirable. Miss Thorpedyke, who had a vivid recollection of the gardens of Luxemburg, spoke of many of their beautiful and classic features which she would recommend for the new park if it were not that they would cost so much money. All these were noted down with great care by Mrs. Cliff, and mentioned to the landscape-constructor the next day.

Thus at home, in church circles, in the society of the town, and in the mental contemplation of the charming landscape which in consequence of her own will and command would soon spread itself out before her windows, Mrs. Cliff was very happy. But among all her sources of enjoyment there was nothing, perhaps, which pleased her better than to think on a cold winter's night, when the piercing winds were roaring about the house, that poor old Nancy Shott was lying warm and comfortable under two of the finest blankets which ever came from Californian looms.

The great object of Willy Croup's thoughts at this time was not the park, — for she could not properly appreciate trees and grass in this shivery weather, — but the entertainment, the grand lunch, or the very high tea which was to be given to Mrs. Buskirk and daughters on the hill. This important event had been postponed because the sleighing had become rather bad and the Buskirks had gone to the city.

But as soon as they returned, Willy hoped with all her heart that Mrs. Cliff would be able to show them what may be done in the line of hospitable entertainment by people who had not only money but something more. There had been a time when Willy thought that when people wished to entertain there was nothing needed but money, but then she had not lived in the house with the Misses Thorpedyke, and had not heard them and Mrs. Cliff discuss such matters.

The peace of mind of Mrs. Cliff was disturbed one day by the receipt of a letter from Mr. Burke, who wrote from New York and informed her that he had found a yacht which he believed would suit her, and he wished very much that she would come and look at it before he completed the purchase.

Mrs. Cliff did not wish to go to New York and look at yachts. She had then under consideration the plan of a semicircular marble terrace which was to overlook one end of a shaded lakelet, which Mr. Humphreys, her professional adviser, assured her she could have just as well as not, by means of a dam, and she did not wish to interrupt this most interesting occupation. Mr. Humphreys had procured photographs of some of the romantic spots of the Luxemburg, and Mrs. Cliff felt within herself the gladdening impulses of a good magician as she planned the imitation of all this classic beauty.

Besides, it was the middle of March, and cold, and not at all the season in which she would be able to properly appreciate the merits of a yacht. Still, as Mr. Burke had found the vessel and wanted her to see it, and as there was a possibility, he had written, that delay might cause her to lose the opportunity of getting what she wanted, and as she was very desirous of pleasing him, she decided that she and Willy would go to New York and look at the vessel.

It would not take long, because, of course, Mr. Burke had already found out everything that was necessary in regard to its sea-going qualities, and a great many other things of which she would not be a judge. In fact, it was not necessary for her to go at all; but as she was to pay for it, Mr. Burke would be better satisfied if first she saw it.

It was very pleasant to think that she could go away whenever she pleased and leave her house in the care of two such ladies as Miss Eleanor Thorpedyke and her sister.

M

CHAPTER XIX

THE "SUMMER SHELTER"

WHEN Mrs. Cliff and Willy, as well wrapped up in handsome furs as Mr. Burke himself, who accompanied them, left their New York hotel to drive over to Brooklyn and examine the yacht which had been selected, Willy's mind vainly endeavored to form within itself an image of the object of the expedition.

She was so thoroughly an inland woman and had so little knowledge of matters connected with the sea, that when she first heard the mention of the yacht it had brought into her mind the idea of an Asiatic animal, with long hair and used as a beast of burden, which she had read about in her school-books. But when she had discovered that the object in question was a vessel and not a bovine ruminant, her mind carried her no farther than to a pleasure boat with a sail to it.

Even Mrs. Cliff, who had travelled, had inadequate ideas concerning a steam yacht. She had seen the small steamers which ran upon the Seine, and she had taken little trips upon them; and if she had given the subject careful consideration she might have thought that the yacht intended for the use of a private individual would be somewhat smaller than one of these.

It would be difficult, therefore, to imagine the surprise and even amazement of Mrs. Cliff and Willy Croup when they beheld the vessel to which Mr. Burke conducted them. It was in fact a sea-going steamer of small comparative size, it is true, but of towering proportions when compared with the ideals in the minds of the two female citizens of Plainton who had come, the one to view it and the other to buy it.

" Before we go on board," said Mr. Burke, as he proudly stood upon the pier, holding fast to his silk hat in the cold breeze which swept along the water front, "I want you to take a general look at her! I don't suppose you know anything about her lines and build, but I can tell you they're all right! But you can see for yourselves that she's likely to be a fine, solid, comfortable craft, and won't go pitchin' and tossin' around like the crafts that some people go to sea in!"

"Why, the name is on it!" cried Willy. "*Summer Shelter!* How did you happen to find one with that name, Mr. Burke?"

"Oh, I didn't!" said he. "She had another name, but I wanted you to see her just as she'd look if she really belonged to you, — so I had the other name painted out and this put on in good big white letters that can be seen for a long distance. If you don't buy her, Mrs. Cliff, of course I'll have the old name put back again. Now what do you think of her, Mrs. Cliff, lookin' at her from this point of view?"

The good lady stood silent. She gazed at the long high hull of the steamer, she looked up at the black smoke-stack, and at the masts which ran up so shapely and so far, and her soul rose higher than it had been uplifted even by the visions of the future Grove of the Incas.

"I think it is absolutely splendid!" said she. "Let us go in!"

"On board, madam," said Burke, gently correcting her. "This way to the gang-plank!"

For nearly two hours Mrs. Cliff and Willy wandered over the upper and lower decks of the yacht; examined its pretty little state-rooms; sat excitedly upon the sofas of its handsomely decorated saloon; examined the folding tables and all the other wonderful things which shut themselves up out of the way when they were not needed; tapped the keys of the piano; investigated the storerooms, lockers, and all the marine domestic conveniences, and forgot it was winter, forgot that the keen wind nearly blew their bonnets off as they walked the upper deck, and felt what a grand thing it would be to sail upon the sea upon such a noble vessel.

To all this there was added in Mrs. Cliff's mind the proud feeling that it would be her own, and in it she could go wherever she pleased and come back again when it suited her.

Willy, who had never been to sea, was perfectly free to form an idea of an ocean voyage as delightful and charming as she pleased, and this she did with great enthusiasm. Even had it been necessary that this perfectly lovely vessel should remain moored at the pier, it would have given joy to her soul to live in it, to sleep in one of those sweet little rooms, and to eat, and read, and sew in that beautiful saloon.

"Mr. Burke," said Mrs. Cliff, "I don't believe you

could find any vessel better suited to our purpose than this one, and I wish you would buy it!"

"Madam," said Burke, "I'll do it immediately! And I tell you, madam, that this is a wonderful chance for this time of the year when yachts and pleasure crafts in this part of the world are generally laid.up and can't be seen properly; and what's more, would have to be docked and overhauled generally before they would be ready for sea. But here is a yacht that's been cruising down south and in the West Indies and has just come up here, and is all ready to go to sea again whenever you like it. If you don't mind going home by yourselves, I'll go to the office of the agent of the owner, and settle the business at once!"

It would have been impossible for any purchase or any possession of palace, pyramid, or principality to make prouder the heart of Mrs. Cliff than did the consciousness that she was the owner of a fine sea vessel worked by steam. She acknowledged to herself that if she had been at home she could not have prevented herself from putting on those airs which she had been so anxious to avoid. But these would wear off very soon she knew, and so long as there was no one, except Willy, to notice a possible change of manner, it did not matter.

Now that Mrs. Cliff and Willy were in New York they both agreed that it would be well for them to attend to some shopping for which they had intended coming to the city later in the spring. It had been found that there were many things wanted to supplement the furnishing of the new house, and to the purchase of these the two ladies now devoted their mornings.

But every afternoon, in company with Mr. Burke, they went on board the *Summer Shelter* to see what he had been doing and to consult with him about what he was going to do. It was astonishing how many little things were needed to be done to a yacht just returned from a cruise, and how interesting all these things were to Mrs. Cliff and Willy, considering that they knew so little about them.

The engineer and fireman had not been discharged, but were acting as watchmen, and Burke strongly recommended that they should be engaged immediately, because, as he said, if Mrs. Cliff were to let them go it would be difficult to get such men again. "It was a little expensive, to be sure, but when a yacht is not laid up," he said, "there should always be men aboard of her." And so the painting, and the cleaning, and the necessary fitting up went on, and Mr. Burke was very happy, and Mrs. Cliff was very proud, although the external manifestation of this feeling was gradually wearing off.

"I don't want to give advice, madam," said Burke one evening, as the little party sat together discussing nautical matters, "but if I was in your place, I wouldn't go back to Plainton before I had taken a little trial trip on the yacht. It doesn't matter a bit about the weather! After we get out to sea it will be only a few days before we find we're in real spring weather and the warm water of the Gulf Stream. We can touch at Savannah, and cruise along the Florida coast, and then go over to the Bahamas, and look around as long as we feel like! And when we get back here it will be beginning to be milder, and then you can go home and arrange for the voyages you're goin' to make in her during the summer!"

Mrs. Cliff considered. This was a tempting proposition. And while she considered, Willy sat and looked at her with glowing cheeks and half-open mouth. It would not have required one second for her to decide such a question.

"You know," said Mr. Burke, "it wouldn't take me long to get her ready for sea. I could soon coal her and put her stores aboard, and as to a crew, I can get one in no time. We could leave port in a week just as well as not!"

"Let's go!" said Willy, seizing the hand of her friend. "It need only be a little trip, just to see how it would all feel."

Mrs. Cliff smiled. "Very good," said she, "we'll take a little trial trip just as soon as you are ready, Captain Burke! That is, if you have not made any plans which will prevent you from accepting the position."

"Madam," said Burke, springing to his feet and standing proudly before Mrs. Cliff, "I'd throw up the command of the finest liner on the Atlantic to be captain of the *Summer Shelter* for this summer! I see far more fun ahead in the cruises that you're going to make than in any voyage I've looked forward to yet; and when people have a chance to mix fun and charity as we're goin' to mix them, I say such people ought to call themselves lucky! This is Wednesday! Well now, madam, by next Wednesday the *Summer Shelter* will be all fitted out for the cruise, and she'll be ready to sail out of the harbor at whatever hour you name, for the tide won't make any difference to her!"

"There is only one thing I don't like about the arrangement," said Mrs. Cliff, when the Captain had left them, "and that is, that we will have to take this trip by ourselves. It seems a pity for three people to go sailing around in a big vessel like that with most of the state-rooms empty; but, of course, people are not prepared yet for country weeks at sea! And it will take some time to make my plans known in the proper quarters."

"I don't suppose," said Willy, "that there's anybody in Plainton that we could send for on short notice. People there want so much time to get ready to do anything!"

"But there is nobody in the town that I would care to take on a first voyage," said Mrs. Cliff. "You know, something might go wrong and we would have to come back, and if it is found necessary to do that, I don't want any Plainton people on board!"

"No indeed!" exclaimed Willy, her mind involuntarily running towards Nancy Shott, to whom a voyage to the West Indies would doubtless be of great service. "Don't let's bother about anything of that kind! Let's make the first trip by ourselves! I think that will be glorious!"

CHAPTER XX

THE SYNOD

As most of Mrs. Cliff's business in New York was now finished, and as she and Willy were waiting there only for the yacht to be made ready for sea, she had a good deal of time on her hands.

On the Saturday following her decision to make a trial trip on the *Summer Shelter*, when returning from the daily visit to the yacht, Mrs. Cliff stopped in at a Brooklyn church in which a Synod was at that time convened. She had read of the proceedings of this body in the papers, and, as the deliberations concerned her own denomination, she thought she would be interested in them. Willy, however, preferred to go on by herself to New York, as she had something to do there which she thought would be more to her taste than the proceedings of a Synod.

It was not long after she had been seated in the church that Mrs. Cliff began to regret that she had not attended some of the earlier meetings, for the questions debated were those in which she took an interest.

After a time she saw near her Mrs. Arkwright, a lady who had visited Mrs. Perley some years before, and with whom she had then become acquainted. Joining her, Mrs. Cliff found Mrs. Arkwright able to give her a great deal of information in regard to the members of the Synod, and as the two sat and talked together in whispers, a desire arose in the mind of Mrs. Cliff that she and her wealth might in some way join in the work in which all these people were engaged. As her mind rested upon this subject, there came into it a plan which pleased her. Here were all these delegates, many of them looking tired and pale, as if they had been hard-worked during the winter, and here was she, the mistress of the *Summer Shelter*, about to take a trip to warm and sunny regions with an almost empty vessel.

As soon as the meeting adjourned, Mrs. Cliff, accompanied by Mrs. Arkwright, made her way to the front, where many of the members were standing together, and was introduced by her friend to several clergymen with whom Mrs. Arkwright was acquainted. As soon as possible Mrs. Cliff referred to the subject which was upon her mind, and informed the gentlemen with whom she had just been made acquainted, that if they thought well of it she would like to invite a party of such of the delegates who would care for such an excursion at this season, to accompany her on a short trip to the West Indies. Her vessel would easily accommodate twelve or fifteen of the gentlemen, and she would prefer to offer her invitation first to the clerical members of the Synod.

The reverend gentlemen to whom this offer was made were a little surprised by it, but they could not help considering it was a most generous and attractive proposition, and one of them undertook to convey the invitation to some of his brethren of the Synod.

Although the Synod had adjourned, many of the delegates remained for a considerable time, during which Mrs. Cliff's invitation was discussed with lively appreci-

MRS. CLIFF'S INVITATION WAS DISCUSSED WITH LIVELY
APPRECIATION

ation, some of the speakers informing her that if they could make the arrangements necessary for their pulpits and their families during a short absence, they would be delighted to accept her invitation. The Synod would finally adjourn on the next Tuesday, and she was promised that before that time she would be informed of the exact number of guests she might expect.

The next morning when Mr. Burke appeared to accompany the ladies to the yacht, he found Willy Croup alone in their parlor.

"Do you know what's happened?" cried Willy, springing towards him as he entered. "Of course you don't, for Mrs. Cliff is going to give the first country week on the *Summer Shelter* to a Synod!"

"To a what?" cried Burke.

"A Synod," explained Willy. "It's a congregation, I mean a meeting, mostly of ministers, come together to settle church matters. She invited the whole lot of them, but of course they all can't come, — for there are more than a hundred of them, — but there will be about a dozen who can sail with us next Wednesday!"

Mr. Burke's jaw dropped. "A dozen ministers!" he exclaimed. "Sail with us! By George! Miss Croup, will you excuse me if I sit down?"

"You know," said Willy, "that the *Summer Shelter* was bought for this sort of thing! That is, to do good to people who can't get that sort of good in other ways! And if Mrs. Cliff takes out poor children from the slums, and hard-working shopgirls, and seamstresses, why shouldn't she take hard-working ministers and give them some fresh air and pleasure?"

"A dozen ministers!" groaned Mr. Burke. "I tell you, Miss Croup, I can't take them in!"

"Oh, there'll be room enough!" said Willy, mistaking his meaning, "for Mrs. Cliff says that each of those little rooms will easily hold two!"

"Oh, it isn't that!" said Burke. his eyes fixed stead-fastly upon a chair near him as if it had been something to look at. "But twelve ministers coming down on me so sudden, rather takes me aback, Miss Croup!"

"I don't wonder." said Willy, "for I don't believe that a Synod ever went out yachting before in a bunch!"

Mr. Burke rose and looked out of the window. "Miss Croup," said he, "do you remember what I said about mixin' fun and charity in these cruises? Well, I guess we'll have to take our charity straight this time!"

But when Mrs. Cliff had come in and had talked with animation and enthusiasm in regard to her plan. the effects of the shock which Mr. Burke had received began to wear off.

"All right, madam!" said he. "You're owner. and I'm Captain, and I'll stand by you! And if you take it into your head to ship a dozen popes on the *Summer Shelter*, I'll take them where you want them to go to, and I'll bring them back safe. I suppose we'll have all sorts of customers on the yacht this season, and if we've got to get used to queer passengers, a Synod will do very well to begin with! If you'll find out who's goin' and

will write to them to be on hand Tuesday night, I'll see
that they're taken care of!"

Mrs. Cliff's whole heart was now in the projected cruise
of the *Summer Shelter.* When she had thought of it
with only Willy and herself as passengers, she could not
help considering it was a great extravagance. Now she
was going to begin her series of sea-trips in a fashion far
superior and more dignified than anything yet thought
of. To be able to give such an invitation to a Synod was
something of which she might well be proud, and she
was proud.

CHAPTER XXI

A TELEGRAM FROM CAPTAIN HORN

IT was early Tuesday morning, and Mrs. Cliff and
Willy having just finished their breakfast, were busily
engaged in packing the two trunks they proposed taking
with them, and the elder lady was stating that although
she was perfectly willing to dress in the blue flannel
suit which had been ordered, she was not willing to wear
a white cap, although Willy urged that this was the
proper thing, as they had been told by the people where
they had bought their yachting suits; and Mrs. Cliff was
still insisting that, although it would do very well for
Willy to wear a white cap, she would wear a hood, — the
same kind of a hood which she had worn on all her other
voyages, which was more like a bonnet and more suitable

to her on that account than any other kind of head covering, when Mr. Burke burst — actually burst — without
knocking, into the room. His silk hat was on the back
of his head, and he wore no overcoat.

"Mrs. Cliff," he exclaimed, "I've just seen Shirley!
You remember Shirley?"

"Indeed, I do," said Mrs. Cliff. "I remember him
very well, and I always thought him to be a remarkably
nice man! But where did you see him, and what in the
world did he tell you to throw you into such a flurry?"

"He said a lot to me!" replied Burke. "And I'll
try to make as straight a tale of it as I can! You
see, about a week ago Shirley got a telegraphic message
from Captain Horn—"

"Captain Horn!" exclaimed Mrs. Cliff. "Where is
he, and what did he say?"

"He's in Mexico," said Burke; "and the telegram
was as long as a letter — that's one advantage in not
being obliged to think of what things cost, — and he
told Shirley a lot—"

"How did they say they were?" asked Mrs. Cliff,
eagerly. "Or did he say anything about Mrs. Horn?
Are they well?"

"Oh, I expect they're all right," said Burke; "but I
don't think he treated that subject. It was all about
that gold, and the part of it that was to go to Peru!

"When the business of dividing up the treasure was
settled in London in the way we know all about, word
was sent to the Peruvian government to tell them what
had happened, and to see what they said about it. And

when they heard the news, they were a good deal more than satisfied, — as they ought to have been, I'm sure, — and they made no bones about the share we took. All they wanted was to have their part sent to them just as soon as could be, and I don't wonder at it; for all those South American countries are as poor as beggars, and if any one of them got a sum of money like that, it could buy up all the others, if it felt like spending the money in that way!

"Those Peruvians were in such a hurry to get the treasure that they wouldn't agree to have the gold coined into money, or to be sent a part at a time, or to take drafts for it; but they wanted it just as it was as soon as they could get it, and, as it was their own, nobody could hinder them from doing what they pleased with it. Shirley and I have made up our minds that most likely the present government thought that they wouldn't be in office when the money arrived if they didn't have it on hand in pretty short order; and, of course, if they got their fingers on that treasure, they could stay in power as long as they pleased.

"It is hard to believe that any government could be such fools, — for they ordered it all shipped on an ordinary merchant vessel, an English steamer, the *Dunkery Beacon*, which was pretty nigh ready to sail for Lima. Now, any other government in this world would have sent a man-of-war for that gold, or some sort of an armed vessel to convoy it, but that wasn't the way with the Peruvians! They wanted their money, and they wanted it by the first steamer which could be got ready to sail. They weren't going to wait until they got one of their cruisers over to England, — not they!

"The quickest way, of course, would have been to ship it to Aspinwall, and then take it by rail to Panama, and from there ship it to Lima, but I suppose they were afraid to do that. If that sort of freight had been carried overland, they couldn't have hindered people from finding out what it was, and pretty nearly everybody in Central America would have turned train-robber. Anyway, the agents over there got the *Dunkery Beacon* to sail a little before her regular time.

"Now here comes the point! They actually shipped a hundred and sixty million dollars' worth of pure gold on a merchant steamer that was going on a regular voyage, and would actually touch at Jamaica and Rio Janeiro on account of her other freight, instead of buying her outright, or sending her on the straightest cruise she could make for Lima! Just think of that! More than that, this business was so talked about by the Peruvian agents, while they were trying to get the earliest steamer possible for it, that it was heard of in a good many more ports than one!

"Well, this steamer with all the gold on board sailed just as soon as it could; and the very next day our London bankers got a telegram from Paris from the head of a detective bureau there to tell them that no less than three vessels were fitting out in the biggest kind of hurry to go after that slow merchant steamer with the millions on board!"

Mrs. Cliff and Willy uttered a simultaneous cry of

horror. "Do you mean they're pirates, and are going to steal the gold?" cried Mrs. Cliff.

"Of course they are!" continued Burke. "And I don't wonder at it! Why, I don't believe such a cargo of gold ever left a port since the beginning of the world! For such a thing as that is enough to tempt anybody with the smallest streak of rascal blood in him and who could get hold of a ship!

"Well, these three vessels were fitting out hard as they could, — two in France, at Toulon and Marseilles, and one in Genoa; and although the detectives were almost positive what their business was, they were not sure that they could get proof enough to stop them. If the *Dunkery Beacon* had been going on a straight voyage, even to Rio Janeiro, she might have got away from them, but, you see, she was goin' to touch at Jamaica!

"And now, now, — this very minute, — that slow old steamer and those three pirates are on the Atlantic Ocean together! Why, it makes your blood creep to think of it!"

"Indeed it does! It's awful!" cried Mrs. Cliff. "And what are the London people going to do?"

"They're not going to do anything so far as I know!" said Burke. "If they could get through with the red-tape business necessary to send any sort of a cruiser or war-vessel after the *Dunkery Beacon* to protect her, — and I'm not sure that they could do it at all, — it would be a precious long time before such a vessel would leave the English Channel! But I don't think

N

that they'll try anything of the sort; all I know is, that the London people sent a cable message to Captain Horn. I suppose that they thought he ought to know what was likely to happen, considerin' that he was the head man in the whole business!"

"And what did the Captain do?" cried Mrs. Cliff. "What could he do?"

"I don't know," answered Burke. "I expect he did everything that could be done in the way of sending messages; and among other things, he sent that telegram, about a thousand words more or less, to Shirley. He might have telegraphed to me, perhaps, but he didn't know my address, as I was wandering around. But Shirley, you know, is a fixture in his shipyard; — and so he sent it to him!"

"I haven't a doubt," said Mrs. Cliff, "that he would have telegraphed to you if he had known where you were!"

"I hope so," said Burke. "And when he had told Shirley all that had happened, he asked him to pull up stakes, and sail by the first steamer he could catch for Jamaica. There was a chance that he might get there before the *Dunkery Beacon* arrived, or while she was in port, and then he could tell everything to make her captain understand that he needn't be afraid to lose anything on account of his ship stopping in Kingston harbor until arrangements could be made for his carrying his gold in safety to Lima. Captain Horn didn't think that the pirates would try to do anything before the *Dunkery Beacon* left Kingston. They would just follow her until she got into the South Atlantic, and then board her, most likely!

"Captain Horn said that he was going to Jamaica too, but as he didn't know how soon he would be able to sail from Vera Cruz, he wanted Shirley to go ahead without losing a minute. And then Shirley he telegraphed to me up at Plainton, — thinking I was there and that I ought to know all about it, and the women at my house took so long forwarding it that I did not get it until yesterday evening, and then I rushed around to where Shirley was staying, and got there just in time to catch him, for the next steamer to Jamaica sailed early this morning. But he had plenty of time to tell me everything.

"The minute he got the Captain's telegram, he just dropped everything and started for New York. And I can tell you, Mrs. Cliff, I'd have done the same, for I don't know what I wouldn't do to get the chance to see Captain Horn again!"

"And you wanted to go with Mr. Shirley?" said Mrs. Cliff, with an eager light in her eyes.

"Indeed I did!" said Burke. "But, of course, I wouldn't think of such a thing as going off and leaving you here with that yacht on your hands, and no knowing what you would do with the people on board, and everything else! So I saw Shirley off about seven o'clock this morning, and then I came to report to you."

"That was too much to expect, Mr. Burke," said Mrs. Cliff, "but it was just like you, and I shall never forget it! But, now tell me one thing, — is Mrs. Horn going to Jamaica with the Captain?"

"I don't know," said Burke, "but, of course, she must be — he wouldn't leave her alone in Mexico!"

"Of course she is!" cried Mrs. Cliff. "And Mr. Shirley will see them! And oh, Mr. Burke, why can't we see them? Of all things in the world I want to see Edna, and the Captain too! And why can't we go straight to Jamaica in the *Summer Shelter* instead of going anywhere else? We may get there before they all leave; don't you think we could do that?"

The eyes of Captain Burke fairly blazed. "Do it!" he cried, springing to his feet. "I believe we can do it; at any rate we can try! The same to you, madam, I would do anything in the world to see Captain Horn, and nobody knows when we will have the chance! Well, madam, it's all the plainest kind of sailing; we can get off at daylight to-morrow morning, and if that yacht sails as they told me she sails, I believe we may overhaul Shirley, and, perhaps, we will get to Kingston before any of them! And now I've got to bounce around, for there's a good deal to be done before nightfall!"

"But what about the Synod?" asked Willy Croup.

"Bless my soul!" exclaimed Mr. Burke, stopping suddenly on his way to the door. "I forgot the Synod."

Mrs. Cliff hesitated for a moment. "I don't think it need make any difference! It would be a great shame to disappoint all those good men; why couldn't we take them along all the same? Their weight wouldn't make the yacht go any slower, would it, Mr. Burke?"

"Not a bit of it!" said he. "But they may not want to go so far. Besides, if we find the Captain at Kingston,

we mayn't feel like going back in a hurry. I'll tell you
what we could do, Mrs. Cliff! We wouldn't lose any
time worth speaking of if we touched at Nassau, — that's
in the Bahamas, and a jolly place to go to. Then we
might discharge our cargo of ministers, and if you paid
their board until the next steamer sailed for New York,
and their passage home, I should think they would be
just as well satisfied as if they came back with us!"

Mrs. Cliff reflected. "That's true!" said she, presently.
"I can explain the case to them, and I don't see why
they should not be satisfied. And as for me, nobody
could be more willing than I am to give pleasure to these
ministers, but I don't believe that I could give up seeing
Edna and Captain Horn for the sake of any members of
any Synod!"

"All right, madam!" cried the impatient Burke.
"You settle the matter with the parsons, and I haven't
a doubt you can make it all right; and I'll be off!
Everything has got to be on board to-night. I'll come
after you early this evening." With this he departed.

When Mr. Burke had gone, Mrs. Cliff, very much
excited by what she had heard and by the thought of
what she was going to do, told Willy that she could go
on with the packing while she herself went over to the
church in Brooklyn and explained matters to the members of the Synod who intended to go with her, and give
them a chance to decide whether or not the plan proposed
by Mr. Burke would suit them.

She carried out this intention and drove to Brooklyn
in a carriage, but, having been delayed by many things

which Willy wanted to know about the packing, and having forgotten in what street the church was situated, she lost a good deal of time; and when she reached her destination she found that the Synod had adjourned *sine die*.

Mrs. Cliff sighed. It was a great pity to have taken so much trouble, especially when time was so precious, but she had done what she could. It would be impossible for her to find the members in their temporary places of abode, and the only thing she could do now was to tell them the change in her plans when they came on board that evening, and then, if they did not care to sail with her, they would have plenty of time to go on shore again.

CHAPTER XXII

THE "SUMMER SHELTER" GOES TO SEA

MR. BURKE did not arrive to escort Mrs. Cliff and Willy Croup to the yacht until nearly nine o'clock in the evening. They had sent their baggage to the vessel in the afternoon, and had now been expecting him, with great impatience, for nearly an hour, but when Mr. Burke arrived, it was impossible to find fault with him, for he had been busy, he said, every minute of the day.

He had made up a full crew; he had a good sailing-master, and the first mate who had been on the yacht before; everything that he could think of in the way of provisions and stores were on board, and there was nothing to prevent their getting out of the harbor early in the morning.

When Mrs. Cliff stepped on board her yacht, the *Summer Shelter*, her first thought was directed towards her guests of the Synod; and when the mate, Mr. Burdette, had advanced and been introduced to her, she asked him if any of the clergymen had yet appeared.

"They're all aboard, madam," said he — "fourteen of them! They came aboard about seven o'clock, and they stayed in the saloon until about half-past nine, and one of them came to me and said that as they were very tired they thought they'd go to bed, thinking, most likely, as it was then so late you wouldn't come aboard until morning. So the steward showed them their state-rooms, and we had to get one more ready than we expected to, and they're now all fast asleep; but I suppose I could arouse some of them up if you want to see them!"

Mrs. Cliff turned to Burke with an expression of despair on her face. "What in the world shall I do?" said she. "I wanted to tell them all about it and let them decide, but it would be horrible to make any of them who didn't care to go to get up and dress and go out into this damp night air to look for a hotel!"

"Well," said Burke, "all that's going ashore has got to go ashore to-night. We'll sail as soon as it is daylight! If I was you, Mrs. Cliff, I wouldn't bother about them. You invited them to go to the Bahamas, and you're going to take them there, and you're going to send them back the best way you can, and I'm willing to bet a clipper ship against your yacht that they will be just as well satisfied to come back in a regular steamer as to come back in this! You might offer to send them over to Savannah, and let them come up by rail, — they might like that for a change! The way the thing looks to me, madam, you're proposing to give them a good deal more than you promised."

"Well," said Mrs. Cliff, "one thing is certain! I'm not going to turn any of them out of their warm beds this night; and we might as well go to our rooms, for it must be a good deal after ten."

When Willy Croup beheld her little state-room, she stood at the door and looked in at it with rapture. She had a beautiful chamber in Mrs. Cliff's new house, fully and elegantly furnished, but there was something about this little bit of a bedroom, with all its nautical conveniences, its hooks, and shelves, and racks, its dear little window, and its two pretty berths, — each just big enough and not a bit too big, — which charmed her as no room she had ever seen had charmed her.

The *Summer Shelter* must have started, Mrs. Cliff thought, before daylight the next morning, for when she was awakened by the motion of the engine it was not light enough to distinguish objects in the room. But she lay quietly in her berth, and let her proud thoughts mount high and spread wide. As far as the possession of wealth and the sense of power could elevate the soul of woman, it now elevated the soul of Mrs. Cliff.

This was her own ship which was going out upon the ocean! This was her engine which was making everything shake and tremble! The great screw which was dashing the water at the stern and forcing the vessel through the waves belonged to her! Everything — the smoke-stacks, the tall masts, the nautical instruments — was her property! The crew and stewards, the engineers, were all in her service! She was going to the beautiful island of the sunny tropics because she herself had chosen to go there!

It was with great satisfaction, too, that she thought of the cost of all this. A great deal of money had been paid for that yacht, and it had relieved, as scarcely any other expenditure she would be likely to make could have relieved, the strain upon her mind occasioned by the pressure of her income. Even after the building of her new apartments her money had been getting the better of her. Now she felt that she was getting the better of her money.

By the way the yacht rolled and, at the same time, pitched and tossed, Mrs. Cliff thought it likely that they must be out upon the open sea, or, at least, well down the outer bay. She liked the motion, and the feeling that her property, moving according to her will, was riding dominant over the waves of the sea, sent a genial glow through every vein. It was now quite light, and when Mrs. Cliff got up and looked out of her round window she could see, far away to the right, the towering lighthouses of Sandy Hook.

About eight o'clock she dressed and went out on deck. She was proud of her good sailing qualities. As she went up the companion-way, holding firmly to the bright brass rail, she felt no more fear of falling than if she had been one of the crew. When she came out on the upper deck, she had scarcely time to look about her, when a man, whom at first sight she took for a stranger, came forward with outstretched hand. But in an instant she saw it was not a stranger, — it was Captain Burke, but not as she had ever seen him before. He was dressed in a complete suit of white duck with gold buttons, and he wore a white cap trimmed with gold, — an attire so different from his high silk hat and the furs that it was no wonder that at first she did not recognize their wearer.

"Why, Captain Burke," she cried, " I didn't know you!"

"No wonder," said he; "this is a considerable change from my ordinary toggery, but it's the uniform of a captain of a yacht; you see that's different from what it would be if I commanded a merchant vessel, or a liner, or a man-of-war!"

"It looks awfully cool for such weather," said she.

"Yes," said the Captain, "but it's the proper thing; and yachts, you know, generally cruise around in warmish weather. However, we're getting south as fast as we can. I tell you, madam, this yacht is a good one! We've just cast the log, and she's doing better than fourteen knots an hour, and we haven't got full steam on, either! It seems funny, madam, for me to command a steamer, but I'll get used to it in no time. If it was a sailing-vessel, it wouldn't be anything out of the way, because I've studied navigation, and I know more about a ship than many a skipper, but a steam yacht is different! However, I've got men under me who know how to do what I order them to do, and if necessary they're ready to tell me what I ought to order!"

"I don't believe there could be a better captain," said Mrs. Cliff, "and I do hope you won't take cold! And now I want to see the ministers as soon as they are ready. I think it will be well for me to receive them up here. I am not sure that I remember properly the names of all of them, but I shall not hesitate to ask them, and then I shall present each one of them to you: it will be a sort of a reception, you know! After that we can all go on pleasantly like one family. We will have to have a pretty big table in the saloon, but I suppose we can manage that!"

"Oh yes," said Mr. Burke; "and now I'll see the steward and tell him to let the parsons know that you're ready to receive them."

About a quarter of an hour after this the steward appeared on deck, and approaching Mrs. Cliff and the Captain, touched his hat. "Come to report, sir," said he, "the ministers are all sea-sick! There ain't none of them wants to get out of their berths, but some of them want tea."

Mrs. Cliff and the Captain could not help laughing, although she declared it was not a laughing matter.

"But it isn't surprising," said the Captain; "it's pretty rough, and I suppose they're all thorough-bred landsmen. But they'll get over it before long, and when they come on deck it's likely it will be pleasanter weather. We're having a considerable blow just now, and it will be worse when we get farther out! So I should say that you and Miss Croup and myself had better have our breakfast."

The steward was still standing by, and he touched his hat again, this time to Mrs. Cliff.

"The other lady is very sea-sick! I heard her groaning fearfully as I passed her door."

"Oh, I must go down to Willy," said Mrs. Cliff. "And, Captain, you and I will have to breakfast together."

As Mrs. Cliff opened the door of Willy Croup's stateroom, a pale white face in the lower berth was turned towards her, and a weak and trembling voice said to her, "Oh, Sarah, you have come at last! Is there any way of getting me out of this horrible little hole?"

For two days Mrs. Cliff and Captain Burke breakfasted, dined, and supped by themselves. They had head-winds, and the sea was very rough, and although the yacht did not make the time that might have been expected of her in fair weather, she did very well, and Burke was satisfied. The two stewards were kept very busy with the prostrate and dejected members of the Synod, and Mrs. Cliff and the stewardess devoted their best efforts to the alleviation of the woes of Willy, which they were glad to see were daily dwindling.

They had rounded Cape Hatteras, the sea was smoother, the cold wind had gone down, and Willy Croup, warmly wrapped up, was sitting in a steamer chair on deck. The desire that she might suddenly be transferred to Plainton or to heaven was gradually fading out of her mind, and the blue sky, the distant waves, and the thought of the

approaching meal were exercising a somewhat pleasur-
able influence upon her dreamy feeling, when Captain
Burke, who stood near with a telescope, announced that
the steamer over there on the horizon line was heading
south and that he had a notion she was the *Antonina*,
the vessel on which Shirley had sailed.

"I believed that we could overhaul her!" said he to
Mrs. Cliff. "I didn't know much about her sailing qualities, but I had no reason to believe she has the speed of
this yacht, and, as we're on the same course, I thought it
likely we would sight her, and what's more, pass her.
We'll change our course a little so that we will be closer
to her when we pass."

Mrs. Cliff, who had taken the glass, but could not see
through it very well, returned it to the Captain and
remarked, "If we can go so much faster than she does,
why can't we take Mr. Shirley on board when we catch
up to her?"

"I don't know about that," said Burke. "To do that,
both vessels would have to lay to and lose time, and she
might not want to do it as she's a regular steamer, and
carries the mail. And besides, if Shirley's under orders,
— that is, the same thing as orders, — to go straight to
Jamaica, I don't know that we have any right to take
him off his steamer and carry him to Nassau. Of course,
he might get to Jamaica just as soon, and perhaps
sooner, if he sailed with us, but we don't know it! We
may be delayed in some way; there're lots of things
that might happen, and anyway, I don't believe in interfering with orders, and I know Shirley doesn't either.

I believe he would want to keep on. Besides, we don't really know yet that that's the *Antonina*."

A couple of hours, however, proved that Captain Burke's surmise had been correct, and it was not long before the two vessels were abreast of each other. The yacht had put on all steam and had proved herself capable of lively speed. As the two vessels approached within hailing distance, Captain Burke went up on the little bridge, with a speaking-trumpet, and it was not long before Shirley was on the bridge of the other steamer, with another trumpet.

To the roaring conversation which now took place, everybody on each vessel who was not too sick, who had no duties, or could be spared from them, listened with the most lively interest. A colloquy upon the lonely sea between two persons, one upon one vessel and the other upon another, must always be an incident of absorbing importance.

Very naturally Shirley was amazed to find it was his friend Burke who was roaring at him, and delighted when he was informed that the yacht was also on its way to Jamaica to meet Captain Horn. After a quarter of an hour of high-sounding talk, during which Shirley was informed of Burke's intention to touch at Nassau, the interview terminated; the *Summer Shelter* shaping her course a little more to the south, by night-fall the *Antonina* had faded out of sight on the northeast horizon.

"I shouldn't wonder," said Captain Burke at dinner, "if we got to Jamaica before her anyway, although we're bound to lose time in the harbor at Nassau."

The company at the dinner-table was larger than it had yet been. Five members of the Synod had appeared on deck during the speaking-trumpet conversation, and feeling well enough to stay there, had been warmly greeted and congratulated by Mrs. Cliff. The idea of a formal reception had, of course, been given up, and there was no need of presenting these gentlemen to the Captain, for he had previously visited all of his clerical passengers in their berths, and was thus qualified to present them to Mrs. Cliff as fast as they should make their appearance. At dinner-time two more came into the saloon, and the next morning at breakfast the delegation from the Synod were all present, with the exception of two whose minds were not yet quite capable of properly appreciating the subject of nutrition.

When at last the *Summer Shelter* found herself in the smoother waters and the warmer air of the Gulf Stream, when the nautilus spread its gay-colored sail in the sunlight by the side of the yacht, when the porpoises flashed their shining black bodies out of the water and plunged in again as they raced with the swiftly moving vessel, when great flocks of flying-fish would rise into the air, skim high above the water, and then all fall back again with a patter as of big rain-drops, and the people on the deck of the *Summer Shelter* took off their heavy wraps and unbuttoned their coats, it was a happy company which sailed with Mrs. Cliff among the beautiful isles of the West Indies.

CHAPTER XXIII

WILLY CROUP COMES TO THE FRONT

THE pleasant rays of the semi-tropical sun so warmed and subsequently melted the varied dispositions of the company on board the *Summer Shelter* that in spite of their very different natures they became fused, as it were, into a happy party of friends.

Willy Croup actually felt as if she were a young woman in a large party of gentlemen with no rivals. She was not young, but many of her youthful qualities still remained with her, and under the influence of her surroundings they all budded out and blossomed bravely. At the end of a day of fine weather there was not a clergyman on board who did not wish that Miss Croup belonged to his congregation.

As for the members of the Synod, there could be no doubt that they were thoroughly enjoying themselves. Tired with the long winter's work, and rejoiced, almost amazed, to be so suddenly freed from the cold wintry weather of their homes, all of their spirits rose and most of their hearts were merry.

There were but few gray heads among these clergymen, and the majority of them were under middle age. Some of them had been almost strangers to each other when they came on board, but now there were no strangers on the *Summer Shelter*. Some of them had crossed the Atlantic, but not one had ever taken a coastwise voyage on a comparatively small vessel, and although the consequence of this new experience, their involuntary seclusion of the first days of the trip, and their consequent unconventional and irregular acceptance of Mrs. Cliff's hospitality, had caused a little stiffness in their demeanor at first, this speedily disappeared, hand in hand with the recollection of that most easily forgotten of human ills which had so rudely interfered with their good manners.

As far as the resources of their portmanteaus would allow, these reverend clergymen dressed themselves simply and in semi-nautical costumes. Some played quoits upon the upper deck, in which sport Willy joined. Others climbed up the shrouds, preferably on the inside, — this method of exercise, although very difficult, being considered safer in case of a sudden lurch of the vessel. And the many other sportive things they did, and the many pleasant anecdotes they told, nearly all relating to the discomfiture of clergymen under various embarrassing circumstances, caused Captain Burke to say to Mrs. Cliff that he had never imagined that parsons were such jolly fellows, and so far as he was concerned, he would be glad to take out another party of them.

"But if we do," he said, "I think we'd better ship them on a tug and let them cruise around the Lightship for two or three days. Then when they hoisted a signal that they were all well on board, we could go out and take them off. In that way, you see, they'd really enjoy a cruise on the *Summer Shelter*."

As the sun went down behind the distant coast of Florida they were boarded by a negro pilot, and in the morning they awoke to find themselves fast to a

o

pier of the city of Nassau, lying white in the early daylight.

The members of the Synod had readily agreed to Mrs. Cliff's plan to leave them at Nassau and let them return by a regular passenger steamer, and they all preferred to go by sea to Savannah and then to their homes by rail. With expenses paid, none but the most unreasonable of men could have objected to such a plan.

As Captain Burke announced that he would stop at Nassau for a day to take in some fresh stores, especially of fruit and vegetables, and to give Mrs. Cliff and Willy Croup an opportunity to see the place, the *Summer Shelter* was soon deserted. But in the evening, everybody returned on board, as the company wished to keep together as long as possible, and there would be plenty of time in the morning for the members of the Synod to disembark and go to the hotel.

Very early in the morning Captain Burke was aroused by the entrance of the sailing-master, Mr. Portman, into his state-room. "'Morning, sir," said Mr. Portman. "I want you to come out here and look at something!"

Perceiving by the manner and tones of the other that there was something important to be looked at, Captain Burke jumped up, quickly dressed himself, and went out on deck. There, fastened against the fore-mast, was a large piece of paper on which were written these words: —

"We don't intend to sail on a filibustering cruise. We know what it means when you take on arms in New York, and discharge your respectable passengers in

THERE, FASTENED AGAINST THE FOREMAST, WAS A LARGE
PIECE OF PAPER

Nassau. We don't want nothing to do with your next lot of passengers, and don't intend to get into no scrapes. So good-bye!   (Signed)   The Crew."

" You don't mean to say," cried Burke, " that the crew has deserted the vessel ?"

"That's what it is, sir," said Mr. Burdette, the first mate, who had just joined them. " The crew has cleared out to a man! Mr. Portman and I are left, the engineer's left and his assistant, — they belonged to the yacht and don't have much to do with the crew, — but the rest's all gone! Deckhands, stewards, and even the cook. The stewardess must have gone too, for I haven't seen her."

" What's the meaning of all this," shouted Burke, his face getting very red. " When did they go, and why did they go ?"

" It's the second mate's watch, and he is off with them," said Mr. Burdette. " I expect he's at the bottom of it. He's a mighty wary fellow. Just as like as not he spread the report that we were going on a filibustering expedition to Cuba, and the ground for it, in my opinion, is those cases of arms you opened the other day !"

" I think that is it, sir," said Mr. Portman. " You know there's a rising in Cuba, and there was lots of talk about filibustering before we left. I expect the people thought that the ladies were going on shore the same as the parsons."

Burke was confounded. He knew not what to say or what to think, but seeing Mrs. Cliff appearing at the head of the companion-way, he thought it his first duty to go and report the state of affairs to her, which he did.   That lady's astonishment and dismay were very great.

"What are we going to do?" she asked.   "And what do you mean by the cases of arms?"

"I'm afraid that was a piece of folly on my part," said Burke.

"I didn't know we had arms on board!"

"Well, what we have don't amount to much," said Burke.   "But this was the way of it.   After I heard the message from Captain Horn about the pirates, and everything, and as I didn't know exactly what sort of craft we would meet round about Jamaica, I thought we would feel a good deal safer, especially on account of you and Miss Croup, if we had some firearms aboard. So I put in some repeating rifles and ammunition, and I paid for them out of my own pocket!   Such things always come in useful, and while I was commanding the vessel on which you were sailing, Mrs. Cliff, I didn't want to feel that I'd left anything undone which ought to be done.   Of course, there was no reason to suppose that we would ever have to use them, but I knew I would feel better if I had them.   But there was one thing I needn't have done, and that was, — I needn't have opened them, which I did the other day in company with Mr. Burdette, because I hadn't had time before to examine them, and I wanted to see what they were. Some of the crew must have noticed the guns, and as they couldn't think why we wanted them, unless we were going on a filibustering expedition, they got that notion into their heads and so cut the ship.   It was easy

enough to do it, for we were moored to a pier, and the
second mate, whose watch they went away in, was most
likely at the head of the whole business!"

"But what are we going to do?" asked Mrs. Cliff.

"I must get another crew just as soon as I can," said
he, "and there isn't a minute to be lost! I was stretching a point when I agreed to stop over a day, but I
thought we could afford that and reach Kingston as soon
as Shirley does, but when he gets there with his message
to the Captain of the *Dunkery Beacon*, I want to be on
hand. There's no knowing what will have to be done,
or what will have to be said. I don't want Shirley to
think that he's got nobody to stand by him!"

"Indeed," said Mrs. Cliff, "we ought to lose no time,
for Captain Horn may be there. It is a most dreadful
misfortune to lose the crew this way! Can't you find
them again? Can't you make them come back?"

"If they don't want to be found," said Burke, "it
will take a good while to find them. But I'm going
on shore this minute, and I wish you would be good
enough to tell Miss Croup and the ministers how matters
stand!"

The news of the desertion of the crew when told by
Mrs. Cliff to those of the passengers who had come on
deck, and speedily communicated by these to their companions, created a great sensation. Willy Croup was so
affected that she began to cry. "Is there any danger?"
she said; "and hadn't we better go on shore? Suppose
some other vessel wanted to come up to this wharf, and
we had to move away,—there's nobody to move us!

And suppose we were to get loose in some way, there's nobody to stop us!"

"You are very practical, Miss Croup," remarked the Reverend Mr. Hodgson, the youngest clergyman on board. "But I am sure you need not have the least fear. We are moored firm and fast, and I have no doubt Captain Burke will soon arrive with the necessary men to take you to Jamaica."

Willy dried her eyes, and then she said, "There's another practical thing I'm thinking of, — there isn't any breakfast, and the cook's gone! But I believe we can arrange that. I could cook the breakfast myself if I had anybody to help me. I'll go speak to Mrs. Cliff."

Mrs. Cliff was decidedly of the opinion that they all ought to have breakfast, and that she and Willy could at least make coffee, and serve the passengers with bread and butter and preserved meats, but she remarked to Mr. Hodgson that perhaps the gentlemen would rather go to their hotels and get their breakfast.

"No indeed," said Mr. Hodgson, a stout, sun-browned fellow, who looked more like a hunter than a clergyman. "We have been talking over the matter, and we are not going to desert you until the new men come. And as to breakfast, here are Mr. Litchfield and myself ready to serve as stewards, assistants, cooks, or in any culinary capacity. We both have camped out and are not green hands. So you must let us help you, and we shall consider it good fun."

"It will be funny," said Willy, "to see a minister

cook! So let's go down to the kitchen. I know where
it is, for I've been in it!"

"I think, Miss Croup," said Mr. Litchfield, a tall
young man with black hair and side whiskers, and a
good deal of manner, "that you should say galley or
caboose, now that we are all nautical together."

"Well, I can't cook nautical," said Willy, "and I
don't intend to try! But I guess you can eat the food
if it isn't strictly naval."

In a few minutes the volunteer cooks were all at
work, and Willy's familiarity with household affairs,
even when exhibited under the present novel condi-
tions, shone out brightly. She found some cold boiled
potatoes, and soon set Mr. Hodgson to work frying
them. Mrs. Cliff took the coffee in hand with all her
ante-millionnaire skill, and Willy skipped from one thing
to another, as happy as most people are whose ability
has suddenly forced them to the front.

"Oh, you ought to see the Synod setting the table!"
she cried, bursting into the galley. "They're getting
things all wrong, but it doesn't matter, and they seem
to be enjoying it. Now then, Mr. Litchfield, I think
you have cut all· the bread that can possibly be
eaten!"

Mr. Burdette had gone on shore with the Captain, and
Mr. Portman considered it his duty to remain on deck,
but the volunteer corps of cooks and stewards did their
work with hearty good-will, and the breakfast would
have been the most jolly meal that they had yet enjoyed
together if it had not been for the uncertainty and

uneasiness naturally occasioned by the desertion of the crew.

It was after ten o'clock when Captain Burke and Mr. Burdette returned. "We're in a bad fix," said the former, approaching Mrs. Cliff, who, with all the passengers, had been standing together watching them come down the pier. "There was a steamer cleared from here the day before yesterday which was short-handed, and seems to have carried off all the available able seamen in the port. But I believe that is all stuff and nonsense! the real fact seems to be, — and Mr. Burdette and I've agreed on that point, — that the report has got out that we're filibusters, and nobody wants to ship with us! Everything looks like it, you see. Here we come from New York with a regular lot of passengers, but we've got arms on board, and we drop the passengers here and let them go home some other way, and we sail on, saying we're bound for Jamaica — for Cuba is a good deal nearer, you know. But the worst thing is this, and I'm bound to tell it so that you can all know how the case stands and take care of yourselves as you think best. There's reason to believe that if the government of this place has not already had its eye on us, it will have its eye on us before very long, and for my part I'd give a good deal of money to be able to get away before they do; but without a crew we can't do it!"

Mrs. Cliff and Burke now retired to consult. "Madam," said he, "I'm bound to ask you as owner, what do you think we ought to do? If you take my advice, the first thing to be done is to get rid of the ministers. You can

settle with them about their travelling and let them go
to their hotels. Then perhaps I can rake up a few
loafers, landsmen, or anybody who can shovel coal or
push on a capstan bar, and by offering them double
wages get them to ship with us. Once in Jamaica, we
shall be all right!"

"But don't you think it will be dangerous," said Mrs.
Cliff, "to go around offering extra pay in this way?"

"That may be," he answered, "but what else is there
to do?"

At this moment Mr. Litchfield approached. "Madam,"
said he, "we have been discussing the unfortunate circumstances in which you find yourself placed, and we
now ask if you have made any plans in regard to your
future action?"

"The circumstances are truly unfortunate," replied
Mrs. Cliff; "for we are anxious to get to Jamaica as
soon as possible on account of very important business,
and I don't see how we are to do it. We have made no
plans, except that we feel it will be well for you gentlemen to leave us and go to your hotel, where you can stay
until the steamer will sail for Savannah day after to-
morrow. As for ourselves, we don't know what we are
going to do. Unless, indeed, some sort of a vessel may
be starting for Jamaica, and in that case we could leave
the *Summer Shelter* here and go on her."

"No," said Burke, "I thought of that and inquired.
Nothing will sail under a week, and in that time everybody we want to see may have left Jamaica!"

"Will you excuse me for a few minutes?" said

Mr. Litchfield, and with that he returned to his companions.

"Captain," said Willy, "won't you come down and have your breakfast? I don't believe you have eaten a thing, and you look as if you needed it!"

Captain Burke really did look as if he needed a good many things, — among others, a comb and a brush. His gold-trimmed cap was pushed on the back of his head; his white coat was unbuttoned, and the collar turned in; and his countenance was troubled by the belief that his want of prudence had brought Mrs. Cliff and her property into a very serious predicament.

"Thank you," said he, "but I can't eat. Breakfast is the last thing I can think of just now!"

Now approached Mr. Litchfield, followed by all his clerical brethren. "Madam," said he, "we have had a final consultation and have come to make a proposition to you and the Captain. We do not feel that we would be the kind of men we would like to think we are, if, after all your kindness and great consideration, we should step on shore and continue the very delightful programme you have laid out for us, while you are left in doubt, perplexity, and perhaps danger, on your yacht. There are five of us who feel that they cannot join in the offer which I am about to make to you and the Captain, but the rest of us wish most earnestly and heartily to offer you our services — if you think they are worth anything — to work this vessel to Jamaica. It is but a trip of a few days I am told, and I have no doubt that we can return to New York from Kingston almost as conveniently as we can from here. We can all write home and arrange for any contingencies which may arise on account of the delay in our return. In fact, it will not be difficult for most of us to consider this excursion as a part, or even the whole, of our annual vacation. Those of us who can go with you are all able-bodied fellows, and if you say so, Captain, we will turn in and go to work this moment. We have not any nautical experience, but we all have powers of observation, and so far as I am able to judge, I believe I can do most of the things I have seen done on this vessel by your common seamen, if that is what you call them!"

Mrs. Cliff looked at Captain Burke, and he looked at her. "If it was a sailin'-vessel," he exclaimed, "I'd say she couldn't be worked by parsons, but a steamer's different! By George! madam, let's take them, and get away while we can!"

CHAPTER XXIV

CHANGES ON THE "SUMMER SHELTER"

WHEN Captain Burke communicated to Mr. Portman and Mr. Burdette the news that nine of their passengers had offered to ship as a crew, the sailing-master and the first mate shook their heads. They did not believe that the vessel could be worked by parsons.

"But there isn't anybody else!" exclaimed Burke.

" We've got to get away, and they're all able-bodied, and they have more sense than most landsmen we can ship. And besides, here are five experienced seamen on board, and I say, let's try the parsons."

" All right," said Mr. Burdette. " If you're willing to risk it, I am."

Mr. Portman also said he was willing, and the engineer and his assistant, who were getting very nervous, agreed to the plan as soon as they heard of it.

Captain Burke shook himself, pulled his cap to the front of his head, arranged his coat properly and buttoned it up, and began to give orders. "Now, then," said he, " all passengers going ashore, please step lively !" And while this lively stepping was going on, and during the leave-taking and rapid writing of notes to be sent to the homes of the clerical crew, he ordered Mr. Burdette to secure a pilot, attend to the clearance business, and make everything ready to cast off and get out of the harbor as soon as possible.

When the five reverend gentlemen who had decided not to accompany the *Summer Shelter* in her further voyaging had departed for the hotel, portmanteaus in hand, and amply furnished by Mrs. Cliff with funds for their return to their homes, the volunteer crew, most of them without coats or waistcoats, and all in a high picnic spirit, set to work with enthusiasm, doing more things than they knew how to do, and embarrassing Mr. Burdette a good deal by their over-willingness to make themselves useful. But this untrained alacrity was soon toned down, and early in the afternoon, the hawsers of the *Summer Shelter* were cast off, and she steamed out of the eastern passage of the harbor.

There were remarks made in the town after the departure of the yacht; but when the passengers who had been left behind, all clergymen of high repute, had related the facts of the case, and had made it understood that the yacht, whose filibustering purpose had been suspected by its former crew, was now manned by nine members of the Synod recently convened in Brooklyn, and under the personal direction of Mrs. Cliff, an elderly and charitable resident of Plainton, Maine, all distrust was dropped, and was succeeded in some instances by the hope that the yacht might not be wrecked before it reached Jamaica.

The pilot left the *Summer Shelter ;* three of the clergymen shovelled coal; four of them served as deck hands; and two others ran around as assistant cooks and stewards ; Mr. Portman and Mr. Burdette lent their hands to things which were not at all in their line of duty; Mrs. Cliff and Willy pared the vegetables, and cooked without ever thinking of stopping to fan themselves; while Captain Burke flew around like half-a-dozen men, with a good word for everybody, and a hand to help wherever needed. It was truly a jolly voyage from Nassau to Kingston.

The new crew was divided into messes, and Mrs. Cliff insisted that they should come to the table in the saloon, no matter how they looked or what they had been doing: on her vessel a coal-heaver off duty was as good as a Captain, — while the clergymen good-humoredly endeavored to preserve the relative lowliness of their positions, each actuated by a zealous desire to show what a good deck hand or steward he could make when circumstances demanded it.

Working hard, laughing much, eating most heartily, and sleeping well, the busy and hilarious little party on board the *Summer Shelter* steamed into the harbor of Kingston, after a much shorter voyage than is generally made from Nassau to that port.

"If I could get a crew of jolly parsons," cried Captain Burke, "and could give them a month's training on board this yacht, I'd rather have them than any crew that could be got together from Cape Horn to the North Pole!"

"And by the time you had made able seamen of them," said Mr. Burdette, who was of a conventional turn of mind, "they'd all go back to their pulpits and preach!"

"And preach better!" said Mr. Litchfield, who was standing by. "Yes, sir, I believe they would all preach better!"

When the anchor was dropped, not quite so promptly as it would have been done if the clerical crew had had any previous practice in this operation, Mr. Burke was about to give orders to lower a boat, — for he was anxious to get on shore as soon as possible, — when he perceived a large boat rowed by six men and with a man in the stern, rapidly approaching the yacht. If they were port officials, he thought, they were extremely prompt, but he soon saw that the man in the stern, who stood up and waved a handkerchief, was his old friend Shirley.

"He must have been watching for us," said Captain Burke to Mrs. Cliff, "and he put out from one of the wharves as soon as we hove in sight. Shirley is a good fellow! You can trust to him to look out for his friends!"

In a very short time the six powerful negro oarsmen had Shirley's boat alongside, and in a few seconds after that, he stood upon the deck of the *Summer Shelter*. Burke was about to spring forward to greet his old comrade, but he stepped back to give way to Mrs. Cliff, who seized the hand of Shirley and bade him a most hearty welcome, although, had she met him by herself elsewhere, she would not have recognized him in the neat travelling suit which he now wore.

Shirley was delighted to meet Burke and Mrs. Cliff, he expressed pleasure in making the acquaintance of Miss Croup, who, standing by Mrs. Cliff's side, was quickly introduced, and he looked with astonishment at the body of queer-looking men who were gathered on the deck, and who appeared to be the crew of the yacht. But he wasted no time in friendly greetings nor in asking questions, but quickly informed Burke that they were all too late, and that the *Dunkery Beacon* had sailed two days before.

"And weren't you here to board her?" cried Burke.

"No," said Shirley; "our steamer didn't arrive until last night!"

Burke and Mrs. Cliff looked at each other in dismay. Tears began to come into Willy Croup's eyes, as they nearly always did when anything unusual suddenly happened, and all the members of the Synod, together with Mr. Portman and Mr. Burdette, and even the two engineers, who had come up from below, pressed close around Shirley, eager to hear what next should be said.

Everybody on board had been informed during the trip from Nassau of the errand of the yacht, for Mrs. Cliff thought she would be treating those generous and kind-hearted clergymen very badly if she did not let them know the nature of the good work in which they were engaged. And so it had happened that everybody who had sailed from Nassau on the yacht had hoped, — more than that, had even expected, — for the *Dunkery Beacon* was known to be a very slow steamer, — to find her in the harbor of Kingston taking on goods or perhaps coaling, and now all knew that even Shirley had been too late.

"This is dreadful!" exclaimed Mrs. Cliff, who was almost on the point of imitating Willy in the matter of tears. "And they haven't any idea, of course, of the dangers which await them."

"I don't see how they could know," said Shirley, "for of course if they had known, they wouldn't have sailed!"

"Did you hear anything about her?" asked Burke. "Was she all right when she arrived?"

"I have no doubt of that!" was the answer. "I made inquiries last night about the people who would most likely be consignees here, and this morning I went to a house on Harbor Street, — Beaver & Hughes. This house, in a way, is the Jamaica agent of the owners. I got there before the office was open, but I didn't find out much. She delivered some cargo to them and had sailed on time!"

"By George!" cried Burke, "Captain Horn was right! They could hardly get a chance to safely interfere with her until she had sailed from Kingston, and now I bet they are waiting for her outside the Caribbees!"

"That's just what I thought," said Shirley; "but of course I didn't say anything to these people, and I soon found out they didn't know much except so far as their own business was concerned. It's pretty certain from what I have heard that she didn't find any letters here that would make her change her course or do anything out of the way, — but I did find something! While I was talking with one of the heads of the house, the mail from New York, which had come over in my steamer too late to be delivered the night before, was brought in, and one of the letters was a cable message from London to New York to be forwarded by mail to Jamaica, and it was directed to 'Captain Hagar, of the *Dunkery Beacon*, care of Beaver & Hughes.' As I had been asking about the steamer, Beaver or Hughes, whichever it was, mentioned the message. I told him on the spot that I thought it was his duty to open it, for I was very sure it was on important business. He considered for a while, saying that perhaps the proper thing was to send it on after Captain Hagar by mail; but when he had thought about it a little he said perhaps he had better open it, and he did. The words were just these: —

"'On no account leave Kingston Harbor until further orders. — Blackburn.' Blackburn is the head owner."

P

"What did you say then," asked Mrs. Cliff, very earnestly, "and what did he say?"

"I didn't say anything about her being a treasure ship," replied Shirley. "If it was not known in Jamaica that she was carrying that gold, I wasn't going to tell it; for there are as many black-hearted scoundrels here as in any other part of the world! But I told the Beaver & Hughes people that I also had a message for Captain Hagar, and that a friend of mine was coming to Kingston in a yacht, and that if he arrived soon I hadn't a doubt that we could overhaul the *Dunkery Beacon*, and give the Captain my message and the one from London besides, and that we'd try to do it, for it was very important. But they didn't know me, and they said they would wait until my friend's yacht should arrive, and then they would see about sending the message to Captain Hagar. Now, I've done enough talking, and we must do something!"

"What do you think we ought to do?" asked Burke.

"Well, I say," answered Shirley, "if you have any passengers to put ashore here, put them ashore, and then let's go after the *Dunkery Beacon* and deliver the message. A stern chase is a long chase, but if I'm to judge by the way this yacht caught up to the *Antonina* and passed her, I believe there's a good chance of overhauling the *Dunkery Beacon* before the pirates get hold of her. Then all she's got to do is to steam back to Kingston."

"But suppose the pirates come before she gets back," said Mrs. Cliff.

"Well, they won't fool with her if she is in company," replied Shirley. "Now, and what do you say?" he asked, addressing Burke, but glancing around at the others. "I don't know how this ship's company is made up, or how long a stop you are thinking of making here, or anything about it! But you're the owner, Mrs. Cliff, and if you lend Burke and me your yacht, I reckon he'll be ready enough to steam after the *Dunkery Beacon* and deliver the messages. It's a thing which Captain Horn has set his heart upon, and it's a thing which ought to be done if it can be done, and this yacht, I believe, is the vessel that can do it!"

During this speech Mr. Burke, generally so eager to speak and to act, had stood silent and troubled. He agreed with Shirley that the thing to do was to go after the *Dunkery Beacon* at the best speed the yacht could make. He did not believe that Mrs. Cliff would object to his sailing away with her yacht on this most important errand, — but he remembered that he had no crew. These parsons must be put off at Kingston, and although he had had no doubt whatever that he could get a crew in this port, he had expected to have a week, and perhaps more, in which to do it. To collect in an hour or two a crew which he could trust with the knowledge which would most likely come to them in some way or other that the steamer they were chasing carried untold wealth, was hardly to be thought of.

"As far as I am concerned," cried Mrs. Cliff, "my yacht may go after that steamer just as soon as she can be started away!"

"And what do you say, Burke ?" exclaimed Shirley.

Burke did not answer. He was trying to decide whether or not he and Shirley, with Burdette and Portman, and the two engineers could work the yacht. But before he had even a chance to speak, Mr. Hodgson stepped forward and exclaimed : —

"I'll stick to the yacht until she has accomplished her business ! I'd just as soon make my vacation a week longer as not. I can cut it off somewhere else. If you are thinking about your crew, Captain, I want to say that so far as I am concerned, I am one volunteer !"

"And I am another !" said Mr. Litchfield. "Now that I know how absolutely essential it is that the *Dunkery Beacon* should be overtaken, I would not for a moment even consider the surrender of my position upon this vessel, which I assure you, madam, I consider as an honor !"

Mr. Shirley stared in amazement at the speaker. What sort of a seaman was this ? His face and hands were dirty, but he had been shovelling coal ; but such speech Shirley had never heard from mariners' lips. The rest of the crew seemed very odd, and now he noticed for the first time that although many of them were in their shirt sleeves, nearly all wore black trousers. He could not understand it.

"Mr. Litchfield, sir," said a large, heavy man with a nose burned very red, a travelling cap upon his head, and wearing a stiffly starched shirt which had once been white, no collar, and a waistcoat cut very straight in front, now opened, but intended to be buttoned up very high, "I believe Mr. Litchfield has voiced the sentiments of us all. As he was speaking, I looked from one brother to another, and I think I am right."

"You are right!" cried every one of the sturdy fellows who had so recently stepped from Synod to yacht.

"I knew it!" exultingly exclaimed the speaker. "I felt it in my heart of hearts! Madam, and Captain, knowing what we do we are not the men to desert you when it is found necessary to continue the voyage for a little!"

"And what would happen to us if we did leave the yacht?" said another. "We might simply have to remain at Kingston until you returned. Oh no, we wouldn't think of it!"

"Burke," said Shirley, in a low tone, "who are these people?"

"Can't tell you now," said Burke, his eyes glistening, "you might tumble overboard backwards if I did! Gentlemen," he cried, turning to his crew, "you're a royal lot! And if any of you ever ask me to stand by you, I'll do it while there's breath in my body! And now, madam," said he, his doubt and perplexity gone and his face animated by the necessity of immediate action, "I can't now say anything about your kindness in lending us your yacht, but if you and Miss Croup want to go ashore, here is a boat alongside."

"Go ashore!" screamed Mrs. Cliff. "What are you talking about? If anybody stays on this yacht, I do! I wouldn't think of such a thing as going ashore!"

"Nor I!" cried Willy. "What's got into your head, Mr. Burke, — do you intend to go without eating?"

"Ladies," cried Burke, "you are truly trumps, and that's all I've got to say! And we'll get out of this harbor just as fast as we can!"

"Look here," cried Shirley, running after Burke to the captain's room; "I've got to go ashore again and get that cable message! We must have authority to turn that steamer back if we overhaul her, and I've got to have somebody to go with me. But before we do anything you must take time to tell me who these queer-looking customers are that you've got on board."

Burke shut the door of his room, and in as few words as possible he explained how some of the members of the recent Synod happened to be acting as crew of the yacht. Shirley was a quiet and rather a sedate man, but when he heard this tale, he dropped into a chair, leaned back, stretched out his legs, and laughed until his voice failed him.

"Oh, it's all funny enough," said Burke, almost as merry as his friend, "but they're good ones, I can tell you that! You couldn't get together a better set of landsmen, and I tell you what I'll do. If you want anybody to go with you to certify that you are all right, I'll send a couple of parsons!"

"Just what I want!" cried Shirley.

Burke quickly stepped out on deck, and calling the mate, "Mr. Burdette," he said, "I want you to detail the Reverend Charles Attlebury and Reverend Mr. Gillingham to go ashore with Mr. Shirley. Tell them to put on their parson's toggery, long coats, high hats, and white cravats, and let each man take with him the address of his church on a card. They are to certify to Mr. Shirley. Tell them to step round lively — we have no time to lose!"

Soon after the boat with Shirley and the clergymen had pulled away from the yacht, two of the clerical crew came to Mrs. Cliff, and told her that they were very sorry indeed to say, that having consulted the sailing-master, and having been told by him that it was not at all probable that the yacht would be able to return to Kingston in a week, they had been forced to the conclusion that they would not be able to offer her their services during the voyage she was about to make. Important affairs at home would make it impossible for them to prolong their most delightful vacation, and as they had been informed that the *Antonina* would return to New York in a few days, it would be advisable for them to leave the yacht and take passage to New York in her. They felt, however, that this apparent desertion would be of less importance than it would have been if it had occurred in the port of Nassau, because now the crew would have the assistance of Mr. Shirley, who was certainly worth more than both of them together.

When Burke heard this, he said to Mrs. Cliff that he was not sure but what the parsons were quite correct, and although everybody was sorry to lose two members of the party, it could not be helped, and all who had letters to send to New York went to work to scribble them as fast as they could. Mrs. Cliff also wrote a note to Captain Horn, informing him of the state of affairs, and of their reasons for not waiting for him, and this the departing clergymen undertook to leave with Beaver & Hughes, where Captain Horn would be sure to call.

When Shirley reached the counting-house of Beaver & Hughes, he found that it was a great advantage to be backed up by a pair of reverend clergymen, who had come to Kingston in a handsome yacht. The message for Captain Hagar was delivered without hesitation, and the best wishes were expressed that they might be able to overtake the *Dunkery Beacon.*

"Her course will be south of Tobago Island," said Mr. Beaver, "and then if your yacht is the vessel you say it is, I should say you ought to overtake her before she gets very far down the coast. I don't know that Captain Hagar will turn back when he gets this message, having gone so far, but, of course, if it is important, I am glad there is a vessel here to take it to him."

"What sort of a looking vessel is the *Dunkery Beacon?*" asked Shirley.

"She is about two thousand tons," said the other, "has two masts which do not rake much, and her funnel is painted black and white, the stripes running up and down. There are three steamers on the line, and all their funnels are painted that way."

"We'll be apt to know her when we see her," said Shirley, and with a hurried leave, he and his companions hastened back to the wharves.

But on the way a thought struck Shirley, and he

determined to take time to go to the post-office.
There might be something for him, and he had not
thought of it before. There he found a telegraphic
message addressed to him and sent from Vera Cruz to
New York, and thence forwarded by mail. It was from
Captain Horn, and was as long as an ordinary business
note, and informed Shirley that the Captain expected to
be in Jamaica not long after this message reached
Kingston. There was no regular steamer which would
reach there in good time, but he had chartered a
steamer, the *Monterey*, which was then being made
ready for sea as rapidly as possible, and would probably clear for Kingston in a few days. It urged
Shirley not to fail to keep the *Dunkery Beacon* in port
until he arrived.

Shirley stood speechless for some minutes after he had
read this message. This telegram had come with him
on the *Antonina* from New York! What a fool he had
been not to think sooner of the post-office — but what
difference would it have made? What could he have
done that he had not done? If the Captain sailed in a
few days from the time he sent the message, he would
be here very soon, for the distance between Kingston
and Vera Cruz was less than that from New York. The
Captain must have counted on Shirley reaching Jamaica
very much sooner than he really did arrive. Puzzled,
annoyed, and disgusted with himself, Shirley explained
the message to his companions, and they all hastened
back to the yacht. There a brief but very hurried consultation was held, in which nearly everybody joined.

The question to be decided was, should they wait for Captain Horn?

A great deal was said in a very short time, and in the midst of the confused opinions, Mrs. Cliff spoke out, loudly and clearly. "It is my opinion," said she, "that we should not stop. If fitting out a steamer is like fitting out anything else in this world that I know of, it is almost certain to take more time than people expect it to take. If Captain Horn telegraphed to us this minute, I believe he would tell us to go after that ship with the gold on board, just as fast as we can, and tell them to turn back."

This speech was received with favor by all who heard it, and without a word in answer to Mrs. Cliff, Captain Burke told Mr. Burdette that they would clear for a cruise and get away just as soon as they could do it.

When the yacht had been made ready to start, the two clergymen descended into the boat, which was waiting alongside, and the *Summer Shelter* steamed out of the harbor of Kingston, and headed away for Tobago Island.

CHAPTER XXV

A NOTE FOR CAPTAIN BURKE

NOTWITHSTANDING the fact that the *Summer Shelter* made very good time, that she had coaled at Nassau, and was therefore ready for an extended cruise, it was impossible for any of those on board of her to conceal from themselves the very strong improbability of sighting the *Dunkery Beacon* after she had got out upon the wide Atlantic, and that she would pass the comparatively narrow channel south of Tobago Island before the yacht reached it, was almost a foregone conclusion.

Mr. Burke assured Mrs. Cliff and his passengers that although their chase after the steamer might reasonably suggest a needle and a haystack, still, if the *Dunkery Beacon* kept down the coast in as straight a line as she could for Cape St. Roque, and if the *Summer Shelter* also kept the same line, and if the yacht steamed a great deal faster than the other vessel, it stood to reason that it could not be very long before the *Summer Shelter* overhauled the *Dunkery Beacon*.

But those who consulted with Mr. Portman were not so well encouraged as those who pinned their faith upon the Captain. The sailing-master had very strong doubts about ever sighting the steamer that had sailed away two days before they left Kingston. The ocean being so very large, and any steamer being so very small comparatively, if they did not pass her miles out of sight, and if they never caught up to her, he would not be in the least surprised.

Four days had passed since they left Kingston, when Burke and Shirley stood together upon the deck, scanning the horizon with a glass. "Don't you think it begins to look like a wild goose chase?" said the latter.

Burke thrust his hands into the pockets of his jacket. "Yes," said he, "it does look like that! I did believe that we were going to overhaul her before she got out-side the Caribbees, but she must be a faster vessel than I thought she was."

"I don't believe she's fast at all," said Shirley. "She's had two days' start, and that's enough to spoil our business, I'm afraid!"

"But we'll keep on," said Burke. "We're not going to turn back until our coal bunkers tell us we've got to do it!"

Steamers they saw, sometimes two in an hour, — sail-ing-vessels were sighted, near by or far away; — schoon-ers, ships, or brigs, and these were steaming and sailing this way and that, but never did they see a steamer with a single funnel painted black and white, with the stripes running up and down.

It was very early next morning after the conversation between Burke and Shirley that the latter saw a long line of smoke just above the horizon which he thought might give him reason for looking out for the steamer of which they were in quest; but when he got his glass, and the masts appeared above the horizon, he saw that this vessel was heading eastward, perhaps a little northeast, and therefore was not likely to be the *Dunkery Beacon*. But in half an hour his glass showed him that there were stripes on the funnel of this steamer which ran up and down, and in a moment Burke was called, and was soon at his side.

"I believe that's the *Dunkery !*" cried the Captain, with the glass to his eye. "But she's on the wrong course! It won't take us long to overhaul her. We'll

head the yacht a few points to the east. Don't say anything to anybody, — we don't want to disappoint them."

"Oh, we can overhaul her," said Shirley, who now
had the glass, "for it isn't a stern chase by any means."

In less than half an hour everybody on board the
Summer Shelter knew that the large steamer, which
they could plainly see on the rolling waves to the
south, must be the *Dunkery Beacon*, unless, indeed, they
should find that this was one of her sister ships coming north. There was great excitement on board the
yacht. The breakfast, which was in course of prepara-
tion, was almost entirely forgotten by those who had it
in charge, and everybody who could possibly leave duty
crowded to the rail, peering across the waves to the
southward. It was not long before Shirley, who had
the best eyes on board, declared that he could read
with his glass the name *Dunkery Beacon* on the port
bow.

"That's not where we ought to see it," cried Burke;
"we ought to see it on the stern! But we've got her,
boys! — and then he remembered himself, and added,
— "ladies; and now let's give three good cheers!"

Three rousing cheers were given by all on board with
such good-will that they would have been heard on the
other steamer had not the wind been pretty strong from
the west.

The *Summer Shelter* gained upon the larger vessel,
and Burke now ran up signals for her to lay to, as he
wished to speak with her. To these signals, however,
the *Dunkery* paid no immediate attention, keeping stead-

ily on, although altering her course towards the southeast.

"What does that mean, Mr. Shirley?" asked Mrs.
Cliff. "Mr. Burke wants her to stop, doesn't he?"

"Yes," said Shirley, "that is what the signal is for."

"But she doesn't stop!" said Mrs. Cliff. "Do you
think there is any chance of her not stopping at all?"

"Can't say, madam," he answered. "But she's got
good reason for keeping on her way; a vessel with all
that treasure on board could hardly be expected to lay to
because a strange vessel that she knows nothing about
asked her to shut off steam."

"That seems to me very reasonable, indeed," said
Mr. Litchfield, who was standing by. "But it would be
very bad fortune, if, after all the trouble and anxiety
you have had in overtaking this vessel, she should
decline to stop and hear the news we have to tell."

There was a strong breeze and a good deal of sea, but
Burke determined to get near enough to hail the *Dunkery Beacon* and speak to her. So he got round on her
weather quarter, and easily overtaking her, he brought
the *Summer Shelter* as near to the other vessel as he
considered it safe to do. Then he hailed her, "*Dunkery
Beacon*, ahoy! Is that Captain Hagar?"

The wind was too strong for the Captain of the other
vessel to answer through his trumpet, but he signalled
assent. Then Burke informed him that he wished him
to lay to in order that he might send a boat on board;
that he had very important orders to Captain Hagar
from his owners, and that he had followed him from

Jamaica in order to deliver them. For some time there was no answer whatever to these loudly bellowed remarks, and the two vessels kept on side by side.

" Anyway," said Burke to Mr. Burdette, "she can see that we're a lot faster than she is, and that she can't get away from us!"

"It may be that she's afraid of us," said the mate, "and thinks we're one of the pirates."

"That can't be," said Burke, "for she doesn't know anything about the pirates! I'll hail her again, and tell her what we are, and what our business is. I think it won't be long before she lays to just to see what we want."

Sure enough, in less than fifteen minutes the *Dunkery Beacon* signalled that she would lay to, and before long the two vessels, their engines stopped and their heads to the wind, lay rising and falling on the waves, and near enough to speak to each other.

"Now, then, what do you want?" shouted the Captain of the *Dunkery*.

"I want to send a boat aboard with an important message from Blackburn!"

After a few minutes the answer came, " Send a boat!"

Orders were given to lower one of the yacht's boats, and it was agreed that Shirley ought to be the man to go over to the *Dunkery Beacon*. "Who do you want to go with you?" asked Burke.

"Nobody but the boat's crew," he answered. "I can explain things better by myself. Captain Hagar seems to be an obstinate fellow, and it won't be easy to turn

him back on his course.   But if I want anybody to stand
by me and back me up in what I say, you might let
some of the clergymen come over.   He might believe
them, and wouldn't me.   But I'll talk to him first by
myself."

Every member of the Synod declared that he was perfectly willing to go to the other vessel if he should be
needed, and Mrs. Cliff assured Burke that if she could
be of any good in making the Captain of the *Dunkery
Beacon* understand that he ought to turn back, she would
be perfectly willing to be rowed over to his vessel.

"I don't think it will be necessary to put a lady into a
boat on such a sea as this," said Burke.   "But when he
hears what Shirley has to tell him, that Captain will
most likely be glad enough to turn back."

Captain Burke was afraid to trust any of his clerical
crew to row a ship's boat on such a heavy sea, and
although he would be perfectly willing to go himself as
one of the oarsmen, he would not leave the yacht so
long as Mrs. Cliff was on board; but Mr. Burdette, the
sailing-master, and the assistant engineer volunteered
as crew of the boat, while Shirley himself pulled an
oar.

When the boat reached the *Dunkery Beacon*, Shirley
was soon on board, while the three men in the boat,
holding to a line which had been thrown them, kept
their little craft from bumping against the side of the
big steamer by pushing her off with their oars.   On board
the *Summer Shelter* everybody stood and gazed over
the rail, staring at the other steamer as if they could

hear with their eyes what was being said on board of her. After waiting about twenty minutes, a note was passed down to the men in the boat, who pushed off and rowed back with it to the *Summer Shelter.*

The note, which Captain Burke opened and read as soon as he could lay hold of it, ran as follows :

"To Captain Burke of the 'Summer Shelter' :

"It's my opinion that you're trying to play a beastly trick on me ! It isn't like my owners to send a message to me off the coast of South America. If they wanted to send me a message, it would have been waiting for me at Kingston. I don't know what sort of a trick you are trying to play on me, but you can't do it. I know my duties, and I'm going to keep on to my port. And what's more, I'm not going to send back the man you sent aboard of me. I'll take him with me to Rio Janeiro, and hand him over to the authorities. They'll know what to do with him, but I don't intend to send him back to report to you whatever he was sent aboard my vessel to find out.

"I don't know how you came to think I had treasure on board, but it's none of your business anyway. You must think I'm a fool to turn back to Kingston because you tell me to. Anybody can write a telegram. So I'm going to get under way, and you can steam back to Kingston, or wherever you came from.

"Captain Hagar."

Captain Burke had hardly finished reading this extraordinary letter when he heard a cry from the boat

Q

lying by the side of the yacht in which the three men were waiting, expecting to go back to the other vessel with an answer. "Hello!" cried Mr. Burdette. "She's getting under way! That steamer's off!"

And at this a shout arose from everybody on board the *Summer Shelter*. The propeller of the *Dunkery Beacon* was stirring the water at her stern, and she was moving away, her bow turned southward. Burke leaned over the rail, shouted to his men to get on board and haul up the boat, and then he gave orders to go ahead full speed.

"What does all this mean?" cried Mrs. Cliff. "What's in that letter, Mr. Burke? Are they running away with Mr. Shirley?"

"That's what it looks like!" he cried. "But here's the letter. You can all read it for yourselves!" and with that he dashed away to take charge of his vessel.

All now was wild excitement on board the *Summer Shelter*, but what was to be done or with what intention they were pursuing the *Dunkery Beacon* and rapidly gaining upon her, no one could say, not even Captain Burke himself. The yacht was keeping on the weather quarter of the other vessel, and when she was near enough, he began again to yell at her through his speaking-trumpet, but no answer or signal came back, and everybody on board the larger vessel seemed to be attending to his duties as if nothing had happened, while Mr. Shirley was not visible.

While the Captain was roaring himself red in the face, both Mrs. Cliff and Willy Croup were crying, and the face of each clergyman showed great anxiety and trouble. Presently Mrs. Cliff was approached by the Reverend Mr. Arbuckle, the oldest of the members of the late Synod who had shipped with her.

"This is a most unfortunate and totally unexpected outcome of our expedition," said he. "If Mr. Shirley is taken to Rio Janeiro and charges made against him, his case may be very serious. But I cannot see what we are to do! Don't you believe it would be well to call a consultation of those on board?"

Mrs. Cliff wiped her eyes, and said they ought to consult. If anything could be done, it should be done immediately.

Captain Burke put the yacht in charge of the mate, and came aft where five of the clergymen, the sailing-master, and Mrs. Cliff and Willy were gathered together. "I'm willing to hold council," said he, "but at this minute I can't give any advice as to what ought to be done. The only thing I can say, is that I don't want to desert Shirley. If I could do it, I would board that vessel and take him off, but I don't see my way clear to that just yet. I'm not owner of this yacht, but if Mrs. Cliff will give the word, I'll follow that steamer to Rio Janeiro, and if Shirley is put on shore and charges made against him, I'll be there to stand by him!"

"Of course, we will not desert Mr. Shirley," cried Mrs. Cliff. "This yacht shall follow that vessel until we can take him on board again. I can't feel it in my heart, gentlemen, to say to you that I'm willing to turn back and take you home if you want to go. It may be very hard to keep you longer, but it will be a great deal harder if we are to let the Captain of that ship take poor Mr. Shirley to Rio Janeiro and put him into prison, with nobody to say a word for him!"

"Madam," said Mr. Arbuckle, "I beg that you will not speak of the question of an immediate return on our account. This is in every way a most unfortunate affair, but we all see what ought to be done, what it is our duty to do, and we will do it! Can you give me an idea, Mr. Portman, of the length of time it would probably require for us to reach Rio Janeiro?"

"I think this yacht could get there in a week," said the sailing-master; "but if we're to keep company with that hulk over there, it will take us ten days. We may have trouble about coal, but if we have good winds like these, we can keep up with the *Dunkery Beacon* with half steam and our sails."

"Mr. Litchfield," said Mrs. Cliff, "the Captain is up in the pilot house. I can't climb up there, but won't you go and tell him that I say that we must stand by Mr. Shirley no matter what happens, nor where we have to go to!"

CHAPTER XXVI

"WE'LL STICK TO SHIRLEY!"

WHEN night began to fall, the *Dunkery Beacon* was still keeping on her course, — a little too much to the eastward, Mr. Portman thought, — and the *Summer Shelter* was still accompanying her almost abreast, and less

than half a mile away. During the day it had been sel-
dom that the glasses of the yacht had not been directed
upon the deck of the larger vessel. Several times Mr.
Shirley had been seen on the main deck, and he had frequently waved his hat. It was encouraging to know that
their friend was in good condition, but there were many
hearts on board the *Summer Shelter* which grew heavier
and heavier as the night came on.

Burke and Burdette stood together in the pilot house.
" Suppose she gets away from us in the night? " said the
mate.

" I don't intend to let her do it," replied his Captain.
" Even if she douses every glim on board, I'll keep her
in sight! It will be starlight, and I'm not afraid, with a
vessel as easily managed as this yacht, to lie pretty close
to her."

" Then there's another thing," said Burdette.

" You're thinking they may get rid of him? " asked
Burke.

" Yes," said the other, " I was thinking of that!"

The Captain did not reply immediately. " That came
across my mind too," said he, " but it's all nonsense! In
the first place, they haven't got any reason for wanting
to get rid of him that way, and besides, they know that if
they went into Rio Janeiro without Shirley, we could
make it very hot for them!"

" But he's a queer one — that Captain Hagar!" said
Burdette. " What was he doing on that easterly course?
I think he's a scaly customer, that's what I think!"

" Can't say anything about that," answered Burke.

"But one thing I know,— I'm going to stick to him like a thrasher to a whale!"

Very early the next morning Mr. Hodgson came aft where Captain Burke was standing with the sailing-master. "Sir," said he, "I am a clergyman and a man of peace, but I declare, sir, that I do not think any one, no matter what his profession, should feel himself called upon to submit to the outrageous conduct of the Captain of that vessel! Is there no way in which we could approach her and make fast to her, and then boldly press our way on board in spite of objection or resistance, and by force, if it should be necessary, bring away Mr. Shirley, whose misfortune has made us all feel as if he were not only our friend, but our brother. Then, sir, I should let that vessel go on to destruction, if she chooses to go."

Burke shook his head. "You may be sure if I considered it safe to run the two vessels together I would have been on board that craft long ago! But we couldn't do it,— certainly not with Mrs. Cliff on the yacht!"

"No indeed!" added Mr. Portman. "Nobody knows what damage they might do us. For my part, I haven't any faith in that vessel. I believe she's no better than a pirate herself!"

"Hold on!" exclaimed Burke. "Don't talk like that! It wouldn't do for the women to get any such notions into their heads!"

"But it is in your head, isn't it, sir?" said Mr. Hodgson.

" Yes," said Burke, "something of the sort. I don't mind saying that to you."

" And I will also say to you," replied the young clergyman, "that we talked it over last night, and we all agreed that the actions of the *Dunkery Beacon* are very suspicious. It does not seem at all unlikely that the great treasure she carries has been too much of a temptation for the Captain, and that she is trying to get away with it."

" Of course, I don't know anything about that Captain," said Burke, "or what he is after, but I'm pretty sure that he won't dare to do anything to Shirley as long as I keep him in sight. And now I'm going to bear down on him again to hail him ! "

The *Summer Shelter* bore down upon the other steamer, and her Captain hailed and hailed for half an hour, but no answer came from the *Dunkery Beacon.*

Willy Croup was so troubled by what had happened, and even more by what was not happening, — for she could not see any good which might come out of. this persistent following of the one vessel by the other, — that her nerves disordered and tangled themselves to such a degree that she. was scarcely able to cook.

But Mrs. Cliff kept up a strong heart. She felt that a great deal depended upon her. At any moment an emergency might arise when she would be called upon, as owner of the yacht, to decide what should be done. She hoped very earnestly that if the Captain of the *Dunkery Beacon* saw that the *Summer Shelter* was determined to follow him wherever he went, and whatever he might do, he would at last get tired of being nagged in that way, and consent to give up Mr. Shirley.

About eight o'clock in the morning, all belief in the minds of the men on board the yacht that the *Dunkery Beacon* intended to sail to Rio Janeiro entirely disappeared, for that steamer changed her course to one considerably north of east. A little after that a steamer was seen on the horizon to the north, and she was bearing southward. In the course of half an hour it seemed as if this new steamer was not only likely to run across the course of the *Dunkery Beacon*, but was trying to do it.

"Captain," exclaimed Mrs. Cliff, grasping Burke by the arm, "don't you think it looks very much as if that Captain Hagar was trying to run away with the treasure which has been entrusted to him?"

"I didn't intend to say anything to you about that," he replied, "but it looks like it most decidedly!"

"If that should be the case," said Mrs. Cliff, "don't you think Mr. Shirley's situation is very dangerous?"

"Nobody knows anything about that, madam," said he, "but until we get him back on this yacht, I'll stick to her!"

Burke could not make out the new-comer very well, but he knew her to be a Mediterranean steamer. She was of moderate size, and making good headway. "I haven't the least bit of a doubt," said he to Burdette, "that that's the pirate vessel from Genoa!"

"I shouldn't wonder if you're right!" said the mate, taking the glass. "I think I can see a lot of heads in

her bow, and now I wonder what is going to happen
next ! "

" That nobody knows," said Burke, " but if I had Shirley on board here, I'd steam away and let them have it
out. We have done all we're called upon to do to keep
those Peruvian fools from losing that cargo of gold ! "

The strange vessel drew nearer and nearer to the
Dunkery Beacon, and the two steamers, much to the
amazement of the watchers on the yacht, now lay to and
seemed prepared to hail each other. They did hail, and
after a short time a boat was lowered from the stranger,
and pulled to the *Dunkery Beacon*. There were but
few men in the boat, although there were many heads on
the decks from which they had come.

" This beats me ! " ejaculated Burke. " They seem
willing enough to lay to for her ! "

" It looks to me," said Mr. Burdette, " as if she wanted
to be captured ! "

" I'd like to know," said the Captain, " what's the
meaning of that queer bit of blotched bunting that's been
run up on the *Dunkery ?* "

" Can't tell," said the other, " but there's another one
like it on the other steamer ! "

" My friends," said Mr. Arbuckle, standing in a group
of his fellow-clergymen on the main deck, " it is my earnest opinion that those two ships are accomplices in a
great crime."

" If that be so," said another, " we are here in the position of utterly helpless witnesses. But we should not
allow ourselves to look on this business from one point

of view only.   It may be that the intentions of that recently arrived vessel are perfectly honorable.   She may
bring later orders from the owners of the *Dunkery Beacon*, and bring them too with more authority than did
Mr. Shirley, who, after all, was only a volunteer!"

The yacht was lying to, and at this moment the lookout announced a sail on the starboard quarter.   Glancing
in that direction, nearly everybody could see that another
steamer, her hull well up in view, was coming down from
the north.

"By George!" cried Burke, "most likely that's another
of the pirates!"

"And if it is," said his mate, "I think we'll have to
trust to our heels!"

Burke answered quietly, "Yes, we'll do that when
we've got Shirley on board, or when it's dead sure we
can't get him!"

The people from the Mediterranean steamer did not
remain on board the *Dunkery Beacon* more than half
an hour, and when they returned to their vessel, she
immediately started her engines and began to move
away.   Making a short circuit, she turned and steamed
in the direction of the distant vessel approaching from
the northward.

"There," cried Burke, "that steamer off there is another of the pirates, and these scoundrels here are going
to meet her.   They've got the whole thing cut and dried,
and I'll bet my head that the *Dunkery Beacon* will
cruise around here until they're ready to come down and
do what they please with her!"

The actions of the treasure ship now seemed to indicate that Mr. Burke was correct in his surmises. She steamed away slowly towards the south, and then making a wide sweep, she steered northward, directing her course toward the yacht as if she would speak with it.

CHAPTER XXVII

ON BOARD THE "DUNKERY BEACON"

WHEN Edward Shirley stepped on board the big steamer which he had so earnestly and anxiously followed from Kingston, and was received by her captain, it did not take him long to form the opinion that Captain Hagar belonged to a disagreeable class of mariners. He was gruff, curt, and wanted to know in the shortest space of time why in the name of his Satanic Majesty he had been asked to lay to, and what message that yacht had for him.

Shirley asked for a private interview, and when they were in the Captain's room he put the whole matter into as few words as possible, showed the cablegram from Blackburn, and also exhibited his message from Captain Horn. The other scrutinized the papers very carefully, asked many questions, but made few remarks in regard to his own opinion or intentions.

When he had heard all that Shirley had to tell him, and had listened to some very earnest advice that he should immediately turn back to Kingston, or at least run into Georgetown, where he might safely lie in harbor until measures had been taken for the safe conveyance of the treasure to Peru, the Captain of the *Dunkery Beacon* arose, and asking Shirley to remain where he was until he should go and consult with his first mate, he went out, closing the door of the room behind him.

During this absence he did not see the first mate, but he went to a room where there was pen, ink, and paper, and there he wrote a note to Captain Burke of the *Summer Shelter*, which note, as soon as he had signed it, he gave to the men in the small boat waiting alongside, telling them that it was from their mate who had come on board, and that he wanted an answer just as soon as possible.

Mr. Burdette, Mr. Portman, and the assistant engineer having no reason whatever to suspect treachery under circumstances like these, immediately rowed back to the *Summer Shelter*. And, as we already know, it was not long before the *Dunkery Beacon* was steaming away from the yacht.

The moment that Shirley, who was getting a little tired of waiting, felt the movement of the engines, he sprang to the door, but found it locked. Now he began to kick, but in a very few moments the Captain appeared.

"You needn't make a row," said he. "Nobody's going to hurt you. I have sent a note to your skipper, telling him I'm going to keep you on board a little while until I can consider this matter. My duty to my owners wouldn't allow me to be a-layin' to here — but I'll think over the business and do what I consider right. But

I've got to keep on my course — I've got no right to lose time whether this is all a piece of foolin' or not."

"There's no fooling about it," said Shirley, warmly. "If you don't turn back you will be very likely to lose a good deal more than time. You may lose everything on board, and your lives too, for all you know."

The Captain laughed. "Pirates!" said he. "What stuff! There are no pirates in these days!" and then he laughed again. "Well, I can't talk any more now," said he, "but I'll keep your business in my mind, and settle it pretty soon. Then you can go back and tell your people what I'll do. You had better go on deck and make yourself comfortable. If you'll take my advice, you won't do any talking. The people on this vessel don't know what she carries, and I don't want them to know! So if I see you talking to anybody, I'll consider that you want to make trouble — and I can tell you, if some of these people on board knew what was in them boxes in the hold, there would be the worst kind of trouble. You can bet your head on that! So you can go on and show yourself. Your friends won't be worried about you — I've explained it all to them in my note!"

When Shirley went on deck he was very much pleased to see that the *Summer Shelter* was not far away, and was steaming close after the larger vessel. He waved his hat, and then he turned to look about him. There seemed to be a good many men on the steamer, a very large crew, in fact ; and after noticing the number of sailors who were at work not far away from him, Shirley came to the conclusion that there were more reasons than one why he would not hold conversation with them.

From their speech he thought that they must all be foreigners — French, or Italians, he could scarcely tell which. It did not seem to him that these belonged to the class of seamen which a careful captain of a British merchantman would wish to ship when carrying a cargo of treasure to a distant land, but then all sorts of crews were picked up in English ports. Her Captain, in fact, surprised Shirley more than did the seamen he had noticed. This Captain must, of course, be an Englishman, for the house of Blackburn Brothers would not be likely to trust one of their vessels, and such an important one, to the charge of any one but an Englishman. But he had a somewhat foreign look about him. His eyes and hair were very black, and there was a certain peculiarity in his pronunciation that made Shirley think at first that he might be a Welshman.

While Shirley was considering these matters, the *Summer Shelter* was rapidly gaining on the other steamer and was now alongside and within hailing distance, and Burke was on the bridge with a trumpet in his hand. At this moment Shirley was accosted by the Captain. "I've got something to say to you," said he; "step in my room. Perhaps we can give your friend an answer at once."

Shirley followed the other, the door was shut, and the Captain of the *Dunkery Beacon* began to tell how extremely injudicious it would be, in his opinion, to turn

WHEN SHIRLEY WENT ON DECK HE WAS MUCH PLEASED
TO SEE THE SUMMER SHELTER

back, for if pirates really were following him, — although he did not believe a word of it, — he might run right into their teeth, whereas, by keeping on his course, he would most likely sail away from them, and when he reached Rio Janeiro, he could make arrangements there for some sort of a convoy, or whatever else was considered necessary.

"I'll go and hail my skipper," said Shirley, "if you'll let me have a speaking-trumpet."

"No," said the other, "I don't want you to do that. I don't mind tellin' you that I don't trust you. I've got very heavy responsibility on me, and I don't know who you are no more than if you was a porpoise come a-bouncin' up out of the sea. I don't want you and your skipper holdin' no conversation with each other until I've got this matter settled to my satisfaction, and then I can put you on board your vessel, and go ahead on my course, or I can turn back, just whichever I make up my mind to do. But until I make up my mind, I don't want no reports made from this vessel to any other, and no matter what you say when you are hailin', how do I know what you mean, and what sort of signals you've agreed on between you?"

Shirley was obliged to accept the situation, and when Burke had ceased to hail, he was allowed to go on deck. Then, after waving his hat to the yacht, — which was now at a considerable distance, although within easy range of a glass, — Shirley lighted his pipe, and walked up and down the deck. He saw a good many things to interest him; but he spoke to no one, and endeavored to assume the demeanor of one who was much interested in his own affairs, and very little in 'what was going on about him.

But Shirley noticed a great many things which made a deep impression upon him. The crew seemed to be composed of men not very well disciplined, but exceedingly talkative, and although Shirley did not understand French, he was now pretty sure that all the conversation he heard was in that tongue. Then, again, the men did not appear to be very well acquainted with the vessel — they frequently seemed to be looking for things, the position of which they should have known. He could not understand how men who had sailed on a vessel from Southampton should show such a spirit of inquiry in regard to the internal arrangements of the steamer. A boatswain, who was giving the orders to a number of men, seemed more as if he were instructing a class in the nautical management of a vessel than in giving the ordinary everyday orders which might be expected on such a voyage as this. Once he saw the Captain come on deck with a book in his hand, apparently a log-book, and he showed it to one of the mates. These two stood turning over the leaves of the book as if they had never seen it before, and wanted to find something which they supposed to be in it.

It was not long after this that Shirley said to himself that he could not understand how such a vessel, with such a cargo, could have been sent out from Southampton in charge of such a captain and such a crew as this. And then, almost immediately, the idea came to him in a flash that perhaps this was not the crew with which the *Dunkery Beacon* had sailed! Now he seemed to see the whole state of affairs as if it had been printed on paper. The *Dunkery Beacon* had been captured by one of the pirates, probably not long after she got outside the Caribbees, and that instead of trying to take the treasure on board their own vessel, the scoundrels had rid the *Dunkery* of her captain and crew, and had taken possession of the steamer and everything in it. This would explain her course when she was first sighted from the yacht. She was not going at all to Rio Janeiro — she was on her way across the Atlantic.

Now everything that he had seen, and everything that he had heard, confirmed this new belief. Of course the pirate Captain did not wish to lay to when he was first hailed, and he probably did so at last simply because he found he need not be afraid of the yacht, and that he could not rid himself of her unless he stopped to see what she wanted. Of course this fellow would not have him go back to the yacht and make a report. Of course this crew did not understand how things were placed and stored on board the vessel, for they themselves had been on board of her but a very short time. The Captain spoke English, but he was not an Englishman.

Shirley saw plainer and plainer every second that the *Dunkery Beacon* had been captured by pirates; that probably not a man of her former crew was on board, and that he was here a prisoner in the hands of these wretches — cut-throats for all he knew, and yet he did not reproach himself for having run into such a trap. He had done the proper thing, in a proper, orderly, and seamanlike way. He had had the most unexpected bad luck, but he did not in the least see any reason to blame himself.

He saw, however, a great deal of reason to fear for himself, especially as the evening drew on. That black-headed villain of a Captain did not want him on board, and while he might not care to toss him into the sea in view of a vessel which was fast enough to follow him wherever he might go, there was no reason why he should not do what he pleased, if, under cover of the night, he got away from that vessel.

The fact that he was allowed to go where he pleased, and see what he pleased, gave much uneasiness to Shirley. It looked to him as if they did not care what he might say, hear, or see, for the reason that it was not intended that he should have an opportunity of making reports of any sort. Shirley had his supper to himself, and the Captain showed him a bunk. "They can't do much talkin' to you," he said. "I had to sail ahead of time, and couldn't ship many Englishmen."

"You liar," thought Shirley, "you didn't ship any!"

Shirley was a brave man, but as he lay awake in his bunk that night, cold shivers ran down his back many times. If violence were offered to him, of course he could not make any defence, but he was resolved that if an attack should be made upon him, there was one thing he would try to do. He had carefully noted the location of the companion-ways, and he had taken off only such clothes as would interfere with swimming. If he were attacked, he would make a bolt for the upper deck, and then overboard. If the yacht should be near enough to hear or see him, he might have a chance. If not, he would prefer the ocean to the *Dunkery Beacon* and her crew.

But the night passed on, and he was not molested. He did not know, down there below decks, that all night the *Summer Shelter* kept so close to the *Dunkery Beacon* that the people in charge of the latter cursed and swore dreadfully at times when the yacht, looking bigger and blacker by night than she did by day, rose on the waves in their wake, so near that it seemed as if a sudden squall might drive the two vessels together.

But there was really no reason for any such fear. Burke had vowed he would stick to Shirley, and he also stuck to the wheel all night, with Burdette or the sailing-master by his side. And there was not an hour when somebody, either a mariner or a clergyman, did not scan the deck of the *Dunkery Beacon* with a marine glass.

Shirley was not allowed to go on deck until quite late the next morning, after Burke had given up his desperate attempt to communicate with the *Dunkery Beacon;* and when he did come up, and had assured himself at a glance that the *Summer Shelter* still hung upon the heels of the larger steamer, and had frantically waved his hat, the next thing he saw was the small Mediterranean steamer which was rapidly coming down from the north, while the *Dunkery Beacon* was steaming northeast. He also noticed that some men near him were running up a queer little flag or signal, colored irregularly red and yellow, and then he saw upon the approaching steamer a bit of bunting which seemed to resemble the one now floating from the *Dunkery*. Of course, under the circumstances, there was nothing for him to believe but that this approaching vessel was one of the pirate ships, and that she was coming down not to capture the *Dunkery Beacon*, but to join her.

Now matters were getting to be worse and worse, and as Shirley glanced over at the yacht, — still hovering on the weather quarter of the *Dunkery*, ready at any time to swoop down and hail her if there should be occasion, — he trembled for the fate of his friends. To be sure these two pirate vessels — for surely the *Dunkery Beacon* now belonged to that class — were nothing but merchantmen. There were no cannon on this steamer, and as the other was now near enough for him to see her decks as she rolled to windward, there was no reason to suppose that she carried guns. If these rascals wished to attack or capture a vessel, they must board her, but before they could do that they must catch her, and he knew well enough that there were few ordinary steamers which could overhaul the *Summer Shelter*. If it were not for his own most unfortunate position, the yacht could steam away in safety and leave these wretches to their own devices, but he did not believe that his old friend would desert him. More than that, there was no reason to suppose that the people on the *Summer Shelter* knew that the *Dunkery Beacon* was now manned

by pirates, although it was likely that they would suspect the character of the new-comer.

But Shirley could only stand, and watch, and wait.
Once he thought that it might be well for him to jump
overboard and strike out to the yacht. If he should be
seen by his friends — and this he believed would happen
— and if he should be picked up, his report would turn
back into safer waters this peaceful pleasure vessel, with
its two ladies and its seven clergymen. If he should be
struck by a ball in the back of the head before he got
out of gunshot of the *Dunkery's* crew, then his friends
would most likely see him sink, the reason for their
remaining in the vicinity of these pirates would be at
an end, and they might steam northward as fast as they
pleased.

The strange vessel came on and on, and soon showed
herself to be a steamer of about nine hundred tons, of a
model with which Shirley was not familiar, and a great
many men on board. The *Dunkery Beacon* lay to, and
it was not long before this stranger had followed her
example, and had lowered a boat. When three or four
men from this boat had scrambled to the deck of the
Dunkery Beacon, they were gladly welcomed by the
black-headed fellow who had passed himself off as Captain Hagar, and a most animated conversation now took
place. Shirley could not understand anything that was
said, and he had sense enough not to appear to be trying
to do so; but no one paid any attention to him, nor
seemed to care whether he knew what was going on or
not.

At first the manner of the speakers indicated that they were wildly congratulating each other, but very soon it was evident that the *Summer Shelter* was the subject of their discourse. They all looked over at the yacht, some of them even shook their fists at her, and although Shirley did not understand their language, he knew very well that curses, loud and savage, were pouring over the bulwarks in the direction of his friends and their yacht.

Then the subject of the conference changed. The fellows began to gaze northward, a glass was turned in that direction, the exclamations became more violent than before, and when Shirley turned, he saw for the first time the other vessel which was coming down from the north. This was now far away, but she was heading south, and it could not be long before she would arrive on the scene.

Now Shirley's heart sank about as far down as it would go. He had no doubt that this very vessel was another of the pirates. If she carried a gun, even if it were not a heavy one, he might as well bid good-bye to the *Summer Shelter*. The pirates would not allow her to go to any port to tell her tale.

The noisy conference now broke up. The boat with its crew returned to the other vessel, which almost immediately started, turned, and steamed away to the north, in the direction of the approaching steamer. This settled the matter. She was off to join her pirate consort. Now the *Dunkery Beacon* started her engines, and steamed slowly in the direction of the yacht, as if

she wished to hail her. Shirley's heart rose a little.
If there was to be a parley, perhaps the pirates had
decided to warn the yacht to stop meddling, and to take
herself away, and if, by any happy fortune, it should be
decided to send him to his friends, he would implore
them, with all his heart and soul, to take the advice
without the loss of a second.

CHAPTER XXVIII

THE PEOPLE ON THE "MONTEREY"

THE vessel which had last appeared upon the scene
and which was now steaming down towards the *Dunkery Beacon* and the *Summer Shelter*, while the small
steamer from the Mediterranean was making her
way northward to meet her, was the *Monterey* of Vera
Cruz, and carried Captain Philip Horn and his wife
Edna.

As soon as Captain Horn had heard of the danger
which threatened the treasure which was on its way
from London to the Peruvian government, — treasure
which had cost him such toil, anxiety, and suffering, and
in the final just disposition of which he felt the deepest
interest and even responsibility, — although, in fact, the
care and charge of which had passed entirely out of his
hands, — he determined not only to write to Shirley to
go to Jamaica, but to go there himself without loss of
time, believing from what he had heard that he could

surely reach Kingston before the arrival there of the *Dunkery Beacon*.

But that steamer started before her time, and when he reached Vera Cruz, he found it impossible to leave immediately for his destination. And when at last he bought a steamer, and arrived at Kingston, the *Dunkery Beacon* and the yacht *Summer Shelter* had both departed. But the Captain found the letter from Mrs. Cliff, and while this explained a great deal, it also puzzled him greatly.

His wife and Mrs. Cliff had corresponded with some regularity, but the latter had never mentioned the fact that she was the owner of a yacht. Mrs. Cliff had intended to tell Edna all about this new piece of property, but when she looked at the matter from an outside point of view, it seemed to her such a ridiculous thing that she should own a yacht that she did not want to write anything about it until her plans were perfected, and she could tell just what she was going to do. But when she suddenly decided to sail for Jamaica, her mind was so occupied with the plans of the moment that she had no time to write.

Therefore it was that Captain and Mrs. Horn wondered greatly what in the name of common sense Mrs. Cliff was doing with a yacht. But they knew that Shirley and Burke were on board, and that they had sailed on the track of the *Dunkery Beacon*, hoping to overtake her and deliver the message which Shirley carried. The Captain decided that it was his duty to follow these two vessels down the coast of South America.

The *Monterey* was a large steamer sailing in ballast, and of moderate speed, and the Captain had with him — besides his wife and her maid — the three negro men whom he had brought up from South America and who were now his devoted personal attendants, and a good-sized crew. Captain Horn had little hope of overhauling the two steamers, for even the yacht, which he had heard was a fast-sailing vessel, had had twenty-four hours' start of him; but he had reason to hope that he might meet one or both of them on their return; for if the yacht should fail to overhaul the *Dunkery Beacon*, she would certainly turn back to Kingston.

Edna was as enthusiastic and interested in this voyage as her husband. She sympathized in all his anxiety in regard to the safety of the treasure, but even stronger than this was her desire to see once more her dear friend, whom she had come to look upon almost as an elder sister.

During each day the Captain and his wife were almost constantly on deck, their glasses sweeping the south-eastern horizon, hoping for the sight of two steamers coming back to Kingston. They saw vessels coming and going, but they were not the craft they looked for, and after they left the Caribbean Sea the sail became fewer and fewer. On the second day after they left Tobago Island they fell in with a small steamer apparently in distress, for she was working her way under sail and against head-winds towards the coast.

When the Captain spoke this steamer, he received a request to lower a boat and go on board of her. There he found an astonishing state of affairs. The steamer was from a French port, she carried no cargo, and she was commanded and manned by Captain Hagar and the crew of the English ship *Dunkery Beacon*. Captain Hagar's story was not a long one, and he told it as readily to Captain Horn as he would to any other friendly mariner who might have boarded him.

He had left Kingston with his vessel as he left it many times before, and the Caribbees were not half a day behind him when he was hailed by a steamer, — the one he was now on, which had been following him for some time. He was told that this steamer carried a message from his owners, and without suspecting anything, he lay to, and a boat came to him from the other ship. This boat had in it a good many more men than was necessary, but he suspected no evil until half-a-dozen men were on his deck and half-a-dozen pistols were pointed at the heads of himself and those around him. Then two more boats came over, more men boarded him, and without a struggle, or hardly a cross word, — as he expressed it, — the *Dunkery Beacon* was in the hands of sea-robbers.

Captain Hagar was a mild-mannered man, an excellent seaman, and of good common sense. He had before found orders waiting for him at Jamaica, and had not thought it surprising that orders should now have been sent after him. He had firearms on board and might have defended himself to a certain extent, but he had suspected no evil, and when the pirates had boarded him it was useless to think of arms or defence.

The men who had captured the *Dunkery Beacon* made very short work of their business. They simply exchanged vessels. They commanded Captain Hagar and all his men to go over to the French steamer, while they all came on board the *Dunkery Beacon*, bringing with them whatever they cared for. Captain Hagar was told that he could work his new vessel to any port in the world which suited him best, and then the *Dunkery Beacon* was headed southward and steamed away.

When Captain Hagar's engineers attempted to start the engines of their vessel, they found it impossible to do so. Several important pieces of the machinery had been taken out, hoisted on deck, and dropped overboard. Whatever port they might make, they must make it under sail.

A broken-hearted and dejected man was Captain Hagar. He had lost a vast treasure which had been entrusted to him, and he had not ceased to wonder why the pirates had not murdered him and all his crew, and thrown them overboard. He hoped that in time he and his men might reach Georgetown, or some other port, but it would be slow and disheartening work under the circumstances.

Captain Horn was also greatly cast down by the news he had received. With the least possible amount of trouble, the pirates had carried off, not only the treasure, but the ship which conveyed it, and now in all probability were far away with their booty. He could understand very well why they would not undertake such wholesale crime as the murder of all the people on the

Dunkery, for it is probable that there were men among them who could not be trusted even had the leaders been willing to undertake such useless bloodshed. If Captain Hagar and his men were set adrift on a steamer without machinery, it would be long before they could reach any port, and even if they should soon speak a vessel and report their misfortune, where was the policeman of the sea who would have authority to sail after the stolen vessel, or, if he had, would know on what course to follow her?

Captain Horn gave up the treasure as lost. The *Dunkery Beacon* was probably shaping her course for the coast of Africa, and even if he had a swifter vessel and could overhaul her, what could he do?

But now he almost forgot his trouble about the treasure, in his deep concern in the fate of Mrs. Cliff and her yacht. He had made up his mind that his friends on board that little vessel — he had very shadowy ideas as to what sort of a yacht it was — had embarked upon this cruise entirely for his sake. They knew that he took such a deep personal interest in the safety of the *Dunkery Beacon;* they knew that he had done everything possible to detain that vessel at Jamaica, and that now, for his peace of mind, for the gratification of his feelings of honor, — no matter how exaggerated they might consider them, — they were following in a little pleasure craft a steamer which they supposed to be a peaceful merchantman, but which was in fact a pirate ship manned by miscreants without conscience.

His plan was soon decided upon. He told Captain

Hagar that he would take him and his men on his own vessel, and that he would carry them with him on his search for the yacht on which his friends had sailed. Captain Hagar agreed in part to this proposition. He would be glad to go with Captain Horn, for it was possible he might hear news of his lost vessel, but he did not wish to give up the French steamer. She was worth money, and if she could be got into port, he felt it his duty to get her there. So he left on board a crew sufficient to work her to Georgetown, but with the majority of his crew came on board the *Monterey*, and Captain Horn continued on his southern course.

When on the following morning Captain Horn perceived far away to the south a steamer which Captain Hagar, standing by with a glass to his eye, declared to be none other than his old vessel, the *Dunkery Beacon*, and when, not long afterwards, he made out a smaller vessel, apparently keeping company with the *Dunkery Beacon*, with another steamer lying off to the eastward, he was absolutely amazed and confounded. He could not comprehend the state of affairs. What was the *Dunkery Beacon* doing down south, when by this time she ought to be far away to the east, if she were running away with the treasure, and what were those two other vessels keeping so close to her?

He could not imagine what they could be, unless, indeed, they were her pirate consorts. "If that's the case," thought Captain Horn, but saying no word to any one, "this is not a part of the sea for my wife to sail upon!"

Still he knew nothing, and he could decide upon nothing. He could not be sure that one of those vessels was not the yacht which had sailed from Kingston with Mrs. Cliff, and Burke, and Shirley on board, and so the *Monterey* did not turn back, but steamed on slowly towards the distant steamers.

CHAPTER XXIX

THE "VITTORIO" FROM GENOA

WHEN Captain Horn on the *Monterey* perceived that one of the vessels he had sighted was steaming northward with the apparent intention of meeting him, his anxieties greatly increased. He could think of no righteous reason why that vessel should come to meet him. He had made out that this vessel with the two others had been lying to. Why should it not wait for him if it wished to speak with him? The course of this stranger looked like mischief of some sort, and the Captain could think of no other probable mischief than that which had been practised upon the *Dunkery Beacon*.

The steamer which he now commanded carried a treasure far more valuable than that which lay in the hold of the *Dunkery*, and if she had been a swifter vessel he would have turned and headed away for safety at the top of her speed. But he did not believe she could outsail the steamer which was now approaching, and safety by flight was not to be considered.

There was another reason which determined him not to change his course. The observers on the *Monterey* had now decided that the small vessel to the westward of the *Dunkery Beacon* was very like a yacht, and the Captain thought that if there was to be trouble of any sort, he would like to be as near Shirley and Burke as possible. Why that rapidly approaching steamer should desire to board him as the *Dunkery Beacon* had been boarded he could not imagine, unless it was supposed that he carried part of the treasure, but he did not waste any time on conjectures. It was not likely that this steamer carried a cannon, and if she intended to attack the *Monterey*, it must be by boarding her; probably by the same stratagem which had been practised before.

But Captain Horn determined that no man upon any mission whatever should put his foot upon the deck of the *Monterey* if he could prevent it. Since he had taken on board Captain Hagar and his men, he had an extraordinarily large crew, and on the number of his men he depended for defence, for it was impossible to arm them as well as the attacking party would probably be armed, if there should be an attacking party.

Captain Horn now went to Edna and told her of the approaching danger, and for the second time in his life he gave her a pistol and requested her to use it in any way she thought proper if the need should come. He asked her to stay for the present in the cabin with her maid, promising to come to her again very shortly.

Then he called all the available men together, and

addressed them very briefly.　It was not necessary to tell the crew of the *Dunkery Beacon* what dangers might befall them if the pirates should come upon them a second time, and the men he had brought with him from Vera Cruz now knew all about the previous affair, and that it would probably be necessary for them to stand up boldly for their own defence.

The Captain told his men that the only thing to be done was to keep the fellows on that approaching steamer from boarding the *Monterey* whether they tried to do so by what might look like fair means or by foul means.　All the firearms of every kind which could be collected were distributed around among those who it was thought could best use them, while the rest of the men were armed with belaying pins, handspikes, hatchets, axes, or anything with which a blow could be struck, and they were ranged along the bulwarks on each side of the ship from bow to stern.

The other steamer was now near enough for her name, *Vittorio*, to be read upon her bow.　This and her build made the captain quite sure that she was from the Mediterranean, and without doubt one of the pirates of whom he had heard.　He could see heads all along her rail, and he thought it possible that she might not care to practise any trick upon him, but might intend a bold and undisguised attack.　She had made no signal, she carried no colors or flag of any kind, and he thought it not unlikely that when she should be near enough, she would begin operations by a volley of rifle shots from her deck.　To provide against this danger he made most of his men crouch down behind the bulwarks, and ordered all the others to be ready to screen themselves. A demand to lie to, and a sharp fusillade might be enough to insure the immediate submission of an ordinary merchantman, but Captain Horn did not consider the *Monterey* a vessel of this sort.

He now ran down to Edna, and was met by her at the cabin door. She had had ideas very like his own. " I shouldn't wonder if they would fire upon us," she said, her face very pale; " and I want you to remember that you are most likely the tallest man on board. No matter what happens, you must take care of yourself, — you must never forget that! "

" I will take care of you," he said, with his arms about her, " and I will not forget myself. And now keep close, and watch sharply. I don't believe they can ever board us, — we're too many for them ! "

The instant the Captain had gone, Edna called Maka and Cheditafa, the two elderly negroes who were the devoted adherents of herself and her husband. " I want you to watch the Captain all the time," she said. " If the people on that ship fire guns, you pull him back if he shows himself. If any one comes near him to harm him, use your hatchets; never let him out of your sight, follow him close, keep all danger from him."

The negroes answered in the African tongue. They were too much excited to use English, but she knew what they meant, and trusted them. To Mok, the other negro, she gave no orders. Even now he could speak but lit-

8

tle English, and he was in the party simply because her
brother Ralph — whose servant Mok had been — had
earnestly desired her to take care of him until he
should want him again, for this coal-black and agile
native of Africa was not a creature who could be left
to take care of himself.

The *Vittorio*, which was now not more than a quarter of
a mile away, and which had slightly changed her course,
so that she was apparently intending to pass the *Monterey*, and continue northward contented with an observation of the larger vessel, was a very dangerous pirate
ship, far more so than the one which had captured the
Dunkery Beacon.   She was not more dangerous because
she was larger or swifter, or carried a more numerous
or better-armed crew, but for the reason that she had on
board a certain Mr. Banker who had once belonged to a
famous band of desperadoes, called the "Rackbirds," well-
known along the Pacific coast of South America.   He
had escaped destruction when the rest of his band were
drowned in a raging torrent, and he had made himself
extremely obnoxious and even dangerous to Mrs. Horn
and to Captain Horn when they were in Paris at a very
critical time of their fortunes.

This ex-Rackbird Banker had had but a very cloudy
understanding of the state of affairs when he was endeavoring to blackmail Mrs. Horn, and making stupid
charges against her husband.   He knew that the three
negroes he had met in Paris in the service of Mrs. Horn
had once been his own slaves, held not by any right of
law, but by brutal force, and he knew that the people

with whom they were then travelling must have been
in some way connected with his old comrades, the Rackbirds. He had made bold attempts to turn this scanty
knowledge to his own benefit, but had mournfully failed.

In the course of time, however, he had come to know
everything. The news of Captain Horn's great discovery
of treasure on the coast of Peru had gone forth to the
public, and Banker's soul had writhed in disappointed
rage as he thought that he and his fellows had lived and
rioted like fools for months, and months, and months,
but a short distance from all these vast hoards of gold.
This knowledge almost maddened him as he brooded
over it by night and by day. When he had been set
free from the French prison to which his knavery had
consigned him, Banker gave himself up body and soul
to the consideration of the treasure which Captain
Horn had brought to France from Peru. He considered
it from every possible point of view, and when at last he
heard of the final disposition which it had been determined to make of the gold, he considered it from the point
of his own cupidity and innate rascality.

He it was who devised the plan of sending out a swift
steamer to overhaul the merchantman which was to
carry the gold to Peru, and who, after consultation with
the many miscreants whom he was obliged to take into
his confidence and to depend upon for assistance, decided
that it would be well to fit out two ships, so that if one
should fail in her errand, the other might succeed. The
steamers from Genoa and Toulon were fitted out and
manned under the direction of Banker, but with the one

which sailed from Marseilles he had nothing to do. This expedition was organized by men who had quarrelled with him and his associates, and it was through the dissension of the opposing parties in this intended piracy that the detectives came to know of it.

Banker had sailed from Genoa, but the Toulon vessel had got ahead of him. It had sighted the *Dunkery Beacon* before she reached Kingston; it had cruised in the Caribbean Sea until she came sailing down towards Tobago Island; it had followed her out into the Atlantic, and when the proper time came it had taken her — hull, engine, gold, and everything which belonged to her, except her captain and her crew, and had steamed away with her.

Banker did not command the *Vittorio*, for he was not a seaman, but he commanded her captain, and through him everybody on board. He directed her course and her policy. He was her leading spirit and her blackest devil.

It had been no part of Banker's intentions to cruise about the South Atlantic and search for a steamer with black and white stripes running up and down her funnel. His plan of action was to be the same as that of the other pirate, and the *Vittorio* therefore steamed for Kingston as soon as she could manage to clear from Genoa. His calculations were very good ones, but there was a flaw in them, for he did not know that the *Dunkery Beacon* sailed three days before her regular time. Consequently, the *Vittorio* was the last of the four steamers which reached Jamaica on business connected with the Incas' treasure.

The *Vittorio* did not go into Kingston Harbor, but Banker got himself put on shore and visited the town. There he not only discovered that the *Dunkery Beacon* had sailed, that an American yacht had sailed after her, but that a steamer from Vera Cruz, commanded by Captain Horn, now well known as the discoverer of the wonderful treasure, had touched here, expecting to find the *Dunkery Beacon* in port, and had then, scarcely twelve hours before, cleared for Jamaica.

The American yacht was a mystery to Banker. It might be a pirate from the United States for all he knew, but he was very certain that Captain Horn had not left Kingston for any reason except to accompany and protect the *Dunkery Beacon*. If a steamer commanded by this man, whom Banker now hated more than he hated anybody else in the world, should fall in and keep company with the steamer which was conveying the treasure to Peru, it might be a very hard piece of work for him or his partner in command of the vessel from Toulon to get possession of that treasure, no matter what means they might employ, but all Banker could do was to swear at his arch-enemy and his bad luck, and to get away south with all speed possible. If he could do nothing, he might hear of something. He would never give up until he was positive there was no chance for him.

So he took the course that the *Dunkery Beacon* must have taken, and sailed down the coast under full head of steam. When at last he discovered the flag of his private consort hoisted over the steamer which carried the golden prize, and had gone on board the *Dunkery Beacon* and had heard everything, his Satanic delight blazed high and wild. He cared nothing for the yacht which hung upon the heels of the captured steamer, — it would not be difficult to dispose of that vessel, — but his turbulent ecstasies were a little dampened by the discovery of a large steamer bearing down from the north. This he instantly suspected to be the *Monterey*, which must have taken a more westerly course than that which he had followed, and which he had therefore passed without sighting.

The ex-Rackbird did not hesitate a moment as to what ought to be done. That everlastingly condemned meddler, Horn, must never be allowed to put his oar into this business. If he were not content with the gold which he had for himself, he should curse the day that he had tried to keep other people from getting the gold that they wanted for themselves. No matter what had to be done, he must never reach the *Dunkery Beacon* — he must never know what had happened to her. Here was a piece of work for the *Vittorio* to attend to without the loss of a minute.

When Banker gave orders to head for the approaching steamer he immediately began to make ready for an attack upon her, and, as this was to be a battle between merchant ships, neither of them provided with any of the ordinary engines of naval warfare, his plan was of a straightforward, old-fashioned kind. He would run his ship alongside the other; he would make fast, and then his men, each one with a cutlass and a pistol, should swarm over the side of the larger vessel and cut down and fire until the beastly hounds were all dead or on their knees. If he caught sight of Captain Horn, — and he was sure he would recognize him, for such a fellow would be sure to push himself forward no matter what was going on, — he would take his business into his own hands. He would give no signal, no warning. If they wanted to know what he came for, they would soon find out.

Before he left Genoa he had thought that it was possible that he might make this sort of an attack upon the *Dunkery Beacon*, and he had therefore provided for it. He had shipped a number of grappling-irons with long chains attached which were run through ring-bolts on his deck. With these and other appliances for making fast to a vessel alongside, Banker was sure he could stick to an enemy or a prize as long as he wanted to lie by her.

Everything was now made ready for the proposed attack, and all along the starboard side of the *Vittorio* mattresses were hung in order to break the force of the shock when the two vessels should come together. Every man who could be spared was ordered on deck, and fully armed. The men who were to make fast to the other steamer were posted in their proper places, and the rest of his miscreants were given the very simple orders to get on board the *Monterey* the best way they could and as soon as they could, and to cut down or shoot every man they met without asking questions or saying a word. Whether or not it would be necessary to dispose of all the crew which Captain Horn might have on board, Banker had not determined. But of one thing he was certain: he would leave no one on board of her to work her to the nearest port and give news of what had happened. One mistake of that kind was enough to make, and his stupid partner, who had commanded the vessel from Toulon, had made it.

CHAPTER XXX

THE BATTLE OF THE MERCHANT SHIPS

WHEN the *Vittorio* showed that in veering away from the *Monterey* she had done so only in order to make a sweep around to the west, and when she had headed south and the mattresses lowered along her starboard side showed plainly to Captain Horn that she was about to attack him and how she was going to do it, his first thought was to embarrass her by reversing his course and steering this way and that, but he instantly dismissed this idea. The pirate vessel was smaller and faster than his own, and probably much more easily managed, and apart from the danger of a collision fatal to his ship, he would only protract the conflict by trying to elude her. He was so sure that he had men enough to beat down the scoundrels when they tried to board that he thought the quicker the fight began, the better. If only he had Shirley and Burke with him, he thought;

but although they were not here, he had Edna to fight for, and that made three men of himself.

With most of his men crouching behind his port bulwarks, and others protected by deck houses, smokestack, and any other available devices against gunshots, Captain Horn awaited the coming of the pirate steamer, which was steaming towards him as if it intended to run him down. As she came near, the *Vittorio* slowed up, and the *Monterey* veered to starboard; but, notwithstanding this precaution and the fact that they sailed side by side for nearly a minute without touching, the two vessels came together with such force that the *Monterey*, high out of water, rolled over as if a great wave had struck her. As she rolled back, grappling-irons were thrown over her rail, and cables and lines were made fast to every available place which could be reached by eager hands and active arms. Some of the grappling-irons were immediately thrown off by the crew of the *Monterey*, but the chains of others had been so tightened as the vessel rolled back to an even keel that it was impossible to move them.

The *Monterey's* rail was considerably higher than that of the *Vittorio*, and as none of the crew of the former vessel had shown themselves, no shots had yet been fired, but with the activity of apes the pirates tried to scramble over the side of the larger vessel. Now followed a furious hand-to-hand combat. Blows rained down on the heads and shoulders of the assailants, some of whom dropped back to the deck of their ship, while others drew their pistols and fired right and left at the heads and arms they saw over the rail of the *Monterey.*

The pirate leaders were amazed at the resistance they met with. They had not imagined that Captain Horn had so large a crew, or that it was a crew which would fight. But these pirates had their blood up, and not one of them had any thought of giving up their enterprise on account of this unexpected resistance. Dozens of them at a time sprang upon the rail of their own vessel, and, with cutlass or pistol in one hand, endeavored to scramble up the side of the *Monterey;* but although the few who succeeded in crossing her bulwarks soon fell beneath the blows and shots of her crew, the attack was vigorously kept up, especially by pistol shots.

Whenever there was a chance, a pirate hand would be raised above the rail of the *Monterey* and a revolver discharged upon her rail, and every few minutes there would be a rush to one point or another and a desperate fight upon the rail. The engines of both vessels had been stopped, and the screaming and roaring of the escaping steam gave additional horror to this fearful battle. Not a word could be heard from any one, no matter how loudly it might be shouted.

Whatever firearms were possessed by the men on the *Monterey* were used with good effect, but in this respect they were vastly inferior to the enemy. When they had fired their pistols and their guns, some of them had no more ammunition, and others had no opportunity to reload. The men of the *Vittorio* had firearms in abundance and pockets full of cartridges. Consequently it

was not long before Captain Horn's men were obliged to
rely upon their hatchets, their handspikes, their belay-
ing-pins, and their numbers.

Banker was in a very furious state of mind. He had
expected to board the *Monterey* without opposition, and
now he had been fighting long and hard, and not a man
of his crew was on board the other vessel. He had soon
discovered that there were a great many men on board
the *Monterey*, but he believed that the real reason for the
so far successful resistance was the fact that Captain
Horn commanded them.

Several times he mounted the upper deck of the *Vittorio*, and with a rifle in hand endeavored to get a
chance to aim at the tall figure of which he now and
then caught sight, and who he saw was directing everything that was going on. But every time he stood out
with his rifle a pistol ball whizzed by him, and made
him jump back. Whoever fired at him was not a good
shot, but Banker did not wish to expose himself to any
kind of a shot. Once he got a chance of taking aim at
the Captain from behind the smokestack, but at that
moment the Captain stepped back hurriedly out of
view, as if somebody had been pulling him by the
coat, and a ball rang against the funnel high above
his own head. It was plain he was watched, and would
not expose himself.

But that devil Horn must be killed, and he swore
between his grinding teeth that he himself would do it.
His men, many of them with bloody heads, were still
fighting, swearing, climbing, and firing. None of them

had been killed except those who had gained the deck of the other vessel, but Banker did not believe that they would be able to board the *Monterey* until its captain had been disposed of. If he could put a ball into that fellow, the fight would be over.

Banker now determined to lead a fresh attack instead of simply ordering one. If he could call to his men from the deck of the *Monterey*, they would follow him. The *Vittorio* lay so that her bow was somewhat forward of that of the *Monterey*, and as the rails at the bows of the two vessels were some distance apart, there was no fighting forward. The long boom of the fore-mast of the *Vittorio* stretched over her upper deck, and, crouching low, Banker cut all the lines which secured it. Then with a quick run he seized the long spar near its outer end, and thus swinging it out until it struck the shrouds, he found himself dangling over the forward deck of the *Monterey*, upon which he quickly dropped.

It so happened that the fight was now raging aft, and for a moment Banker stood alone looking about him. He believed his rapid transit through the air had not been noticed. He would not call upon his men to follow as he had intended. Without much fear of detection he would slip quietly behind the crew of the *Monterey*, and take a shot at Captain Horn the moment he laid eyes on him. Then he could shout out to his men to some purpose.

Banker moved on a few steps, not too cautiously, for he did not wish to provoke suspicion, when suddenly a hand was placed upon his chest. There was nobody in front of him, but there was the hand, and a very big one it was, and very black. Like a flash Banker turned, and beheld himself face to face with the man Mok, the same chimpanzee-like negro who had been his slave, and with whom in the streets of Paris he had once had a terrible struggle, which had resulted in his capture by the police and his imprisonment. Here was that same black devil again, his arms about him as if they had been chain-cables on a windlass.

Banker had two pistols, but he had put them in his pockets when he made his swing upon the boom, and he had not yet drawn them, and now his arms were held so tightly to his sides that he could not get at his weapons. There was no one near. Banker was wise enough not to call out or even to swear an oath, and Mok had apparently relapsed into the condition of the speechless savage beast. With a wrench which might have torn an ordinary limb from its socket, Banker freed his left arm, but a black hand had grasped it before he could reach his pistol.

Then there was a struggle — quick, hard, silent, and furious, as if two great cobras were writhing together, seeking each other's death. Mok was not armed. Banker could not use knife or pistol. They stumbled, they went down on their knees, they rose and fell together against the rail. Instantly Banker, with his left arm and the strength of his whole body, raised the negro to the rail and pushed him outward. The action was so sudden, the effort of the maddened pirate was so great, that Mok could not resist it — he went over the side. But his hold upon Banker did not relax even in the moment when he felt himself falling, and his weight was so great and the impetus was so tremendous that Banker could not hold back, and followed him over the rail. Still clutching each other tightly, the two disappeared with a splash into the sea.

Fears were beginning to steal into the valiant heart of Captain Horn. The pirates were so well armed, they kept up such a savage fire upon his decks, that although their shots were sent at random, several men had been killed, and others — he knew not how many — wounded, that he feared his crew, ordinary sailors and not accustomed to such savage work as this, might consider the contest too unequal, and so lose heart. If that should be the case, the affair would be finished.

But there was still one means of defence on which he thought he might rely to drive off the scoundrels. The *Monterey* had been a cotton ship, and she was provided with hose by which steam could be thrown upon her cargo in case of fire, and Captain Hagar had undertaken to try to get this into condition to use upon the scoundrels who were endeavoring to board the vessel. By this time two heavy lines of hose had been rigged and attached to the boiler, and the other ends brought out on deck — one forward and the other amidships.

Captain Hagar was a quiet man, and in no way a fighter, but now he seemed imbued with a reckless courage; and without thinking of the danger of exposing himself to pistol or to rifle, he laid the nozzle of his hose over the rail and directed it down upon the deck

BANKER COULD NOT HOLD BACK

below. As soon as the hot steam began to pour upon
the astonished pirates there were yells and execrations,
and when another scalding jet came in upon them over
the forward bulwarks of the *Monterey,* the confusion
became greater on the pirate ship.

It was at this moment, as Edna, her face pale and
her bright eyes fixed upon the upper deck of the *Vittorio,* stood with a revolver in her hand at the window
of her cabin, which was on deck, that her Swedish maid,
trembling so much that she could scarcely stand, approached her and gave her notice that she must quit
her service. Edna did not hear what she said. "Are
you there?" she cried. "Look out — tell me if you
can see Captain Horn!"

The frightened girl, scarcely knowing what she did,
rushed from the cabin to look for Captain Horn, not so
much because her mistress wanted information of him
as because she thought to throw herself upon his protection. She believed that the Captain could do anything
for anybody, and she ran madly along the deck on the
other side from that on which the battle was raging,
and meeting no one, did not stop until she had nearly
reached the bow. Then she stopped, looked about her,
and in a moment was startled by hearing herself called
by her name. There was no one near her; she looked
up, she looked around.

Then again she heard her name, "Sophee! Sophee!"
Now it seemed to come from the water, and looking over
the low rail she beheld a black head on the surface of
the sea. Its owner was swimming about, endeavoring

to find something on which he could lay hold, and he had seen the white cap of the maid above the ship's side. Sophia and Mok were very good friends, for the latter had always been glad to wait upon her in every way possible, and now she forgot her own danger in her solicitude for the poor black man.

"Oh, Mok! Mok!" she cried, "can't you get out of the water? Can I help you?"

Mok shouted out one of his few English words. "Rope! rope!" he said. But Sophia could see no rope except those which were fast to something, and in her terror she ran aft to call for assistance.

There was now not so much noise and din. The steam was not escaping from the boilers of the *Monterey*, for it was needed for the hose, and there were no more shots fired from the *Vittorio*. The officers of the pirate ship were running here and there looking for Banker, that they might ask for orders, while the men were crowding together behind every possible protection, and rushing below to escape the terrible streams of scalding steam.

Now that they could work in safety, the *Monterey's* men got their handspikes under the grappling-irons, and wrenched them from their holes, and leaning over the side they cut the ropes which held them to the pirate ship. The two vessels now swung apart, and Captain Horn was on the point of giving orders to start the engines and steam ahead, when the maid, Sophia, seized him by the arm. "Mrs. Horn wants you," she said, "and Mok's in the water!"

"Mok!" exclaimed the Captain.

"Yes, here! here!" cried Sophia, and running to the side, she pointed to where Mok's black head and waving arms were still circling about on the surface of the sea.

When a rope had been cast to Mok, and he had been hauled up the side, the Captain gave orders to start ahead, and rushed to the cabin where he had left Edna; but it was not during that brief interval of thankfulness that he heard how she had recognized the Rackbird, Banker, on the pirate ship, and how she had fired at him every time he had shown himself.

The *Monterey* started southward towards the point where they had last seen the yacht and the *Dunkery Beacon*, and the pirate ship, veering off to the southeast, steamed slowly away. The people on board of her were looking everywhere for Banker, for without him they knew not what they ought to do, but if their leader ever came up from the great depth to which he had sunk with Mok's black hands upon his throat, his comrades were not near the spot where, dead or alive, he floated to the surface.

CHAPTER XXXI

"SHE BACKED!"

WHEN Captain Burke observed the *Dunkery Beacon* steaming in his direction, and soon afterwards perceived a signal on this steamer to the effect that she wished to speak with the yacht, he began to hope that he was

T

going to get out of his difficulties. The natural surmise was that as one of the pirates had gone to join another just arriving upon the scene, the *Dunkery Beacon* — the Captain and crew of which must have turned traitors — was now coming to propose some arrangement, probably to give up Shirley if the yacht would agree to go its way and cease its harassing interference.

If this proposition should be made, Burke and Mrs. Cliff, in conference, decided to accept it. They had done all they could, and would return to Kingston to report to Captain Horn what they had done, and what they had discovered. But it was not long before the people on the yacht began to wonder very much at the conduct of the great steamer which was now rapidly approaching them, apparently under full head of steam.

The yacht was lying to, her engines motionless, and the *Dunkery Beacon* was coming ahead like a furious ram on a course, which, if not quickly changed, would cause her to strike the smaller vessel almost amidships. It became plainer and plainer every second that the *Dunkery* did not intend to change her course, and that her object was to run down the yacht.

Why the *Dunkery Beacon* should wish to ram the *Summer Shelter* nobody on board the yacht considered for a moment, but every one, even Willy Croup, perceived the immediate necessity of getting out of the way. Burke sprang to the wheel, and began to roar his orders in every direction. His object was to put the yacht around so that he could get out of the course of the *Dunkery Beacon* and pass her in the opposite direction to which she was going, but nobody on board seemed to be sufficiently alive to the threatening situation, or to be alert enough to do what was ordered at the very instant of command; and Burke, excited to the highest pitch, began to swear after a fashion entirely unknown to the two ladies and the members of the Synod. His cursing and swearing was of such a cyclonic and all-pervading character that some of those on board shuddered almost as much on account of his language as for fear of the terrible crash which was impending.

"This is dreadful!" said one of the clergymen, advancing as if he would mount to the pilot house.

"Stop!" said Mr. Arbuckle, excitedly placing his hand upon the shoulder of the other. "Don't interfere at such a moment. The ship must be managed."

In a very short time, although it seemed like long, weary minutes to the people on the yacht, her engines moved, her screw revolved, and she slowly moved around to leeward. If she could have done this half a minute sooner, she would have steamed out of the course of the *Dunkery Beacon* so that that vessel must have passed her, but she did not do it soon enough. The large steamer came on at what seemed amazing speed, and would have struck the yacht a little abaft the bow had not Burke, seeing that a collision could not be avoided, quickly reversed his helm. Almost in the next second the two vessels came together, but it was the stem of the yacht which struck the larger steamer abaft the bow.

The shock to the *Summer Shelter* was terrific, and having but little headway at the moment of collision she was driven backward by the tremendous momentum of the larger vessel as if she had been a ball struck by a bat. Every person on board was thrown down and hurled forward. Mrs. Cliff extended herself flat upon the deck, her arms outspread, and every clergyman was stretched out at full length or curled up against some obstacle. The engineer had been thrown among his levers and cranks, bruising himself badly about the head and shoulders, while his assistant and Mr. Hodgson, who were at work below, were jammed among the ashes of the furnace as if they were trying to stop the draught with their bodies.

Mr. Burdette was on the forward deck, and if he had not tripped and fallen, would probably have been shot overboard; and the sailing-master was thrown against the smokestack with such violence that for a few moments he was insensible.

Burke, who was at the wheel, saw what was coming and tried to brace himself so that he should not be impaled upon one of the handles, but the shock was too much for him and he pitched forward with such force that he came near going over the wheel and out of the window of the pilot house. As soon as Captain Burke could recover himself he scrambled back to his position behind the wheel. He had been dazed and bruised, but his senses quickly came to him and he comprehended the present condition of affairs.

The yacht had not only been forced violently backward, but had been veered around so that it now lay with its broadside towards the bow of the other steamer.

In some way, either unwittingly by the engineer or by the violence of the shock, her engine had been stopped and she was without motion, except the slight pitching and rolling occasioned by the collision. The *Dunkery Beacon* was not far away, and Burke saw to his horror that she was again moving forward. She was coming slowly, but if she reached the yacht in the latter's present position, she would have weight and force enough to turn over the smaller vessel.

Immediately Burke attempted to give the order to back the yacht. The instant performance of this order was the only chance of safety, but he had been thrown against the speaking-tube with such violence that he had jammed it and made it useless. If he pulled a bell the engineer might misunderstand. She must back! She could not pass the other vessel if she went ahead. He leaned out of the door of the pilot house and yelled downward to the engineer to back her; he yelled to somebody to tell the engineer to back her; he shouted until his shouts became screams, but nobody obeyed his orders, no one seemed to hear or to heed. But one person did hear.

Willy Croup had been impelled out of the door of the saloon and had slid forward on her knees and elbows until she was nearly under the pilot house. At the sound of Burke's voice, she looked up, she comprehended that orders were being given to which no attention was paid. The wild excitement of the shouting Captain filled her with an excitement quite as wild. She heard the name of the engineer, she heard the order, and without taking time to rise to her feet, she made a bound in the direction of the engine room.

Thrusting her body half through the doorway she yelled to the engineer, who, scarcely conscious of where he was or what he was doing, was pushing himself away from among his bars and rods. "Back her!" screamed Willy, and without knowing what she said or did, she repeated this order over and over again in a roaring voice which no one would have supposed her capable of, and accompanied by all the oaths which at that moment were being hurled down from the pilot house.

The engineer did not look up; he did not consider himself nor the situation. There was but one impression upon his mind made by the electric flash of the order backed by the following crash of oaths. Instinctively he seized his lever, reversed the engine, and started the *Summer Shelter* backward. Slowly, very slowly, she moved. Burke held his breath!

But the great steamer was coming on slowly. Her motion was increasing, but so was that of the yacht, and when, after some moments of almost paralyzing terror, during which Willy Croup continued to hurl her furious orders into the engine room, not knowing they had been obeyed, the two vessels drew near each other, the *Dunkery Beacon* crossed the bow of the *Summer Shelter* a very long biscuit-toss ahead.

"Miss Croup," said Mr. Litchfield, his hand upon her shoulder, "that will do! The yacht is out of immediate danger."

Willy started up. Her wild eyes were raised to the

face of the young clergyman, the roar of her own invectives sounded in her ears. Tears poured from her eyes.

"Mercy on me, Mr. Litchfield," she exclaimed, "what have I been saying?"

"Never mind now, Miss Croup," said he. "Don't think of what you said. She backed!"

CHAPTER XXXII

A HEAD ON THE WATER

WITH her engines in motion and her wheel in the hands of Captain Burke, the *Summer Shelter* was in no danger of being run into by the *Dunkery Beacon*, for she was much the more easily managed vessel.

As soon as they had recovered a moderate command of their senses, Burdette and Portman hurried below to find out what damage had been sustained by the yacht; but, although she must have been greatly strained and might be leaking through some open seams, the tough keelson of the well-built vessel, running her length like a stiff backbone, had received and distributed the shock, and although her bowsprit was shivered to pieces and her cut-water splintered, her sides were apparently uninjured. Furniture, baggage, coils of rope, and everything movable had been pitched forward and heaped in disordered piles all over the vessel. A great part of the china had been broken. Books, papers, and ornaments littered the floors, and even the coal was heaped up in the forward part of the bunkers.

Burke gave the wheel to Burdette and came down, when Mrs. Cliff immediately rushed to him. She was not hurt, but had been dreadfully shaken in body and mind. "Oh, what are we going to do?" she cried. "They are wretched murderers! Will they keep on trying to sink us? Can't we get away?"

"We can get away whenever we please," said Burke, his voice husky and cracked. "If it wasn't for Shirley, I'd sail out of their sight in half an hour."

"But we can't sail away and leave Mr. Shirley," said she. "We can't go away and leave him!"

But little effort was made to get anything into order. Bruised heads and shoulders were rubbed a little, and all on board seemed trying to get themselves ready for whatever would happen next. Burke, followed by Portman, ran to the cases containing the rifles, and taking them out, they distributed them, giving one to every man on board. Some of the clergymen objected to receiving them, and expostulated earnestly and even piteously against connecting themselves with any bloodshed. "Cannot we leave this scene of contention?" some of them said. "Not with Shirley on that steamer," said Burke, and to this there was no reply.

Burke had no definite reason for thus arming his crew, but with such an enemy as the *Dunkery Beacon* had proved herself to be, lying to a short distance away, two other vessels, probably pirates, in the vicinity, and the strong bond of Shirley's detention holding the yacht where she was, he felt that he should be prepared for every possible emergency. But what to do he did not know. It would be of no use to hail the *Dunkery* and demand Shirley. He had done that over and over again before that vessel had proved herself an open enemy. He stood with brows contracted, rifle in hand, and his eyes fixed on the big steamer ahead. The two other vessels he did not now consider, for they were still some miles away.

Willy Croup was sitting on the floor of the saloon, sobbing and groaning, and Mrs. Cliff did not know what in the world was the matter with her. But Mr. Litchfield knew, and he knew also that it would be of no use to try to comfort her with any ordinary words of consolation. He was certain that she had not understood anything that she had said, not even, perhaps, the order to back the yacht, but the assertion of this would have made but little impression upon her agitated mind. But a thought struck him, and he hurried to Burke and told him quickly what had happened. Burke listened, and could not even now restrain a smile. "It's just like that dear Willy Croup," said he; "she's an angel!"

"Will you be willing," said Mr. Litchfield, "to come and tell her that your orders could not have been forcibly and quickly enough impressed upon the engineer's mind in any other way?"

Without answering, Burke ran to where Willy was still groaning. "Miss Croup," he exclaimed, "we owe our lives to you! If you hadn't sworn at the engineer, he never would have backed her in time, and we would all have been at the bottom of the sea!"

Mrs. Cliff looked aghast, and Willy sprang to her feet. "Do you mean that, Mr. Burke?" she cried.

"Yes," said he, "in such desperate danger you had to do it. It's like a crack on the back when you're choking. You were the only person able to repeat my orders, and you were bound to do it!"

"Yes," said Mr. Litchfield, "and you saved the ship!"

Willy looked at him a few moments in silence, then wiping her eyes, she said, "Well, you know more about managing a ship than I do, and I hope and trust I'll never be called upon to back one again!"

Burke and most of the other men now gathered on deck, watching the *Dunkery Beacon*. She was still lying to, blowing off steam, and there seemed to be a good deal of confusion on her deck. Suddenly Burke saw a black object in the water near her starboard quarter. Gazing at it intently, his eyes began to glisten. In a few moments he exclaimed, "Look there! It's Shirley! He's swimming to the yacht!"

Now everybody on deck was straining his eyes over the water, and Mrs. Cliff and Willy, who had heard Burke's cry, stood with the others. "Is it Shirley, really?" exclaimed Mrs. Cliff. "Are you sure that's his head in the water?"

"Yes," replied Burke, "there's no mistake about it! He's taking his last chance and has slipped over the rail without nobody knowing it."

"And can he swim so far?" gasped Willy.

"Oh, he can do that," answered Burke. "I'd steam up closer if I wasn't afraid of attracting attention. If they'd get sight of him they'd fire at him, but he can do it if he's let alone!"

Not a word was now said. Scarcely a breath seemed to come or go. Everybody was gazing steadfastly and rigidly at the swimmer, who with steady, powerful strokes was making a straight line over the gently rolling waves towards the yacht. Although they did not so express it to themselves, the coming of that swimmer meant everything to the pale, expectant people on the *Summer Shelter*. If he should reach them, not only would he be saved, but they could steam away to peace and safety.

On swam Shirley, evenly and steadily, until he had nearly passed half the distance between the two vessels, when suddenly a knot of men were seen looking over the rail of the *Dunkery*. Then there was a commotion. Then a man was seen standing up high, a gun in his hand. Willy uttered a stifled scream, and Mrs. Cliff seized her companion by the arm with such force that her nails nearly entered the flesh, and almost in the same instant there rang out from the yacht the report of eight rifles.

Every man had fired at the fellow with the gun, even Burdette in the pilot house. Some of the balls had gone high up into the rigging, and some had rattled against the hull of the steamer, but the man with the gun disappeared in a flash. Whether he had been hit or frightened, nobody knew. Shirley, startled at this tremendous volley, turned a quick backward glance and then dived, but soon reappeared again, striking out as before for the yacht.

"Now, then," shouted Burke, "keep your eyes on the rail of that steamer! If a man shows his head, fire at it!"

If this action had been necessary, very few of the rifles in the hands of the members of the late Synod would have been fired, for most of them did not know how to recharge their weapons. But there was no need even for Burke to draw a bead on a pirate head, for now not a man could be seen on the *Dunkery Beacon*. They had evidently been so surprised and astounded by a volley of rifle shots from this pleasure yacht, which they had supposed to be as harmless as a floating log, that every man on deck had crouched behind the bulwarks.

Now Burke gave orders to steam slowly forward, and for everybody to keep covered as much as possible; and when in a few minutes the yacht's engine stopped and Shirley swam slowly around her stern, there was a rush to the other side of the deck, a life preserver was dropped to the swimmer, steps were let down, and the next minute Shirley was on deck, Burke's strong arm fairly lifting him in over the rail. In a few moments the deck of the yacht was the scene of wild and excited welcome and delight. Each person on board felt as if a brother had suddenly been snatched from fearful danger and returned to their midst.

"I can't tell you anything now," said Shirley. "Give me a dram, and let me get on some dry clothes!

And now all of you go and attend to what you've got to do. Don't bother about that steamer — she'll go down in half an hour! She's got a big hole stove in her bow!"

With a cry of surprise Burke turned and looked out at the *Dunkery Beacon*. Even now she had keeled over to starboard so much that her deck was visible, and her head was already lower than her stern. "She'll sink," he cried, "with all that gold on board!"

"Yes," said Shirley, turning with a weak smile as he made his way to the cabin, accompanied by Mr. Hodgson, "she'll go down with every bar of it!"

There was great commotion now on the *Dunkery Beacon*. It was plain that the people on board of her had discovered that it was of no use to try to save the vessel, and they were lowering her boats. Burke and his companions stood and watched for some minutes. "What shall we do!" exclaimed Mr. Arbuckle, approaching Burke. "Can we offer those unfortunate wretches any assistance?"

"All we can do," said Burke, "is to keep out of their way. I wouldn't trust one of them within pistol shot." Now Shirley reappeared on deck — he had had his dram, and had changed his clothes. "You're right," said he, "they're a set of pirates — every man of them! If we should take them on board, they'd cut all our throats. They've got boats enough, and the other pirates can pick them up. Keep her off, Burke; that's what I say!"

There was no time now for explanations or for any

story to be told, and Burke gave orders that the yacht should be kept away from the sinking steamer and her boats. Suddenly Burdette, from the pilot house, sung out that there was a steamer astern, and the eyes which had been so steadfastly fixed upon the *Dunkery Beacon* now turned in that direction. There they saw, less than a mile away, a large steamer coming down from the north.

Burke's impulse was to give orders to go ahead at full speed, but he hesitated, and raised his glass to his eye. Then in a few moments he put down his glass, turned around, and shouted, "That's the *Monterey!* The *Monterey!* and Captain Horn!"

CHAPTER XXXIII

11° 30' 19" N. LAT. BY 56° 10' 49" W. LONG.

THE announcement of the approach of Captain Horn created a sensation upon the *Summer Shelter* almost equal to that occasioned by any of the extraordinary incidents which had occurred upon that vessel. Burke and Shirley were wild with delight at the idea of meeting their old friend and commander. Willy Croup had never seen Captain Horn, but she had heard so much about him that she considered him in her mind as a being of the nature of a heathen deity who rained gold upon those of whom he approved, and utterly annihilated the unfortunates who incurred his displeasure.

As for Mrs. Cliff, her delight in the thought of meeting Captain Horn, great as it was, was overshadowed by her almost frantic desire to clasp once more in her arms her dear friend Edna. The clergymen had heard everything that the *Summer Shelter* people could tell them about Captain Horn and his exploits, and each man of them was anxious to look into the face and shake the hand of the brave sailor, whom they had learned to look upon as a hero; and one or two of them thought that it might be proper, under the circumstances, to resume their clerical attire before the interview. But this proposition, when mentioned, was discountenanced. They were here as sailors to work the yacht, and they ought not to be ashamed to look like sailors. The yacht was now put about and got under headway, and slowly moved in the direction of the approaching steamer.

When Captain Horn had finished the fight in which he was engaged with the *Vittorio*, and had steamed down in the direction of the two other vessels in the vicinity, it was not long before he discovered that one of them was an American yacht. Why it and the *Dunkery Beacon* should be lying there together he could not even imagine, but he was quite sure that this must be the vessel owned by Mrs. Cliff, and commanded by his old shipmate, Burke.

When at last the *Monterey* and the *Summer Shelter* were lying side by side within hailing distance, and Captain Horn had heard the stentorian voice of Burke roaring through his trumpet, he determined that he and Edna would go on board the yacht, for there were dead men and wounded men on his own vessel, and the condition of his deck was not such as he would wish to be seen by Mrs. Cliff and whatever ladies might be with her.

When Captain Horn and his wife, with Captain Hagar, rowed by four men, reached the side of the *Summer Shelter*, they were received with greater honor and joy than had ever been accorded to an admiral and his suite. The meeting of the five friends was as full of excited affection as if they were not now standing in the midst of strange circumstances, and, perhaps, many dangers of which none of them understood but a part.

Captain Horn seized the first opportunity which came to him to ask the question, "What's the matter with your yacht? You seem to have had a smash-up forward."

"Yes," said Burke, "there's been a collision. Those beastly hounds tried to run us down, but we caught her squarely on her bow."

At this moment the conversation was interrupted by a shout from Captain Hagar, who had taken notice of nobody on the yacht, but stood looking over the water at his old ship. "What's the matter," he cried, "with the *Dunkery Beacon?* Has she sprung a leak? Are those the pirates still on board?"

Captain Horn and the others quickly joined him. "Sprung a leak!" cried Shirley. "She's got a hole in her bow as big as a barrel. I've been on board of her, but I can't tell you about that now. There's no use to think of doing anything. Those are bloody pirates that are lowering the boats, and we can't go near them. Besides, you can see for yourself that that steamer is settling down by the head as fast as she can."

Captain Horn was now almost as much excited as the unfortunate commander of the *Dunkery Beacon*. "Where's that gold?" he cried. "Where is it stowed?"

"It is in the forward hold, with a lot of cargo on top of it!" groaned Captain Hagar.

Shirley now spoke again. "Don't think about the gold!" he said. "I kept my eyes opened and my ears sharpened when I was on board, and although I didn't understand all their lingo, I knew what they were at. When they found there was no use pumping or trying to stop the leak, they tried to get at that gold, but they couldn't do it. The water was coming in right there, and the men would not rig up the tackle to move the cargo. They were all wild when I left."

Captain Horn said no more, but stood with the others, gazing at the *Dunkery Beacon*. But Captain Hagar beat his hands upon the rail and declared over and over again that he would rather never have seen the ship again than to see her sink there before his eyes, with all that treasure on board. The yacht lay near enough to the *Dunkery Beacon* for Captain Hagar to see plainly what was going on on his old ship, without the aid of a glass. With eyes glaring madly over the water, he stood leaning upon the rail, his face pale, his whole form shaking as if he had a chill. Every one on the deck of the yacht gathered around him, but no one said anything. This was no time for asking questions, or making explanations.

The men on the *Dunkery Beacon* were hurrying to leave the vessel. One of the starboard boats was already in the water, with too many men in her. The vessel had keeled over so much that there seemed to be difficulty in lowering the boats on the port side. Everybody seemed rushing to starboard, and two other boats were swinging out on their davits. Every time the bow of the steamer rose and fell upon the swell it seemed to go down a little more and up a little less, and the deck was slanted so much that the men appeared to slide down to the starboard bulwarks.

Now the first boat pushed off from the sinking ship, and the two others, both crowded, were soon pulling after her. It was not difficult to divine their intentions. The three boats headed immediately for the northeast, where, less than two miles away, the *Vittorio* could be plainly seen.

At this moment Captain Hagar gave a yell; he sprang back from the rail, and his eyes fell upon a rifle which had been laid on a bench by one of the clergymen. He seized it and raised it to his shoulder, but in an instant Captain Horn took hold of it, pointing it upward. "What are you going to do?" he said. "Captain, you don't mean to fire at them?"

"Of course I mean it!" cried Captain Hagar. "We've got them in a bunch. We must follow them up and shoot them down like rats!"

HE SEIZED IT AND RAISED IT TO HIS SHOULDER

"We'll get up steam and run them down!" shouted
Burke. "We ought to sink them, one boat after another,
the rascally pirates! They tried to sink us!"

"No, no," said Captain Horn, taking the gun from
Captain Hagar, "we can't do that. That's a little too
cold-blooded. If they attack us, we'll fight them, but
we can't take capital punishment into our own hands."

Now the excited thoughts of Captain Hagar took
another turn. "Lower a boat! Lower a boat!" he
cried. "Let me be pulled to the *Dunkery!* Everything
I own is on that ship, the pirates wouldn't let me take
anything away. Lower a boat! I can get into my
cabin."

Shirley now stepped to the other side of Captain
Hagar. "It's no use to think of that, Captain," he said.
"It would be regular suicide to go on board that vessel.
Those fellows were afraid to stay another minute. She'll
go down before you know it. Look at her bows now!"

Captain Hagar said no more, and the little company
on the deck of the yacht stood pale and silent, gazing
out over the water at the *Dunkery Beacon.* Willy Croup
was crying, and there were tears in the eyes of Mrs.
Cliff and Edna. In the heart of the latter was deep,
deep pain, for she knew what her husband was feeling
at that moment. She knew it had been the high aim of
his sensitive and honorable soul that the gold for
which he had labored so hard and dared so much
should safely reach, in every case, those to whom it had
been legally adjudged. If it should fail to reach them,
where was the good of all that toil and suffering? He

had in a measure taken upon himself the responsibility
of the safe delivery of that treasure, and now here he
was standing, and there was the treasure sinking before
his eyes. As she stood close by him, Edna seized her
husband's hand and pressed it. He returned the pressure, but no word was said.

Now the *Dunkery Beacon* rolled more heavily than
she had done yet, and as she went down in the swell it
seemed as if the water might easily flow over her forward bulwarks; and her bow came up with difficulty, as
if it were sticking fast in the water. Her masts and funnel were slanting far over to starboard, and when, after
rising once more, she put her head again into the water,
she dipped it in so deep that her rail went under and
did not come up again. Her stern seemed to rise in the
air, and at the same time the sea appeared to lift
itself up along her whole length. Then with a dip forward of her funnel and masts, she suddenly went down
out of sight, and the water churned, and foamed, and
eddied about the place where she had been. The gold of
the Incas was on its way to the bottom of the unsounded
sea.

Captain Hagar sat down upon the deck and covered
his face with his hands. No one said anything to
him, — there was nothing to say. The first to speak
was Mrs. Cliff. "Captain Horn," said she, her voice
so shaken by her emotion that she scarcely spoke above
a whisper, "we did everything we could, and this is
what has come of it!"

"Everything!" exclaimed Captain Horn, suddenly

turning towards her. "You have done far more than could be expected by mortals! And now," said he, turning to the little party, "don't let one of us grieve another minute for the sinking of that gold. If any·body has a right to grieve, it's Captain Hagar here. He's lost his ship, but many a good sailor has lost his ship and lived and died a happy man after it. And as to the cargo you carried, my mate," said he, "you would have done your duty by it just the same if it had been pig lead or gold; and when you have done your duty, there's the end of it!"

Captain Hagar looked up, rose to his feet, and after gazing for a second in the face of Captain Horn, he took his extended hand. "You're a good one!" said he; "but you're bound to agree that it's tough. There's no getting around that. It's all-fired tough!"

"Burke," said Captain Horn, quickly, glancing up at the noon-day sun, "put her out there near the wreckage, and take an observation."

It was shortly after this that Mr. Portman, the sailing-master, came aft and reported the position of the yacht to be eleven degrees, thirty minutes, nineteen seconds north latitude by fifty-six degrees, ten minutes, forty-nine seconds west longitude.

"What's the idea," said Burke to Captain Horn, "of steering right to the spot? Do you think there'll ever be a chance of getting at it?"

Captain Horn was marking the latitude and longitude in his note-book. "Can't say what future ages may do in the way of deep-sea work," said he, "but I'd like to put a dot on my chart that will show where the gold went down."

Nothing could be more unprofitable for the shaken and disturbed spirits of the people on the *Summer Shelter* than to stand gazing at the few pieces of wood and the half-submerged hencoop which floated above the spot where the *Dunkery Beacon* had gone down, or to look out at the three boats which the pirates were vigorously rowing towards the steamer in the distance, and this fact strongly impressed itself upon the practical mind of Mrs. Cliff. "Captain Horn," said she, "is there any reason why we should not go away?"

"None in the world," said he, "and there's every reason why your vessel and mine should get under headway as soon as possible. Where are you bound for now?"

"Wherever you say, Captain," she answered. "This is my ship, and Mr. Burke is my captain, but we want you to take care of us, and you must tell us where we should go."

"We'll talk it over," said he, and calling Burke and Captain Hagar, a consultation was immediately held; and it did not take long to come to a decision when all concerned were of the same mind.

It was decided to set sail immediately for Kingston, for each vessel had coal enough, with the assistance of her sails, to reach that port. Mrs. Cliff insisted that Edna should not go back to the *Monterey*, and Captain Horn agreed to this plan, for he did not at all wish any womankind on the *Monterey* in her present condition.

The yacht had been found to be perfectly seaworthy, and although a little water was coming in, her steam pump kept her easily disposed of it. Edna accepted Mrs. Cliff's invitation, provided her husband would agree to remain on the yacht, and, somewhat to her surprise, he was perfectly willing to do this. The idea had come to him that the best thing for all parties, and especially for the comfort and relief of the mind of Captain Hagar, was to put him in command of a ship and give him something to think about other than the loss of his vessel.

While they were talking over these matters, and making arrangements to send to the *Monterey* for Edna's maid and some of her baggage, Captain Horn sought Burke in his room. "I want to know," said he, "what sort of a crew you've got on board this yacht? One of them — a very intelligent-looking man, by the way, with black trousers on — came up to me just now and shook hands with me, and said he was ever so much pleased to make my acquaintance and hoped he would soon have some opportunities of conversation with me. That isn't the kind of seaman I'm accustomed to."

Burke laughed. "It's the jolliest high-toned, upper-ten crew that ever swabbed a deck or shoveled coal. They're all ministers."

"Ministers!" ejaculated Captain Horn, absolutely aghast. Then Burke told the story of the Synod. Captain Horn sank into a chair, leaned back, and laughed until the tears ran down his cheeks.

"I didn't suppose," he said presently, "that anything

could make me laugh on a day like this, but the story
of those Synod gentlemen has done it! But, Burke,
there's no use of their serving as seamen any longer.
Let them put on their black clothes and be comfortable
and happy. I've got a double crew on board the *Monterey*, and can bring over just as many men as are needed
to work this yacht. I'll go over myself and detail a
crew, and then, when everything is made ready, I'll
come on board here myself. And after that I want you to
remember that I'm a passenger and haven't anything to
do with the sailing of this ship. You're Captain and
must attend to your own vessel, and I'm going to make
it my business to get acquainted with all these clergymen, and that lady I see with Mrs. Cliff. Who is
she?"

"By George!" exclaimed Burke, "she's the leading
trump of the world! That's Willy Croup!"

There was no time then to explain why Willy was a
leading trump, but Captain Horn afterwards heard the
story of how she backed the ship, and he did not wonder
at Burke's opinion.

When the *Summer Shelter*, accompanied by the *Monterey*, had started northward, Burke stood by Shirley on
the bridge. Mr. Burdette had a complete crew of able
seamen under his command; there was a cook in the
kitchen, and stewards in the saloons, and there was a
carpenter with some men at work at a spare spar which
was to be rigged as a bowsprit.

"I'm mighty glad to lay her course for home," said
Burke, "for I've had enough of it as things are; but if

things were not exactly as they are, I wouldn't have enough of it."

"What do you mean?" said Shirley.

"I mean this," was the answer. "If this was my yacht, and there was no women on board, and no ministers, I would have put on a full head of steam, and I would have gone after those boats, and I would have run them down, one after another, and drowned every bloody pirate on board of them. It makes my blood boil to think of those scoundrels getting away after trying to run us down, and to shoot you!"

"It would have served them right to run them down, you know," said Shirley, "but you couldn't do it, and there's no use talking about it. It would have been a cold-blooded piece of business to run down a small boat with a heavy steamer, and I don't believe you would have been willing to do it yourself when you got close on to them! But the Captain says if we get to Kingston in good time, we may be able to get a cable message to London, and set the authorities at every likely port on the lookout for the *Vittorio*."

The voyage of the *Summer Shelter* to Kingston was uneventful, but in many respects a very pleasant one. There had been a great disappointment, there had been a great loss, and, to the spirits of some of the party, there had been a great shock, but every one now seemed determined to forget everything which had been unfortunate, and to remember only that they were all alive, all safe, all together, and all on their way home.

The clergymen, relieved of their nautical duties, shone

out brightly as good-humored and agreeable companions. Their hardships and their dangers had made them so well acquainted with each other, and with everybody else on board, and they had found it so easy to become acquainted with Captain and Mrs. Horn, and they all felt so much relieved from the load of anxiety which had been lifted from them, that they performed well their parts in making up one of the jolliest companies which ever sailed over the South Atlantic.

At Kingston the *Summer Shelter* and the *Monterey* were both left, — the former to be completely repaired and brought home by Mr. Portman, and the other to be coaled and sent back to Vera Cruz, with her officers and her crew, — and our whole party, including Captain Hagar, sailed in the next mail steamer for New York.

CHAPTER XXXIV

PLAINTON, MAINE

IT was late in the summer, and Mrs. Cliff dwelt happy and serene in her native town of Plainton, Maine. She had been there during the whole warm season, for Plainton was a place to which people came to be cool and comfortable in summer-time, and if she left her home at all, it would not be in the months of foliage and flowers. It might well be believed by any one who would look out of one of the tall windows of her drawing-room that Mrs. Cliff did not need to leave home for the mere sake of rural beauty. On the other side of the street, where once stretched a block of poor little houses and shops, now lay a beautiful park, The Grove of the Incas.

The zeal of Mr. Burke and the money of Mrs. Cliff had had a powerful influence upon the minds of the contractors and landscape-gardeners who had this great work in hand, and the park, which really covered a very large space in the village, now appeared from certain points of view to extend for miles, so artfully had been arranged its masses of obstructing foliage, and its open vistas of uninterrupted view. The surface of the ground, which had been a little rolling, had been made more unequal and diversified, and over all the little hills and dells, and upon the wide, smooth stretches there was a covering of bright green turf. It had been a season of genial rains, and there had been a special corps of workmen to attend to the grass of the new park.

Great trees were scattered here and there, and many people wondered when they saw them, but these trees, oaks and chestnuts, tall hickories and bright cheerful maples, had been growing where they stood since they were little saplings. The people of Plainton had always been fond of trees, and they had them in their side yards, and in their back yards, and at the front of their houses; and when, within the limits of the new park, all these yards, and houses, and sheds, and fences had been cleared away, there stood the trees. Hundreds of other trees, evergreens and deciduous, many of them of good size, had been brought from the adjacent coun-

try on great wheels, which had excited the amazement
of the people in the town, and planted in the park.

Through the middle of the grounds ran a wide and
turbulent brook, whirling around its rocks and spreading out into its deep and beautiful pools, and where once
stood the widow Casey's little house, — which was built
on the side of a bank, so that the Caseys went into the
second story when they entered by the front, — now
leaped a beautiful cataract over that very bank, scat-
tering its spray upon the trunks of the two big chestnuts, one of which used to stand by the side of Mrs.
Casey's house, and the other at the front.

In the shade of the four great oak trees which had
stood in William Hamilton's back yard, and which he
intended to cut down as soon as he had money enough
to build a long cow-stable, — for it was his desire to go
into the dairy business, — now spread a wide, transparent
pool, half surrounded at its upper end by marble terraces,
on the edges of which stood tall statues with their white
reflections stretching far down into the depths beneath.
Here were marble benches, and steps down to the water,
and sometimes the bright gleams of sunshine came flit-
tering through the leaves, and sometimes the leaves
themselves came fluttering down and floated on the surface of the pool. And when the young people had stood
upon the terraces, or had sat together upon the wide marble steps, they could walk away, if they chose, through
masses of evergreen shrubbery, whose quiet paths seemed
to shut them out from the world.

On a little hill which had once led up to Parson's barn,

but now ended quite abruptly in a little precipice with
a broad railing on its edge and a summer-house a little
back, one could sit and look out over the stretch of bright
green lawns, between two clumps of hemlocks, and
over a hedge which concealed the ground beyond, along
the whole length of the vista made by Becker Street,
which obligingly descended slightly from the edge of
the park so that its houses were concealed by the hemlocks, and then out upon the country beyond, and to the
beautiful hills against the sky; and such a one might
well imagine, should he be a stranger, that all he saw
was in the Grove of the Incas. Upon all the outer edges
of this park there were masses of shrubbery, or little lines
of hedge, irregularly disposed, with bits of grass opening
upon the street, and here and there a line of slender iron
railing with a group of statuary back of it, and so the
people when they walked that way scarcely knew when
they entered the park, or when they left it.

The home of Mrs. Cliff, itself, had seemed to her to be
casting off its newness and ripening into the matured
home. Much of this was due to work which had been
done upon the garden and surrounding grounds, but
much more was due to the imperceptible influence of the
Misses Thorpedyke. These ladies had not only taken
with them to the house so many of the time-honored
objects which they had saved from their old home, but
they had brought to bear upon everything around them
the courtly tastes of the olden time.

Willy Croup had declared, as she stood in the hall
gazing up at the staircase, that it often seemed to her,

since she came back, as if her grandfather had been in the habit of coming down those stairs. "I never saw him," she said, "and I don't know what sort of stairs he used to come down, but there's something about all this which makes me think of things far back and grand, and I know from what I've heard of him that he would have liked to come down such stairs."

Mrs. Horn and her husband had made a long visit to Mrs. Cliff, and they had departed early in the summer for a great property they had bought in the West, which included mountains, valleys, a cañon, and such far extending groves of golden fruit that Edna already called the Captain "The Prince of Orange."

Edna's brother, Ralph, had also been in Plainton. He had come there to see his sister and Captain Horn, and that splendid old woman, Mrs. Cliff, but soon after he reached the town it might well be supposed it was Mr. Burke whom he came to visit. This worthy mariner and builder still lived in Plainton. His passion for an inland residence had again grown upon him, and he seemed to have given up all thoughts of the sea. He and Ralph had royal times together, and if the boy had not felt that he must go with Captain Horn and his sister to view the wonders of the far West, he and Burke would have concocted some grand expedition intended for some sort of an effect upon the civilization of the world.

But although Mrs. Cliff, for many reasons, had no present desire to leave her home, she did not relinquish the enterprise for which the *Summer Shelter* had been designed. When Captain Hagar had gone to London and had reported to his owners the details of his dire and disastrous misfortune, he had been made the subject of censure and severe criticism; but while no reason could be found why he should be legally punished for what had happened, he was made to understand that there was no ship for him in the gift of the house he had so long served.

When Mrs. Cliff heard of this, — and she heard of it very soon, through Captain Horn, — she immediately offered Captain Hagar the command of the *Summer Shelter*, assuring him that her designs included cruises of charity in the North in summer and in tropical waters in the winter-time, and that of all men she knew of, he was the Captain who should command her yacht. He was, indeed, admirably adapted to this service, for he was of a kind and gentle nature, and loved children, and he had such an observing mind that it frequently happened when he had looked over a new set of passengers, and had observed their physical tendencies, that he did not take a trip to sea at all, but cruised up the smooth quiet waters of the Hudson.

As soon as it could possibly be done, Captain Horn caused messages to be sent to many ports on the French and Spanish coast and along the Mediterranean, in order that if the *Vittorio* arrived in any of these harbors, her officers and men might be seized and held; but it was a long time before there was any news of the pirate ship, and then she was heard of at Mogador, a port on the western coast of Morocco, where she had been sold under very peculiar circumstances and for a very small price by the men who had come there in her, and who had departed north at different times on trading-vessels which were bound for Marseilles and Gibraltar.

More definite information was received of the third of the pirate vessels which had been fitted out to capture the Peruvians' treasure, for, as this vessel approached the West Indies, she was overhauled by a Spanish cruiser, who, finding her manned by a suspicious crew and well supplied with firearms, had seized her as a filibuster, and had taken her into a Cuban port, where she still remained, with her crew in prison awaiting trial or a tardy release, in case it became inconvenient to detain them longer.

The other pirate vessel, on which Captain Hagar and his men had been placed when they were forced to leave the *Dunkery Beacon*, finally reached Georgetown, British Guiana, where, after a long course of legal action, it was condemned and sold, and as much of the price as was left after costs had been paid, was handed over to the owners of the *Dunkery Beacon*.

Among the reasons which made Mrs. Cliff very glad to remain at Plainton was one of paramount importance. She was now engaged in a great work which satisfied all her aspirations and desires to make herself able to worthily and conscientiously cope with her income.

When, after the party on the *Summer Shelter* had separated at New York, and the ex-members of the Synod had gone to their homes, Mrs. Cliff and her party, which included Shirley as well as Captain Horn and his wife, had reached Plainton, their minds were greatly occupied with the subject of the loss of the Peruvians' share of the Incas' treasures. It was delightful for Mrs. Cliff and Willy to reach again their charming home, and their friends were filled with a pleasure which they could scarcely express to see and enjoy the beauties and the comforts with which Mrs. Cliff had surrounded herself; but there was still upon them all the shadow of that great misfortune which had happened off the eastern coast of South America.

News came to them of what had been said and done in London, and of what had been said and done, not only in Peru, but in other states of South America in regard to the loss of the treasure, but nothing was said or done in any quarter which tended to invalidate their right to the share of the gold which had been adjudged to them. The portion of the treasure allotted to the Peruvian government had been duly delivered to its agents, and it was the fault of those agents, acting under the feverish orders of their superiors, which had been the reason of its injudicious and hasty transportation and consequent loss.

But although the ownership of the treasure which was now in the safe possession of those to whom it had been adjudged was not considered a matter to be questioned or discussed, Mrs. Cliff was not satisfied with the case as it stood, and her dissatisfaction rapidly spread to the other members of the party. It pained her to think that the native Peruvians, those who might be considered the descendants of the Incas, would now derive no benefit from the discovery of the treasure of their ancestors, and

x

she announced her intention to devote a portion of her wealth to the interests and advantage of these natives.

Captain Horn was much impressed with this idea, and agreed that if Mrs. Cliff would take the management of the enterprise into her own hands, he would contribute largely to any plan which she might adopt for the benefit of the Peruvians. Edna, who now held a large portion of the treasure in her own right, insisted upon being allowed to contribute her share to this object, and Burke and Shirley declared that they would become partners, according to their means, in the good work.

There was, of course, a great deal of talk and discussion in regard to the best way of using the very large amount of money which had been contributed by the various members of the party, but before Captain Horn and his wife left Plainton everything was arranged, and Mrs. Cliff found herself at the head of an important and well-endowed private mission to the native inhabitants of Peru. She did not make immediately a definite plan of action, but her first steps in the direction of her great object showed that she was a woman well qualified to organize and carry on the great work in the cause of civilization and enlightenment which she had undertaken. She engaged the Reverend Mr. Hodgson and the Reverend Mr. Litchfield, both young men whose dispositions led them to prefer earnest work in new and foreign lands to the ordinary labors of a domestic parish, to go to Peru to survey the scene of the proposed work, and to report what, in their opinion, ought to be done and how it should be undertaken.

Mrs. Cliff, now in the very maturity of her mental and physical powers, felt that this great work was the most congenial task that she could possibly have undertaken, and her future life now seemed open before her in a series of worthy endeavors in which her conscientious feelings in regard to her responsibilities, and her desire to benefit her fellow-beings should be fully satisfied. As to her fellow-workers and those of her friends who thoroughly comprehended the nature of the case, there was a general belief that those inhabitants of Peru who were rightfully entitled to the benefits of the discovered treasure, would, under her management and direction of the funds in her hands, receive far more good and advantage than they could possibly have expected had the treasure gone to the Peruvian government. In fact, there were those who said that had the *Dunkery Beacon* safely arrived in the port of Callao, the whole of the continent of South America might have been disturbed and disrupted by the immense over-balance of wealth thrown into the treasury of one of its states.

It is true that Mrs. Cliff's plans and purposes did not entirely pass without criticism. "It's all very well," said Miss Nancy Shott to Mrs. Ferguson one morning when the latter had called upon her with a little basket of cake and preserves, "for Mrs. Cliff to be sending her money to the colored poor of South America, but a person who has lived as she has lived in days gone by ought to remember that there are poor people who are not colored, and who live a great deal nearer than South America." Miss Shott was at work as she said this, but she could always talk when she was working. She was busy packing the California blankets, which Mrs. Cliff had given her, in a box for the summer, putting pieces of camphor rolled up in paper between their folds. "If she wanted to find people to give money to, she needn't hire ministers to go out and hunt for them. There are plenty of them here, right under her nose, and if she doesn't see them, it's because she shuts her eyes wilfully, and won't look."

"But it seems to me, Miss Shott," said Mrs. Ferguson, "that Mrs. Cliff has done ever so much for the people of Plainton. For instance, there are those blankets. What perfectly splendid things they are, — so soft and light, and yet so thick and warm! They're all wool, every thread of them, I have no doubt."

"All wool!" said Miss Shott. "Of course they are, and that's the trouble with them. Some of these days they'll have to be washed, and then they'll shrink up so short that I suppose I'll have to freeze either my chin or my toes. And as to her giving them to me, 'turn about's fair play.' I once jined in to give her a pair."

"Oh," said Mrs. Ferguson.

Mr. George Burke was now the only member of our little party of friends who did not seem entirely satisfied with his condition and prospects. He made no complaints, but he was restless and discontented. He did not want to go to sea, for he vowed he had had enough of it, and he did not seem to find any satisfaction in a life on shore. He paid a visit to his mother, but he did not stay with her very long, for Plainton seemed to suit him better. But when he returned to his house in that town, he soon left it to go and spend a few days with Shirley.

When he came back, Mrs. Cliff, who believed that his uneasy state of mind was the result of want of occupation and the monotonous life of a small town, advised him to go out West and visit Captain Horn. There was so much in that grand country to interest him and to occupy him, body and mind; but to this advice Mr. Burke stoutly objected.

"I'm not going out there," he said. "I've seen enough of Captain Horn and his wife. To tell you the truth, Mrs. Cliff, that's what's the matter with me."

"I don't understand you," said she.

"It's simply this," said Burke. "Since I've seen so much of the Captain and his wife, and the happiness they get out of each other, I've found out that the kind of happiness they've got is exactly the kind of happiness I want, and there isn't anything else — money, or land, or orange groves, or steamships — that can take the place of it."

"In other words," said Mrs. Cliff, with a smile, "you want to get married."

"You've hit it exactly," said he. "I want a wife. Of course I don't expect to get exactly such a wife as Captain Horn has — they're about as scarce as buried treasure, I take it — but I want one who will suit me and who is suited to me. That's what I want, and I shall never be happy until I get her."

"I should think it would be easy enough for you to

get a wife, Mr. Burke," said Mrs. Cliff. "You are in the prime of life, you have plenty of money, and I don't believe it would be at all hard to find a good woman who would be glad to have you."

"That's what my mother said," said he. "When I was there she bored me from morning until night by telling me I ought to get married, and mentioning girls on Cape Cod who would be glad to have me. But there isn't any girl on Cape Cod that I want. To get rid of them, I came away sooner than I intended."

"Well then," said Mrs. Cliff, "perhaps there is some one in particular that you would like to have."

"That's it exactly," said Burke, "there is some one in particular."

"And do you mind telling me who it is?" she asked.

"Since you ask me, I don't mind a bit," said he. "It's Miss Croup."

Mrs. Cliff started back astonished. "Willy Croup!" she exclaimed. "You amaze me! I don't think she would suit you."

"I'd like to know why not?" he asked quickly.

"In the first place," said she, "it's a long time since Willy was a girl."

"That's the kind I want," he answered. "I don't want to adopt a daughter. I want to marry a grown woman."

"Well," said Mrs. Cliff, "Willy is certainly grown. But then, it doesn't seem to me that she would be adapted to a married life. I am sure she has made up her mind to live single, and she hasn't been accustomed to manage a house and conduct domestic affairs. She has always had some one to depend upon."

"That's what I like," said he. "Let her depend on me. And as to management, you needn't say anything to me about that, Mrs. Cliff. I saw her bouncing to the galley of the *Summer Shelter*, and if she manages other things as well as she managed the cooking business there, she'll suit me."

"It seems so strange to me, Mr. Burke," said Mrs. Cliff, after a few moments' silence. "I never imagined that you would care for Willy Croup."

Mr. Burke drew himself forward to the edge of the chair on which he was sitting, he put one hand on each of his outspread knees, and he leaned forward, with a very earnest and animated expression on his countenance. "Now, look here, Mrs. Cliff," he said, "I want to say something to you. When I see a young woman, brought up in the very bosom of the Sunday school, and on the quarter deck of respectability, and who never, perhaps, had a cross word said to her in all her life, or said one to anybody, judging from her appearance, and whose mind is more like a clean pocket-handkerchief in regard to hard words and rough language than anything I can think of; — when I see that young woman with a snow-white disposition that would naturally lead her to hymns when-ever she wanted to raise her voice above common con-versation, — when I see that young woman, I say, in a moment of life or death to her and every one about her, dash to the door of that engine room, and shout my orders down to that muddled engineer, — knowing I

" What is it?" said Willy, letting her work drop in her lap.

" Miss Croup," said he, " I heard you swear once, and I never heard anybody swear better, and with more conscience. You did that swearing for me, and now I want to ask you if you will be willing to swear for me again ? "

" No," said Willy, her cheeks flushing as she spoke, " no, I won't! It was all very well for you to tell me that I didn't do anything wrong when I talked in that dreadful way to Mr. Maxwell, and for you to get the ministers to tell me that as I didn't understand what I was saying, of course there was no sin in it; but although I don't feel as badly about it as I did, I sometimes wake up in the night and fairly shiver when I think of the words I used that day. And I've made up my mind, no matter whether ships are to be sunk or what is to happen, I will never do that thing again, and I don't want you ever to expect it of me."

" But, William Croup," exclaimed Mr. Burke, forgetting in his excitement that the full form of her Christian name was not likely to be masculine, " that isn't the way I want you to swear this time. What I want you to do is, to stand up alongside of me in front of a minister and swear you'll take me for your loving husband to love, honor, and protect, and all the rest of it, till death do us part. Now, what do you say to that ? "

Willy sat and looked at him. The flush went out of her cheeks, and then came again, but it was a different kind of a flush this time, and the brightness went out of her eyes, and another light, a softer and a different light, came into them. "Oh! Is that what you want?" she said, presently. "I wouldn't mind that."

THE END

www.ingramcontent.com/pod-product-compliance
Lightning Source LLC
Chambersburg PA
CBHW020942030726
47496CB00005B/1311